Lyndon Publishing

Mr. What's-His-Name

The Texas Serendipity Series
Romance with a twist of humor

JANICE OLSON

Lyndon Publishing

Acknowledgements

A special thanks to my terrific friends and beta readers—Jackie, Jewlene, Ann, and Martha—who were so gracious to give their time and input. You gals are awesome! I appreciate your help more than you'll ever know.

I give God thanks for the words and the stories.

Also, to my dear husband who puts up with me, gives me encouragement, and is my sounding block, thank you.

And last, but not least, where would I be without my loyal fans. Your joy of my books continues to inspire me. Thank you!

Though this book is a departure from my romantic suspense, I hope you will enjoy the first in the series of the "Texas Serendipity" romance with a twist of humor—all in great fun, of course. But don't lose faith … I will continue to write romantic suspense.

Blessings,

Janice Olson

Mailing Address:
Janice Olson
P.O. Box 382380
Duncanville, Texas 75132
            or
Email: Janice@JaniceOlson.com
And as I respect your time, please respect mine. No junk mail please. ☺

Mr. What's-His-Name

The helpless call to him, and he answers;
he saves them from all their troubles. Psalm 34:6 KJV

Chapter 1

I heard the screech of tires. Within nanoseconds, my seatbelt did a chokehold as I flew forward. And because it functioned as designed, the airbag slammed me back in the opposite direction into the not-so-soft faux leather seat of Agnes—my 1992 VW bug.

And why? Because an egotistical, larger-than-life, master-of-the-office, exec thought it his duty to conduct business on his cell phone while driving.

How do I know this?

Seconds before impact, I glanced into my rearview mirror. His was face animated, mouth moving, yet no one else was in the car, unless there was a littler person. And I, Tiffany Gates, not remotely related to Bill Gates of the dot com fame, had to suffer for his neglect.

In the seconds before the cars collided, his eyes locked with mine. Shock registered in his face.

If he was paying attention, he witnessed fear-stricken horror in mine seconds before he proceeded to smash into Agnes' little *bee*-hind.

All the fine officers of the beautiful city of Waxahachie, Texas, should summarily hand out citations to anyone if they see their mouth moving with no one except said driver in said car. Believe me, I would be the first to sign the petition to ban all cell phones in vehicles. I would even stand in a picket line to campaign for reform if asked.

Oh, Agnes, my poor Agnes, what has he done to you?

Here I sit, door open, legs dangling over the side of the car, feet barely touching the street—regardless if Agnes is low to the ground—with a headache the size of Gibraltar. My hand is covering a huge crater—well actually a small cut—as blood oozes through my fingers.

Where my head injury came from, I have no idea. Weren't airbags supposed to stop that sort of thing?

And what was Mr. Business-First doing at this precise moment?

Standing by Agnes' backend on his cellphone.

Really? Apparently, Mr. I'm-To-Important-To-Hang-Up-The-Phone-To-See-How-You're-Doing was talking to his lawyer, if the snippets of conversation filtering to my ears were any indication. Unfortunately, at this moment, I'm not certain my ears can be trusted, what with the loud ringing and buzzing sifting through the canals in my brain.

He spoke quietly, probably thought I couldn't hear him. However, I did.

I heard the word *wreck*, which was entirely his fault—my words, not his.

Lime-green bug, my all-time favorite color and, I might add, one Agnes wears quite well.

I don't think so, came next.

Well, at least he had an opinion.

Me? With my head pounding like a jackhammer gone amuck, I couldn't put a concise thought together if my life depended upon it. Which, come to think of it, might be the case.

Lawsuit.

Surely, he doesn't plan on suing me. My body zinged. I wondered if I could counter sue on grounds of insufficient attention to driving.

The voice came closer. Now I heard all of the one-sided conversation.

"Not much damage to my car. Hers, well, I don't think it's drivable …

Tears smarted. What would I do without a car? I would lose my job.

"No. She doesn't appear to be too badly hurt, thank God."

Oh, great! Just my fortune to have a profane man hit my little Agnes on the *bee*-hind.

"I'll call you back in a few minutes after I see how the woman is doing."

The instant silence, except for the crunch of footsteps, alerted my foggy brain Mr. I'm-Through-With-Business-For-The-Moment was headed in my direction and very close to where I sat nursing my poor brow.

Without offering to look up, I prayed this wouldn't be one of *those* experiences. Neither my body nor my psyche would be able to withstand another blow.

The footsteps stopped.

Spreading my fingers, I peeked through my partially covered eyes.

A pair of imported, handmade, oxblood Italian shoes stopped within the peripheral of my vision, right next to my Payless $9.99, off-the-discount-rack sandals. What a contrast—Mr. Millionaire versus Little Orphan Annie, with *Annie* wishing she were anywhere but here.

"You didn't get hurt from that little tap, did you?"

My blood boiled. I saw red. My jaw clamped down so hard I thought I was going to crack some teeth.

Whipping my gaze upward, I looked right into the face of Mr. Presumption-Personified, which was a big mistake for two reasons. First, I felt woozy. Second, his smile would have melted the ice caps on Mount McKinley. Thankfully, it didn't do a thing for me. Especially, after the crack about *that little tap.*

The overwhelming desire to kick him in the shin, or at the very least, strike him across the chops and wipe that faultless, gleaming smile from his fortune-five-hundred face was almost *too* hard to resist. I would have too, if it hadn't been for all the aches running rampant through my body at that moment. The effort to move or even stand would have been my undoing.

Hurting from head to toe, it felt as if I was in the throws of a bad case of flu or ptomaine poisoning. My legs and arms were still shaking from the experience of my one hundred and ten pounds being slammed back and forth like a punching bag in the car.

In addition, that whole airbag incident—exploding in my face and chest—wasn't the best of experiences either. I don't believe I'll ever be the same, especially in the upper regions where there were slim pickin's to begin with. And, if I'm not graced with two deep, dark purple eye sockets that will eventually turn to a nasty, pukey, mustard color before disappearing altogether, I'll be absolutely shocked.

"Are you hurt?"

A groan, provoked by pain, whooshed out. I lowered my head back in its former position before Mr. Little-Tap had arrived to check on my injuries, if that was what he was doing.

"Are—you—hurt?"

His words, enunciated as if I was a child or a simpleton really stirred my temper.

Did he really just ask that? "No—I—am—fine." I raised my face to give him a *what for.*

Mr. CEO, knees bent, rear resting on his calves, nose level with mine, took my breath away and nearly sent me careening over backwards. Shaking my head to clear the fog or whatever Mr. GQ's close proximity had caused, reinforced my opinion.

I wasn't at all well.

Indignation stirred, simmered, then turned into a full-fledged boil, much like the contents of a pot ready to roll over the top, creep down onto a hot burner and raise an awful stink. I drew in a deep breath to let him have it, but made a fatal error. I gazed into deep pools of pale-green eyes, the color of an Alaskan glacier river and every bit as breathtaking. His were a hairs-breath away from my mouse-colored brown ones. A quiver ran down my spine and had the gall to run right back up.

Boy, was I glad I had brushed my teeth minutes before I left the house. Surely my breath was still in good-smelling order. I squelched the urge to lift my hand and *haaaw* into my palm to make sure the commercial guarantee of twelve-hour, minty freshness was still working.

When it registered that Mr. Glacier-Eyes was waiting for my answer, nothing came to mind. Whether too stunned or overwhelmed by the accident, I'm not sure. It could have been because he was in my personal space.

Isn't there a rule somewhere of how one should never invade another person's space?

If there isn't, there certainly should be. This gorgeous, hunk-of-a-man was definitely in mine, and I didn't like what he was doing to my senses. I felt all gooey and melty inside, like a piece of caramel warmed by the sun.

I glanced down at my hand covered with blood, my own, of course, to avoid his gaze.

"Where did the blood come from? Where are you hurt? Aren't air bags supposed to stop this sort of thing from happening? Or does this little contraption even have airbags?"

He did it again—the personal space thingy. Only closer this time. His questions were coming too fast for my befuddled brain. His mesmerizing gaze searched my face, moving in for the kill.

Strong, well-manicured, manly looking fingers reached out and lifted my hair from my forehead. He grimaced, dropped the hair, that proceeded to plop down in my eyes blinding my vision, which at this point, wasn't all bad if I were to keep my mind off Mr. GQ.

I brushed the now sticky, congealed strands to the side, having to do it several times before my hair would stay put.

Mr. Businessman stood, reached inside his back pocket, dug out a pristine, white handkerchief that looked like it had been pressed by an iron or his ...

Oh, my! I must be worse off than I realized.

Wait a minute. Do men still carry hankies? My father used to when he was alive, but modern GQ men? Really?

I just hope it's clean.

Before he shoved my hand away, I noticed a silk embroidered 'A' in one corner. Then he pressed the cloth to my brow.

Reaching up to take over the chore of holding the hankie, our hands collided—mine and his. I must have taken a harder wallop from the airbag than originally thought. The mere touch of his fingers caused sparks, blazing a trail all the way to the pit of my stomach.

I grimaced and jerked my head back. "Ouch." Pain ricocheted around inside my skull.

Mr. All-Gentle-Concern probably thought I was the type of person who would sue his expensive pants right off his well-shaped derrière.

Well, let him squirm. What he didn't know, I wasn't the suing kind.

"Is there anything I can do for you?"

Whether from his nearness or my injury, I couldn't answer.

"My car is bigger than yours."

He bent down, back in my personal space again. *Comfort zone* didn't mean a thing to this man.

"My seats are supple and soft."

Oh, really. I can imagine they're very supple.

"You could lie down in the back seat of my car until help arrives. Or, if you like, the front seat reclines fully back."

Oh, yeah! I just bet they do, buster. No way are you getting me into your chick magnet. No telling what would happen then.

I shook my head. This time I kept the pain quiet—not even a grimace.

"Surely, there's something I can do to make you more comfortable."

Did Mr. Big-Bucks think me some kind of dimwit?

Mama didn't raise no foolish child. She warned me often about the evils of men and what could happen if I got into a stranger's backseat or front seat for that matter, regardless how well dressed, handsome, or sexy he happened to be.

Did I say sexy? My head injury is definitely worse than I thought.

Why, just last night, Channel 8 News flashed a photo across the TV screen of a good-looking serial killer they'd put in jail. When they interviewed his neighbors and friends, they all said he was a likeable, kind man, willing to do anything for you. None of them wanted to believe he could be such a monster.

No way, was I going to get in his car. I was going stay put in my little beetle, even if she wasn't as large or comfortable as Mr. Millionaire's silver Beamer.

I shook my head again for emphasis and again instantly regretted my action.

He looked agitated, seeing I wasn't about to succumb to his plan of getting a lone female into his Beamer.

Mr.   I-Have-More-Important-People-To-Talk-To flashed a smile somewhere in the vicinity of my forehead. Evidently, he decided I wouldn't expire on the spot.

"If you're sure you're okay and you won't move to my car, I'll step over there and make a few calls." He used his head as a directional signal, nodding toward *Diane's ~ The Answer to All Your Hair, Fingernail & Pedicure Needs* salon.

Oh, wow! Isn't that a shocker. "Please do. I'll be just fine."

"She speaks." A sparkling row of perfect, white teeth, visible between his drop-dead smiling lips, temporarily deprived me of sight. "By the way, I'm Matthew Ainsley."

Matthew Ainsley? Where have I heard that name before?

Then like the early dawn sun breaking through a foggy morning, the haze cleared from my mind.

Surely not *the* Matthew Thomas Ainsley the Third.

Chapter 2

Of all people who could have rear-ended me, why him, Lord?

I knew Matthew Thomas Ainsley the Third. Well, not personally, but I had heard of him, even read about him. Who hadn't?

The aftershock of such news wore off, and my brain began to function again.

"I'm Tiff-Tiffany Gates."

A small twitch appeared at the corner of his mouth. Oh, not like some sort of muscle spasm or hereditary tick. More like he was doing his best not to smile, but couldn't quite hold it back.

There, he did it again. This time he didn't attempt to control the twitch but allowed his lips to do a half turn upward. Then a full blown *I'm-gonna-charm-you* smile swelled across his mug, accompanied by an ever-so-slight lift of his left brow.

"Hi, Tiff-Tiffany Gates. Do you feel up to exchanging information now, or do you want to wait until the police arrive?"

"I'll wait." My mumble was barely audible. I knew I was acting stinky but he'd put my whole internal system off kilter.

His smile disappeared. With it the sun vanished behind the clouds. A perplexed look traveled cross his face.

"Well, if you'd rather not." His gaze searched the street and then the sidewalk. I saw his slight hesitation. "If you're sure you don't need me, I'll make those calls while we're waiting."

Wellll, suuuuprrriize, suuuuprrriize.

"I'll be fine. By all means, redeem the time." The last came out a little too snippish. After all, I wasn't up to my usual pleasant self.

He gave me a piercing look, as if he was trying to figure me out, and then a shrug. "Well, if you want me, I'll be right over there." Mr. All-Business nodded again toward the vicinity of the salon. "You sure you'll be all right?"

I almost didn't answer his question, but I managed to push out, "Yes, I'll be fine. Here." I stuck out the now very blood-soiled hankie.

When he saw what I held in my hand, he waved it off as though it had cooties or something.

"No, you keep it. Your cut may start bleeding again." Shining his every-ready, irresistible smile, he sauntered to the curb.

Though I tried, I couldn't help myself. My gaze followed his well-formed backside as he ambled toward the building, already talking over the Bluetooth attached to his ear—oh, I don't mean permanently, but it might as well have been.

Me? I was out of sight, out of mind.

As much as I hate to admit it, I relished the excellent view his backside afforded. My mind kept going back to *if you need me—if you want me* part of his conversation. I tossed the thought away, but found it came bouncing right back without any choice on my part.

Oh sure, there were thousands of young women who would have lined up to swoon at Mr. Handsome's feet, but I wasn't one of them. Certainly attractive enough, if you like a man six foot plus a couple of inches, broad shoulders, a physique without one ounce of flab, chestnut hair kissed by the sun, and pale green eyes that danced with merriment and caused me to quiver. His smile could knock the wind out of a gal's sails—even if she were the most confirmed man-hater or her sails were a little tattered.

I lowered my head into the palms of my hands. I prayed this morning would hurry up and end before I did something stupid, like drool all over myself, or fall at his feet.

Mr. Exec's sexy-sounding voice rode the wind to my ears. The timbre, without a doubt, would give most women, single or attached, cardiac arrest or at the very least, heart palpitations and hot flashes. At the moment, my whole body was alive and feeling .... *No, I won't go there.*

The rushed breathing and the rapid *dum-dum, dum-dum* of my heart pounding wildly in my chest was purely from the excitement of the wreck, nothing more. This shortness of breath and the jitters I was experiencing had absolutely nothing to do with Mr. Man-of-Every-Woman's-Dream.

With all the conviction within me, I told myself his honey-toned voice didn't do a thing for me. My overheated imagination wouldn't cooperate and continued to force me to sneak several peeks in his direction, straining to hear his voice.

His rapid-fire instructions to someone on the opposite end of the phone had Mr. Exec quite disturbed. Maybe he was checking with his lawyer to make sure I couldn't sue him. Yet, he didn't seem too concerned about me, so I probably wasn't what had him upset.

I perked up, tuning in on the scraps of conversation floating my way. The discussion wasn't about me at all. Something about an acquisition or merger and a very important meeting he had missed due to this *little* fender bender.

Well! It didn't seem like he was sparing one bit of concern over my injuries or for my poor old Agnes. I could have expired right under his nose, and he wouldn't have noticed. No doubt he was more worried if the NASDAC had gone up or down than he was about *my* wellbeing.

Before I could turn away, he looked in my direction. Our gaze locked, causing a great disturbance to my stomach, not like pukey sick, more like a tightening, quivery thing that settled deep inside. My heart raced and zinged. I couldn't catch my breath. Was I having a heart attack right here, right now?

He broke eye contact and continued conducting business once again. My body settled down to normal, if there could be such a thing after today.

Hearing a siren not too far off, I decided it was time to dig out my insurance papers. I needed to be prepared to give my side of the story. As of yet, I hadn't gotten out of my car to take a look at the damage to Agnes. I think I was too afraid I'd be reduced to a blubbering idiot in front of Mr. Studley. Or, maybe I would be too hurt and humiliated by what he referred to as our little fender-bender to my tiny, but comfy auto that meant the world to me.

Agnes was like an old friend. We had been through thick and thin, good times and bad, ups and downs, and now ... *Oh, I just hope she's repairable.*

I leaned over in the passenger seat, reaching to open the glove compartment. The papers were in my grasp, when I felt someone lean into Agnes, grab my shoulders, and pull me upright.

After blinking several times, I found my blurred vision wasn't from the wreck. Our noses were less than an inch apart. I had the overwhelming desire to lean in to feel his lips on mine.

"What are you doing?"

Had he read my mind about the kiss?

I pulled from his grasp, heat rushing to my cheeks. "I might ask you the same. What do you think you are you doing?"

"Are you all right?" He looked perturbed. "I wished you would've listened to me and moved to my car where you could have rested."

"I'm fine." I leaned away, doing my best to put distance between all that animal magnetism seeping from every pore of his body.

"You weren't fine. I saw you go down. You fainted."

I couldn't help the burble of laughter pushing its way through my lips. "I didn't faint. I heard the siren. I was reaching for my insurance papers. See, here they are." I shoved the little clear, see-through pouch containing everything I would need for such an occasion as this, up in his face, waving the packet in the air. "This, Mr. Ainsley. This is why I leaned over."

A bemused, almost embarrassed expression crossed his face. It looked good on him. Come to think of it, everything looked good on him, even worry. "I'm sorry. I saw you go down and …"

"Really, I'm fine. But I'd be better if you would give me some room to stand."

His cheeks went pink.

Even though I wouldn't generally associate pink with men, there it was as plain as day. Flustered is another one, if his quivery, apologetic smile on his delicious looking lips meant anything. He moved back, holding out his hand to help me up.

Paperwork in hand, I stood on my own accord, and then the ground tilted. I would have fallen if it hadn't been for Mr. Quick-To-The-Rescue. One second he was a foot away, the next holding me in his warm arms.

The weak protest on my lips never came, probably due to delirium.

Strong arms scooped me up, then carried me as if I were as light as a pizza to the silver Beamer, and then opened the door to the back seat. For some reason, warning bells went off inside my head, but I couldn't formulate a protest.

Mr. Gorgeous gently deposited me on the soft kid leather seat, positioning my head on something supple but lumpy. He leaned over me. His fingers brushed the hair from my face and his beautiful lips moved, but with the buzzing in my ears and head, I couldn't process his words.

I closed my eyes. Heaven help me, at that moment, I knew without a doubt I could very well be in love with Mr. What's-His-Name, aka, Matthew Thomas Ainsley the Third.

Chapter 3

Voices woke me. They were coming from outside. *Outside where?*

My eyes popped open. My gaze searched my surroundings. That's when I realized I was lying in the very car I swore I would never enter.

Beyond the door, I could see two sets of legs. The one pair I recognized as Mr. Chick-Magnet, the owner of the very same vehicle I presently occupied and was sprawled all over the backseat. The other pair, clad in navy blue, utilitarian cloth, I didn't recognize.

Mr. Ainsley apparently felt the need to bring in reinforcements to back up his story, whatever story that might be.

Alerted by the groan I couldn't repress, my handsome _hittee_ and a young man in an officer's uniform bent down and peered into the backseat.

So I was wrong about the reinforcements. Shoot me. In my present condition, I can't be blamed.

"How are you feeling, Ms. Gates? I'm Officer Tally." This came from the police officer, and by the looks of him, my age, but baby-faced, with dimpled cheeks any mother would be proud to pinch. He had a pleasant smile ... handsome too. There's something about a man in uniform ... who could resist.

First thing when I get home, those romance books have gotta go.

"I'm fine." I pushed upward to sit.

"Oh, no, don't do that." The officer held out his hand to stop me, shaking his head, his concern, genuine.

"Yes, please stay where you are. An ambulance will be here any moment." That came from Mr. Solicitous himself.

"I don't need an ambulance. All I need is to get to work before I lose my job."

I moved to extricate myself from the car, but met resistance when Mr. I'm-In-Command restrained me by a slight pressure on my shoulder and standing in the middle of the doorway.

"You fainted. You need to be examined by a doctor. Stay put!"

I didn't like his authoritative tone. No one has told me what to do for some time now.

"If you won't move, I'll get out on the other side." I shifted in the seat.

"Come here." Mr. Knight-in-Tarnished-Armor motioned, then offered his hand to help me out of his silver Beamer.

"Thank you."

His fingers ... strong as suspected. His touch ... shocking and not expected at all. The jolt went through me, electrifying and turning every nerve in my body on fire, and my mind to putty.

I extricated my hand as quickly as possible, stepped away from him as soon as was respectable and without looking foolish, then wobbled.

His brawny arm snaked around my waist anchoring me to his side. When I gazed up at him, he watched through darkened eyes.

Brawny? From now on, it's Moby Dick or Robinson Crusoe.

I averted my gaze, pulled away, and straightened my clothes as best I could, taking a moment to clear my head from his nearness. Nonetheless, his eyes seemed to blaze a trail through my defenses, marking a path to my heart. I shook my head to get rid of such foolish thoughts.

His hand reached out to steady me.

Those romance novels have affected my brain.

"I'm fine. Really." Careful not to make any sudden moves for fear of a repeat of earlier, I glanced at the policeman. "I had them in my hand. My papers—"

"Are right here." Mr. Take-Charge held up the plastic packet in front of my face.

The nice Officer Tally smiled brightly at me. And of course, I offered one of my best to him.

"I've already seen your insurance card. Mr. Ainsley was good enough to give it to me. All I need from you is your license and your side of the story, if you're up to it."

"Let me get my purse." I moved toward Agnes and took my first real glimpse of my car.

Bumper on the ground. Red deflectors shattered into a million pieces littered the street. Both fenders wrinkled like crinkle fries—the left one sitting lopsided and loose. And her little hood looked like mangled shrink wrap, totally useless.

I couldn't help myself. I cried. Oh, not a *boo-hoo* out loud where anyone could hear me cry, but a deep, gut wrenching wail in my heart. Agnes had been faithful through the years to get me from point A to point B and back again without so much as a scratch, with only oil changes and minor engine repairs, until now. Now she looked forlorn and sad, and a little accusatory.

It wasn't my fault!

I glanced at the Beamer. There were a few surface scratches, a minor dent in one fender and one in the bumper, but other than that, nothing. The BMW must have run up and over Agnes' *bee*-hind.

I guess that's what you get when a luxury car owner can't be bothered to pay attention to his driving. Agnes was just too little to defend against such madness.

Reaching inside the open window for my purse, I found it on the seat. The contents were scattered on the floorboard, but no wallet.

I opened the door and began searching under the seat, behind the seat, on the side of the seat, even the back seat, but it wasn't there.

Gone! As in *nowhere to be found*. As in, *what am I going to do now?* Every last cent I owned was in my wallet—all twenty-five dollars and forty-three cents, everything I had scraped together this morning before leaving for work. The money was supposed to last me until I got my paycheck on Friday.

Pulling my head out of the car, I turned toward the two men. "Did either of you see my wallet? It's not in my car."

They advanced on me with questioning looks, wrinkled foreheads, and partially closed eyelids.

Did they think I was lying?

"What do you mean your wallet's missing?" This came from my new sidekick.

"Just what I said. It's not—"

"I heard you the first time."

"Then why'd you ask?"

He ignored my question. "Did you look under the seat?" Mr. I'm-Much-Smarter-Than-You moved me aside, none to gently I might add, then tried to insert himself into the small confines of Agnes, emitting a sharp groan when he hit his head on the roof. He rummaged about inside my car mumbling the whole time. He finally eased himself back out.

"No wallet."

I plopped my hands on my hips, giving him a squinted, disgusted look. "Isn't that what I just said?"

"There's no call for—"

"Why don't we step over here in the shade?" The sweet officer probably thought to advert a knock-down-drag-out for a minor fender-bender—Mr. Hotshot's reference, not mine.

By now, our little fender-bender had drawn a nice small crowd. Even Diane, from *Diane's' Hair, etc.,* if her embroidered name across her left bosom were any indication of her true identity, stood outside her shop door watching the show. She lifted her bejeweled hand, a green painted nail with a rhinestone on the tip and pointed somewhere down the block.

"Before you got here, I saw a young man by the green bug run and go in that direction. Didn't see him in the car though. Could've been him. It happened while he was putting her in the car." The rhinestone twinkled in Mr. Hittee's direction.

Officer Tally moved over by Diane.

She batted her long lashes at him as her ruby lips turned into a seductive smile. Which, I might add, she did quite nicely and without looking foolish.

If I had tried Diane's maneuver, Officer Tally would have probably hauled me off to jail and charged me for showing disrespect to a law officer.

I advanced on them both, a little wobbly on my legs, when I felt a hand grip my elbow. Though to be truthful, I smelled Mr. GQ's cologne long before his touch. He guided me with expert care.

Again, the rapid heartbeat, the upward spike in blood pressure, and a certain tingly sensation … *I'm a goner for sure.*

"He was about this tall." Diane reached up to Officer Tally's nose, twitched it as she smiled and batted her long come-hither lashes once more. "Had dark hair with bleached streaks. But not nearly as thick as your hair, Officer Tally."

"Why, thank you." He nearly melted on the spot. Much more and he'd be a puddle at her feet.

"He had olive colored skin, and ran like the dogs of Satan were chasing him."

"But, did you see the wallet?" This came from Mr. Sidekick.

Diane shook her head, her huge lashes fluttering in his direction. "No. So I can't be sure it was the young man." She glanced back at the officer, all peaches and cream. "I open my shop at eight in the morning." She winked.

I was afraid her lashes might get stuck together, but, miracle of miracles, they didn't.

Hmm. I wonder if I should ask her about purchasing a pair?

Her words, thick and syrupy as molasses, dripped like honey from her tongue. "I close at six, and leave for home around sevenish, that is if you need to ask me more questions."

My goodness. Diane was a novel waiting to happen. *I might have to write one just for her.*

If Officer Tally didn't get the hint Diane was throwing his way, then he didn't have as much on the ball as I thought.

Ahh, by the sparkle in his eyes, he knew what was what.

"Thanks, Mrs.—"

"*Msssz* Phillips. Never been married. No objection, mind you. Just never quite found someone to meet my requirements." Again the batting of lashes. This woman had it down to a science. She could give lessons in the art of flirting. *I wonder if she ever thought about offering classes.*

"But, I could be persuaded. I've always loved a man in uniform." A throaty, deep chuckle followed her last line.

I coughed.

Mr. Sidekick chuckled under his breath.

I wanted to laugh too, but didn't want to offend sweet Diane.

Since I didn't have a clue who had taken my wallet, my gaze roamed over the crowd wondering if the culprit was standing there enjoying his game of cat and mouse, or hide and seek, or whatever it was he might be playing. How could someone be so despicable to steal from another person who had been incapacitated and out for the count? I guess if a person was going to steal, what better opportunity while everyone else is distracted or unconscious.

Seeing no one of interest, I extracted my arm from Mr. Helpful since *Msssz* Phillips was keeping both men entertained with physical attributes I lacked. I headed over to Agnes to retrieve my cell phone, now resting on the front seat. Not knowing who to call for a tow truck, my finger stopped from dialing information when the sound of a loud diesel and the scraping and screeching gears drew my attention.

An old battered truck with a towing device hanging from the backend pulled in front of Agnes and stopped. The rusty door squealed in protest as a burly man hopped down out of the truck and began to limp in my direction. His beard was as long and white as ZZ Top's, but there the resemblance stopped.

"This here your vehicle?" He gave Agnes the once over, scrunching up his nose as though he sniffed something dead in the air like an old fish.

"Yes, sir." I wasn't sure I wanted to place Agnes in his hands. However, since no one else seemed to be coming to the rescue, this man would have to do.

"*Humph.*" He kicked the tire closest to him.

I wanted to kick his shin.

He brightened when he glanced over at the silver Beamer. "Now that's my idea of a ride."

"I'll bet." I mumbled under my breath.

"What'd you say, little lady."

I ignored his question and asked one of my own. "How much will it cost to tow Ag—my Volkswagen to a car repair place?"

"Well, that'll be seventy-five for the call, and another fifty for the tow, unless you go outside of a twenty-five mile radius, and then it will be a dollar a mile extra— payment on demand without proof of insurance."

"Tow it to the Volkswagen dealership in Dallas." Mr. I'm-In-Charge held out a card. "Here's my insurance information. Call and tell them it was my fault. They'll cover the costs."

Not sure I liked Mr. I'm-In-Charge taking over, I bristled, then thought, *let him. He was responsible and should pay.* I closed my mouth. With my head splitting and shooting pains down the back of my neck, I was in no condition to argue anyway.

After he dispatched the tow truck guy, he turned his mesmerizing gaze on me. "How are you feeling?"

"Not too bad. Just a little achy, which surprises me. I wouldn't think soreness would set in this fast. Almost like I have the beginnings of the flu, which I don't, of course."

"If you won't agree to a doctor taking a look at you, then allow me to drive you where you need to go since my car is still drivable."

He must have seen my look of suspicion.

"I have no designs on your person. You're not my type."

The last was added under his breath, but I heard it just the same. His words put a chink in my well-fortified armor and tarnished his. Talk about making a woman feel ugly and unwanted. *I wanted to ask what's wrong with me? Not rich enough? Not sophisticated? Not model like?* My blood boiled—that's been happening a lot since Mr. Mega-Bucks *tapped* into my little Agnes.

"I can call—" I looked down at my cell phone and found my battery was completely dead. I breathed out heavily. "My battery's dead. I'll accept your offer, if it's not too much trouble."

"Great. Get your things. After I make sure Officer Tally has everything he needs from us, I'll take you wherever you need to go." His smile seemed genuine and not forced, which was a good sign. At least he wasn't making me feel like I was an inconvenience.

My eyes strayed to his backside. *Get over it. He's not your type.*

Oh, yeah, what is my type? Not rich as Midas. More like Average Joe who might afford a night out once a week at the local DQ. Mr. Exec could afford fillet mignon, caviar, or lobster whenever the urge hit.

Tearing my eyes away from the magnificent display of manhood, I found his image lingered in my mind. Desire? Regret? Want? Not me. More like delirium from the wreck because I wasn't one to yearn for something that could never be.

Chapter 4

Though worried awkward silence would prevail, I slid into the small confines of Mr. Matthew Thomas Ainsley the Third's luxurious kid-leather seat as he held open the door. He handed me the seatbelt, as a father would do for a child, deflating my ego even further.

Mr. Manners walked around and then scooted behind the wheel. As soon as he started the ignition, soft music filled the compartment, accompanied only by the faint purr of the car engine. My enigmatic companion fell silent as he pulled away from the curb, his eyes intent on the road.

I leaned my head back, closed my eyes, doing my best to turn off my mind, but found it was difficult to ignore the attraction of the fascinating man less than a foot away.

The soothing strands from the orchestra weaved its magic and lolled me into a state of semi-consciousness. Another time, another place, maybe things would have been different.

Sun glistened off the knight's polished armor as he rode toward Judith. The ground trembled beneath the black stallion's hooves. Upon command from his master, the magnificent animal stiffened his legs and slid to a skidding halt several feet from the tent where Judith sat.

Murmurs rose from her family and from other McKinseys sitting nearby as the dust settled out of the air. The murmurs turned into a loud roar of dissent. Her clansmen had traveled two days to be present at the tournament of their sworn enemy.

The knight lowered his lance in Judith's direction and then waited. His mighty steed pawed at the ground, impatient to get back to the field of battle.

Slurs and insults were hurled at the knight, but he ignored them, his gaze intent on Lady Judith McKinsey.

A hush settled over the spectators. All eyes were turned in Judith's direction. The purple silk, though delicate and soft, seemed to burn her hand as she wove the cloth through her anxious fingers.

To do this deed, Judith knew her family and her clan would be lost to her forever. She'd be expunged completely, her name never to be spoken again. Her clan would be her enemy.

A silence, more deafening than the cheers seconds ago, mocked her spirit. Right or wrong, her heart wept for the choice she was about to make. Filled with bleak sadness, her arms protested as she lifted them, knotting the silk to the lance.

The deed was done. No turning back. She had made her choice.

A unified rumble of hate tore through those standing around Judith as cheers from across the field rent the air. Tears fell down her cheeks as a portion of her heart rent in two. She looked up at her champion knowing she belonged to him now and forever. The cost ... her family.

The knight snapped his face guard up. Judith witnessed love as she looked into the eyes of—

"Where do I take you?"

My eyes snapped open pulling me out of my story. I looked over at Mr. Hunk and recognized the very face I had envisioned as my hero in my new novel *Surrender at Dusk*.

Shock rendered me speechless. Fortunately, all I saw was his profile, no eye-to-eye contact. I was uncertain what I would have said if Mr. Ruggedly-Handsome had looked at me at that exact moment. I took a second or two to recover from the stunned knowledge—I had put Mr. Tarnished-Knight into Sir Rolf's shoes—or whatever a medieval knight wore on his feet.

Thankfully, I had enough presence of mind to give him the address.

When he said nothing more, I allowed the silence to surround me as music played in the background once again. I gave myself a good mind thrashing for being so foolish to envision Mr. Richie-Rich as Sir Rolf of my book. Once again, the strings of violins seduced me, weaving their magic through my overactive imagination.

I pushed all thoughts aside, closed my eyes, and gave my spirit over to the soft cello strands coming from the surround sound.

Rolf looked deep into Judith's eyes, his promise of undying love was there for all to see. He accepted her favor by the dip of his lance, and then pulled it straight up.

The wind caught the cloth, billowing out the purple silk high above horse and rider. As were good manners, the knight gave a nod of acknowledgement to her father, the chieftain.

A roar of hatred erupted from Judith's father and filled the tent, spilling over to her clansmen as they showed loathing for the knight and her choice.

Another loving glance at Judith, then with a flick of Sir Rolf's finger, the face guard slid back in place. He nudged his black beauty with his knees and rode off to the end of the field to face his next challenger and his—

The blasting sounds of hard rock music jerked me out of my reverie. I glared at my companion alarmed and too shaken to articulate my true feelings on his choice of listening pleasure.

"Sorry about that." A sheepish grin accompanied by a not-so-innocent-look made me wonder if he was truly sorry, or had he planned the chaotic interruption. He touched some buttons, and the music vanished. Silence—an awkward, nail-biting, anxious-filled silence took over.

I glanced out the window.

I shifted in my seat.

I adjusted my blouse.

I smoothed down my pant legs.

I brushed off a wayward piece of nonexistent lint.

I cleared my throat, and, just in time, stopped myself from humming.

"By your insurance card, I noticed you're not a resident of Waxahachie. How long have you lived in Midlothian?"

My natural, God-given radar zinged though my veins pumping anxious blood to my heart. I searched his face for a clue to some nefarious plan he might be hatching. My protective armor clinked back in place. I feverishly tried to decipher what he might be fishing for or where he could be heading with his question.

Certainly not conversation. My address? He already had it because of the wreck. Should I be suspicious? Alarmed?

No. He, Mr. Most-Eligible-Bachelor, wouldn't have any designs on this nondescript little ol' wren—*me.* However, after all those years of mama doing her best to drill into me what to do and not to do, her instructions and training came to the forefront. Let him try. He wasn't about to ferret out much info from me.

"Not long."

My Knight-in-Tarnished-Armor gave a quick, puzzled glance before turning those brilliant green eyes back to the road. "Where did you live before?"

"Here and there."

His brows puckered and he looked incredulous.

"Anywhere specific, like a name of a town?"

Laughter wrinkles appeared, and his small chuckle began to do unmentionable things to my stomach—and I don't mean like when I'm hungry either, more like tying it into knots and all quivery-like. However, by his expression, he seemed to be trying his best to figure me out and hadn't quite gotten there yet.

Figure away, Mister. I'm a tough nut to crack.

"I lived in Dallas before moving to Midlothian."

"What kind of work do you do?"

"Pardon me?" *The man's definitely on a fishing expedition, but looking for what?*

"You mentioned you'd be late for work. Just curious. What do you do?"

Apparently, Mr. Type-A-Personality hadn't recognized the address I had given him. "I work as a clerk at Hadley's Department Store."

"Oh."

Wellll! Talk about sucking all the air out of the car and turning on the deep freeze. Mr. Frost froze me to the bone, along with deflating my ego, if I had one in the beginning. He lost interest quicker than I could flatten a balloon with a pin, if he ever had any interest to begin with.

My career was nothing so glamorous as a model, actress, or even an executive of a corporation. Just a measly little shop clerk, writing romance novels on her off time. For sure, the writing part was something Mr. Uninterested wouldn't pry from my lips, unless I made it to the big times.

> *New York Times Best Seller, Tiffany Ann Gates, writer extraordinaire, author of the year, and notable speaker, has landed a million dollar book contract and a five million dollar movie deal.*

Do writers get paid that much?

Oh, I can see it now, Mr. Matthew Thomas Ainsley the Third in Barnes & Noble looking for a book. There, in front of him, on an easel, is my larger-than-life picture along with the title of my latest novel. The bookshelf beside my photo is full of my novels with people right and left ripping the books off the shelf begging …

Oh, forget it. I'm a long way from being published. And at the moment, what I need most is to give some serious thought to how I'm going to keep my job at Hadley's.

Surely, Mr. Hadley wouldn't fire me. I shoved the nasty thought right out of my mind.

With Mr. Silent next to me showing no interest in furthering *his* conversation, I leaned back against the headrest once again and closed my eyes. No use explaining to Mr. I'm-So-Rich how proud I was to have a job, especially since so few were hiring.

I'm sure he could care less that I've been working my way through college for the last ten years, hoping to set the world on fire upon graduation. Then, with the downturn in the economy, to be reduced to taking whatever job I could find. *Humiliating.* Yet, I'm thankful for the job I do have, even if shop clerk wasn't my first choice—more like my one hundred and ninety-third.

As a clerk at Hadley's the work wasn't bad, the hours weren't great, and the pay was lousy. But it kept the proverbial wolf from my door. However, Mr. Hadley's grandson was the mouse dropping on the cake.

One thing I learned early on in my employment at the store—never get caught in the back stockroom alone when Stewey Hadley was on duty. It took only once to learn that lesson. From that time to this, I have avoided the stock room, fitting room, and any other room. I even checked the lady's restroom before entering. I avoid Stewey like the bubonic plague.

Hands-On is the name the other women dubbed Stewey. In my mind, he's more like an octopus. Most times, it seemed as though he had a dozen arms and hands all moving, grabbing, and reaching at the same time. There are times when it's impossible to avoid him. And he doesn't give up easily either.

Sleazy Hands-On has tried his best to mash me up against the counter, the merchandise rack, even the square post with the fire extinguisher. *The post incident* ... I pulled down the extinguisher and threatened to open fire if he didn't leave me alone.

The slimy guy even went so far as to run his hand across my backside one time—the only escape was to squeeze between the manikin and clothes rack. The manikin's head bounced onto the floor creating a horrible racket.

I could have rectified the incident if the head hadn't rolled down the aisle and stopped at Mr. Hadley's feet. Hands-on Stewey used the diversion to make his escape.

That time, I thought I'd lost my job for sure, but thankfully, I didn't. I believe the man knows what his grandson is—*a pervert.*

The last six months, I've learned some pretty fancy footwork to maneuver around Stewey—footwork the NFL would do well to pay me to incorporate into their plays.

The car slowed. I opened my eyes. The Beamer pulled to the curb in front of Hadley's. Grabbing my purse strap, I made a move to open the door.

"Just a minute." Mr. Silent turned and stretched toward me.

My purse in a death grip against my underly-enhanced chest, I hugged the door with my legs for a ready escape, then noticed he was reaching into the back seat. I relaxed and did as instructed. I waited.

It's a shame, but after today, he'll probably have a permanent imprint of my knee in his cushy, leather door panel.

"Let me give you my card." He grabbed his wrinkled coat from the back seat, the very same one my head had rested upon. Pulling out a silver holder, he retrieved a card, then slipped the small case back inside the pocket. Next, he extracted a money clip, pulled some bills loose, and began shucking off several one hundred dollar bills. He held both card and cash out to me. "I know you don't have any money—"

"No!" The word came out too loud, too vehement. Did he think I was a charity case? I felt my face do a slow burn. My hand shoved the money back toward my philanthropic companion.

"Your wallet was stolen. I feel certain, so were credit and debit cards and your money. Am I correct?"

His eyes delved deep inside me, making me squirm. I couldn't tell a lie, so I nodded. There was no need to tell him I didn't own a credit or debit card. Nor could I say all the money I had in the world until payday was gone along with my wallet. It was none of his business.

"Thought so. This will give you some money for lunch and until you can get to the bank."

Eeeek! What does this man think I eat for lunch? Three hundred dollars would last me a month of Sundays, and I don't mean the ice cream kind either. I knew he could tell I was going to refuse.

"Take it please. It'll tide you over. I'll feel much better knowing you aren't without money." He shoved it toward me again. "You can use this for incidentals. Call it a loan."

"With interest." I was weakening and he knew it.

A smirk road his kissable lips. *Whoa, girl. Get a grip.*

"If you insist. With interest." He nailed me with his brilliant green eyes. And then he placed the money and business card in my hand, his fingers grazing mine ever so slightly.

Again, the rush of excitement zinged though my veins all the way to my toes. "Th-thanks. I-I appreciate the loan."

"If you have any trouble with the insurance paying for your car or doing the work satisfactorily, give me a call." He pointed at the card in my hand. "A car will be delivered within the hour for you to use while yours is being repaired." He gave me a long, hard stare.

I wanted to fidget, slick down my hair, or something, but resisted the urge.

"Are you sure you won't let me take you to a doctor for a checkup?"

"No. I'm fine." I shook my head and gave him what I hoped was a brilliant smile, even though the jackhammer was still pounding in my head.

"All right then. Sorry about the accident." His smile helped to soften the blow I felt over Agnes.

"Thank you for the ride. And I'll have the money returned to you in a few days."

"No rush. Take your time. Let me know if I can be of service."

I scooted out of the car as fast as I could and shut the door. *Be of service* reverberated around in my brain.

Refusing to watch the Silver Bullet pull away from the curb and drive one of the most eligible bachelors in Texas out of my life, I moved toward the entrance of Hadley's. I wasn't going to, but unable to stop myself, I cheated. At the last second, I turned to watch the BMW go around the corner and out of sight.

I'm of weak resolve. I admit it. But how often does a gal get that close to a rich, handsome, no nix that, gorgeous specimen of a man? The kind of man one only dreams about.

Never.

Chapter 5

Entering Hadley's, my eyes slowly adjusted to the light. A couple of the clerks gave me *Uh-oh* looks, as much as to say *you're in trouble* and *what happened to you?*

I glanced to the back of the building where Mr. Hadley stood with a stern, hostile look locked directly on me. I knew this wouldn't be my finest hour.

He raised his hand and crooked his index finger, beckoning me like one of those villains in the old black and whites Grams and Mom used to be fond of watching. The kind of movie where the lady in distress knows full well the outcome won't be good.

"Ms. Gates, I want a word with you in my office." His eyes bugged out more than usual. His face turned several shades of dark, then darker, even thunderous dark, if a dark can be called thunderous.

I drew in a deep breath, squared my shoulders, and then marched like a doomed convict to the execution room. Understanding my employer's zero tolerance for tardiness and messy appearance, I hoped he would listen to my explanation first, accept it for the truth, and not terminate me on the spot.

Courageously, shaking in my shoes, I followed Mr. Hadley, determined to meet my punishment head on.

I need this job! I need this job at least until a better one comes along or one of my books sells and makes the Best Sellers' List, which ain't gonna happen anytime soon.

Mr. Hadley moved up the dark stairwell. Though skinnier than someone on a starvation diet, each rung creaked beneath his feet. How Stewey and he could be related was a mystery.

Wishing I had time to go to the ladies' room and at least make a stab at looking presentable before my interview with death, I followed. The sounds mocked me all the way to the top of the stairs. *Creak-eek. You're fired. Creak-eek. You're fired. Creak-eek* ... all the way to Hadley's office.

The office held a musty, stuffy odor. In contrast to everything downstairs visible to the public, this room looked like it hadn't seen a good cleaning in at least a decade.

Rumpled, discarded McDonald bags littered the floor. Surely, they belonged to the scourge upon the earth, Hands-on Stewey.

Seated at his ancient desk, Mr. Hadley's head peered at me over the stacks of ledgers, files, and mounds of paperwork.

I waited for my punishment, refusing to quake.

"Ms. Gates. I would like an explanation as to your appearance and tardiness."

A squeak, more like what would come from a door in a haunted house, came from Mr. Hadley's chair as he leaned back. He placed his elbows on the cracked leather armrests, then steepled his boney fingers in front of his chest. His beady-eyed stare didn't waver from my face one iota.

I had the feeling I was on trial and subjected to the scrutiny of my executioner. The very thought made me uneasy, wanting to run a finger along the inside of my collar, but I didn't.

I cleared my throat, stood up straight, giving it my best shot.

"Being late was directly due to my wreck on the way to work. Well, sir, come to think of it, that's not exactly correct. A man tail-ended my car. I really had nothing to do with the accident, except for being there at the wrong place, wrong time. He claims all fault for what happened. It was bad enough that a tow truck had to haul Ag—my VW off to the car dealership. So you see, my appearance is a direct result of the wreck." I touched my head gingerly and winced.

When I saw no concern for my welfare in Mr. Hadley's face, I continued. "My head received a cut, but not to worry, I'll be quite all right." I took a calming breath. "A few minute in the ladies' room and I feel sure I can put everything in order and come out looking presentable and ready for work."

Taking a deep breath, I waited for what seemed an eternity as Mr. Hadley rocked back and forth in his chair. *Squeak-squeeeak, squeak-squeeeak.* His gaze turned upward to the ceiling.

"A wreck you say." *Squeak, thump.* The chair plopped upright. Again that stare, but this time, I feel certain, it was to see if I were lying. The *tick, tick, tock* of the antique Regulator clock made my wait seem interminable.

"Very well. I will excuse you *this* time. But in the future, tardiness and a slothful appearance will not be tolerated." His beady eyes looked down his long, narrow nose at me. "I'll give you exactly ten minutes to right yourself and not a minute longer, otherwise …"

His unspoken words hung between us, but I knew their meaning.

"Thank you, sir." I moved with haste out the door, down the stairs, and smack-dab into—*Stewey Hadley*.

"*Wellll*, what have we here. A little worse for wear aren't we?"

His greasy, puffy face looked hot and flushed, like he'd been running a marathon. Probably chasing one of the women clerks in the back room. Several of his red puffy pimples, the size of Mount Vesuvius, looked ready to explode and ooze down his bloated, sweaty face.

Like the villain in those old silent films, Stewey's malicious smile made my stomach churn. Not in the same way it had with Mr. Ainsley. More like regurgitate, deathly ill, ready to vomit kind of churn.

"Excuse me, Stewey. I need to get to work."

I pushed his chest. My hand sunk three inches into his blubbery flesh, but didn't do a thing to move him out of my way. I snatched my fingers back and couldn't wait to wash them.

His intentions were written across his face even before his hands began to move in my direction, closing off my escape.

"How's 'bout you and me doing a little fooling around before work. It looks like you could use a little something to loosen you up a bit." His bushy, caterpillar brows jumped up and down.

I wanted to squash them to see if they would stop wiggling.

"I'm serious Stewey. Get out of my way or I'll scream." I backed up a step and then another.

Hands-On followed, getting closer, the smell of his sickly sweet cologne gagging me.

"Now, honey, you don't want to scream. You don't want Grandpa coming to see what you've been up to, do you? Just a little kiss, then I'll let you pass. Come on, you'll enjoy it."

"In your dreams, you moron. Now move."

He advanced.

I backed up.

He advanced some more.

I backed up some more.

My heel caught in the rug runner and I fell backward. With a vengeance, my rear-end hit the edge of the stair tread and shot more pain up into my already aching body.

Hands-On moved in for the kill. He lunged at me.

I dodged, scampering to one side of the small stairwell, which wasn't easy. Stewey's three hundred plus pounds fell forward, crushing one of my legs beneath his, but the rest of his marshmallow body hit the hard wood surface with a thud. I heard the clunk of his head, along with the full impact of soft flesh meeting hard, unmovable wood. Air whooshed out of his mouth along with a groan.

The smell of stale tuna fish and something else I didn't care to distinguish filled my nostrils.

"*Aughhh!*" I gagged, shoving with all my might. "Get off of me, you pervert."

I freed my leg from beneath the unmoving dead weight, and scrambled to my feet. Stewey stayed in his prone position, moaning and wallowing in pain.

I watched in disgust.

"What is the meaning of this, Ms. Gates?" Mr. Hadley stood at the head of the stairwell looking like an avenging gargoyle, eyes blazing a path down the stairs to where I stood.

Stewey rolled over, lumbered into a sitting position on one of the steps, holding his head in his hands. Another moan, but this time for affect.

"She made a pass at me. When I wouldn't play her little game, she tripped me, Grandfather."

"Why, you liar. I did no such thing." I trembled with indignation, wishing I could roast that no-good, lying marshmallow over an open pit. My hands rolled into tight fists and I gave him a *just you dare me* stare. "You were the one—"

"Enough!" The harsh voice bellowed from the top of the stairs, reaching, without a doubt, all the way to the front door of the store. "Ms. Gates, leave your badge at the front register. You'll get no second chance. You're fired."

"Fired?"

Stewey's smirk went all through me. My hand itched to give him a sucker punch in the middle of his bloated face.

"You're firing me when it's your grandson's fault? It's certainly not for anything I've done except to protect myself from this demented and depraved yellow belly snake who can't keep his hands off any woman under fifty. Let him tell you what he does to all the helpless sales women in the back storeroom. Or how he's—"

"Ms. Gates, that's enough. Leave the premises immediately or I'll call the police."

"I'm going. But I've got a good mind to sue your store for sexual harassment—naming *little* Stewey here in the complaint and you as his accomplice. What do you think about that? Huh?"

"Leave now!"

"I'm going. I'm going."

Mr. Hadley went to his office and slammed the door, certain I would follow his orders.

I hitched the strap of my purse on my shoulder and turned to leave, frustrated beyond reason that I couldn't wipe the arrogant, smug smile off Stewey's face.

"I know you wanted some, Sugar. You shouldn't have played hard to get. Your loss. But then—"

Stewey's nasty whispered comments had me turning around. The vulgar gestures he made with his hands were the last straw.

I raised my arm and swung with all my might. My hand made contact with the side of his red, blotchy face. I felt the sting of the blow all the way to my elbow. Stewey's bellow of pain and whimpers made me feel good from the top of my head to the tip of my toes.

Without a backward glance, I tried not to limp as I made my way through the small gathering in the hall and others who were hovering in the aisle. My leg pained me something awful where Stewey had pinned me against the stairwell.

I was rewarded with silent cheers and pats on my back from my ex-coworkers, which caused me to redden for acting so rashly. But a girl's gotta do what a girl's gotta do to defend her honor. Men like Hands-On Stewey deserved what he got and a whole lot worse.

Stepping outside into the sunshine, for the first time in several months, I felt lighthearted, and ... almost broke down crying.

What am I gonna do?

Chapter 6

Standing out front of Hadley's, I glanced in both directions and realized my day had gone from bad to worse. No job. No car. No money, except for the borrowed three hundred dollars burning a hole in my purse from Mr. Richie-Rich.

What more could happen? Is a meteorite gonna fall from the sky and hit me on the head?

Tears smarted. A heavy knot, the size of an ostrich egg, formed in the pit of my empty stomach. My gut twisted and then twisted again. I chased around one horrible scenario after another.

Even with Mr. Ainsley's three hundred dollars, if my state of unemployment lasted longer than a month, I'd be toast. I'd be out of my little efficiency apartment and on the street. But I refused to give in to worry. If I ever started, I'd never stop.

The money!

I rammed my hand down inside my purse making sure the bills were still where I had put them. Thankfully, I found the money along with *his* card. I ran my finger over the top of the embossed printing, knowing this card didn't come from one of those quickie print places online or do-it-yourself kind where the perforation never tears smoothly and leaves little bumps on the edge—dead give-away it's a do-it-yourself job. No this card was first class and costly, just like everything else belonging to Mr. Big-Bucks.

The money mocked me. I should have never taken the three hundred dollars. What was I thinking? And then to stupidly blurt out *with interest*. My head should be examined. I should have shoved it right back at him.

Mama's words came rushing in and bounced around in my brain … *Pride cometh before a fall.* Oh, boy, had I ever fallen. I didn't have two quarters to rub together, let alone interest for the bills burning their imprint into my palm.

 Maybe he'll let me take what I owed him out in trade. My face burned and not from the sun. *I just bet he would.* But I wasn't about to stoop that low.

The big question … how would I pay him back with interest?

I moved down the street out of sight of Hadley's storefront windows, found a relatively clean spot on the curb out of the direct sun, then plopped down to wait for the promised rental car.

Oh, what I would give for a chocolate bar.

A glance at my watch made me aware I'd been dropped off over an hour ago—yet no rental car. Home was too far to walk, especially in these shoes. I'd be hard put to get there by dark.

If my cell phone had been charged instead of being deader than a rat in a trap, or if my wallet with all my money and change hadn't been stolen by a despicable cretin, I would give Mr. Matthew Thomas Ainsley the Third a call. The urge to succumb to self-pity pricked at my eyelids.

Standing, I brushed my backside off, crossed the street, then headed down the three blocks to the First Bank and Trust. I figured I'd exchange one of the three hundred dollar bills for smaller ones and some change. Then I would give Mr. Exec a call to remind him about the rental car.

Who carries around one hundred dollar bills anyway? Didn't Mr. Big-Bucks know there were other denominations like ones, fives, or tens? Even a little pocket change would have been nice.

Feeling dejected and alone, I did the next best thing. I surrounded my mind with a particularly difficult scene in my novel.

> *The servants removed the last of the trenchers from the table, and with a silent command from Lord Sebastian, the steward poured more wine into Judith's cup until she waved him off. Sebastian moved to her side and slid onto the bench closer to where she sat.*
>
> *"Lady Judith."*
>
> *His oily voice did nothing to alleviate her fear of the man.*
>
> *"My brother, Rolf has requested we become better acquainted. After all, I am your brother, also, since you married Rolf. It makes us kin, you see. We should become good friends, don't you think?"*
>
> *The sickly smile raised goose flesh on Judith's arms. A chill crawled up her spine, tingling the hairs at the back of her neck. She leaned away, putting distance between her and her step-brother-in-law.*
>
> *"Come now, my dear, this is no way to treat kin."*
>
> *He latched onto her upper arm, pulling her back to his side, his putrid breath hot on her turned cheek. She reached for her wine, her hand*

latched onto the goblet. She tried to pull away but when Sebastian didn't allow her to move, she threw the contents—

"Yuck! Disgusting! Who in the world?"

There I stood, splashed and dripping from head to toe in ugly, black, filthy, slimy gunk, comprised of things I shuddered to imagine. I barely held myself back from throwing a temper tantrum right in the middle of the sidewalk. Could things get worse?

You would think the idiot driving could see I was there on the sidewalk and would try to miss the hole filled with putrid muck? Surely he knew I would be splashed? Or did he care?

My rage flared as I rained down curses of the nicest kind on the stupid man's head. I wished I could pound the driver into the ground for his thoughtlessness, or at the very least smear the foul muck all over his face.

Covered from head to toe, I swiped at the stuff dripping from my chin, regurgitated to the point of almost throwing up. As I pulled out what few tissues were in my purse, I gave a quick prayer I wouldn't contract some awful, contagious disease and die from the filth covering me. Or maybe catch some decaying infection that would eat my flesh off down to the bone.

I'm not a hypochondriac or anything, but still the stuff was disgusting and smelled worse. I swiped my face while I continued to mutter horrible curses down on the thoughtless driver.

May he be turned into a toad. May his children track mud all through his house. May he rot in ...

Wiping the nasty stuff from my face as best I could, I heard the screech of tires. I looked up to find the car that had launched all the dreadful filth on me, stop. The driver did a quick U-turn, passed me, and then made another U-turn.

Oh, great! There was still enough muck and sludge left in the street crater for the driver to have another go at me. Maybe the psycho was coming back for a bonus pass to complete the job.

I scurried back away from the street.

The black car pulled over by the curb, stopped with the window making a slow decent into the door cavity.

Shock of shocks. There sat Mr. Neat-'n-Tidy himself.

I seethed inside, wanting to give the guy a good piece of my mind, but afraid if I did, I wouldn't be able to stop. Or better yet, my fingers itched to sling some of the horrible gunk back at him. Instead, I gathered what little sanity I had left and plastered a genuine fake smile on my face.

"Were you the one who so graciously deposited all this wonderful, filthy slime all over me that will no doubt give me some contagious, flesh-eating disease?"

"Sorry. Guilty as charged." Mr. Oops made an adorable sheepish face trying for contrite. He almost managed the feat until a tiny crack of a smile lurked at the edge of his lips and then he started outright laughing.

"I thought that was you. Sorry about all that." He waved his hand like a magician, but nothing disappeared. The gook was still there all over me and my clothes.

"I'm glad you're having a good laugh at my expense."

Mr. Pristine, with his gorgeous smile and twinkling eyes, almost caused my temper to evaporate. Still, I did my best to hold on to a small portion of my righteous anger.

"I tried to avoid the puddle, but I see I didn't quite miss."

"Oh-ho, really?" I did a Vanna White flourish with my hand. "What does a little filthy road film, mud, and who knows what else matter. There's still a little left. Would you like to take another go at it?" Sarcasm dripped like sorghum from my lips.

That's when I remembered my landlady, Mrs. MacIntosh's words—sin in haste, repent in leisure—what does that mean anyway? Take your time repenting? Or, maybe I could kill the guy and then take all the time in the world to think about saying I'm sorry—*what?*

"I think I'll pass. I did enough damage the first go around."

Mr. Non-Repentant smiled again turning my insides out. I took a deep breath, praying for patience, which at this minute was in short supply, then said, "Please forgive my sarcasm. As you well know, this just hasn't been my day."

I hoped Mr. Clean wouldn't recognize how close I had come to losing it altogether. Beneath all the dirt and grime, I wanted to strangle someone. At the moment, Mr. Perfect looked like the ideal candidate, but I kept that last thought to myself.

"You do look a mess. I apologize." Again, he waved his hand sideways, and then up and down, looking more like the pope pronouncing a blessing.

"Gee thanks." My hands swiped downward over my pants, making my slacks turn a pukey vomit-brown. Knowing nothing would help my appearance but a bath and a change of clothes, I gave Mr. Spotless another disgusted look. After which, I received a modicum of pleasure.

"I thought you'd be at work. I did say a car would be delivered to you." He looked a little put out over the trouble I seemed to be causing *him*.

"In an hour."

"What's in an hour?"

"The car was supposed to be delivered to me in an hour. It's—"

"I'm only fifteen minutes late. You should have waited at work. If you had, this would have never happened." He raised his brow along with a competent shrug.

Welll, excuuuuse me! "I would have been at work, but ...." I clamped my mouth shut. I wasn't about to tell Mr. I've-Got-the-World-By-the-Tail I'd been fired. He'd really think I was a loser then.

"I was headed to the bank to cash one of the hundreds you loaned me so I could buy some lunch." The lie slipped off my tongue like sugar from a spoon and, at the same time, chafed like sand inside a bathing suit.

Oh, do I ever need to repent, but not just now—not in front of Mr. My-World-Is-Perfect.

A little attitudinal adjustment wouldn't hurt either.

After a dubious look thrown in my direction, he flashed his pearly-white, orthodontic smile. His parents must have spent thousands to make his teeth perfect and flawless.

"Hop in. I'll ... buy your lunch. That's the least I can do."

And just why the pregnant pause? Second guessing before he spoke? Didn't want the muck in his car?

I had nailed it on the head. I gave him a look of *are you kidding?*

"Or we could grab some take-out, whichever you'd prefer." He leaned over, shoved the passenger door open, waiting for me to slide in.

I gave a momentary pause, then *why not.* After all, he's the one responsible for my messed up clothes and day—well maybe not all. Stewey's part couldn't be discounted.

"Take-out," I said grumpily. Without thinking, I turned my back to him. "Is there any black gunk on my bottom?" As the words left my mouth, I wanted to snatch them back.

A chuckle from inside the car prompted a hurried turn around and a quick scoot into the seat. And furthermore, I didn't care if I wore the muddy mess on my backside or not. He deserved what he got on his upholstery for that chuckle.

Again my face and neck were on fire, probably an adverse reaction from the muddy substance I now wore. *Good grief, now I'm even lying to myself.*

"Take-out it is."

He pulled away from the curb as I fiddled with the seatbelt.

"What kind?"

"What?" This man could make a basket case out of a sane person.

He shook his head. "What kind of food would you like? Or do you want me to choose?"

"You choose." I hoped he would take the matter out of my hands, or maybe change his mind and go back to work. Then I squinted in his direction and gave him a glance of uncertainty. "I thought a person from the rental company would be delivering the car. Why you? Shouldn't you be busy or something—doing mega million dollar deals, or whatever you do?"

He gave me a strange look before flashing that million dollar smile again. "Yes, I'm extremely busy. However, I thought since it was my fault—the wreck that is—I would deliver the car in person. What time do you need to be back at work?"

"Oh, ah-I have the rest of the day off." *And all the other days too, thanks to Stewey.*

"Then, you won't mind dropping me off at my office, once we pick up the food." He raised his brow in question. His eyes twinkled as if enjoying a private joke.

"Sure. That's the least I can do since you're acting delivery boy."

A loud ring came through the car's speaker system. Mr. Swift punched a button on the steering wheel. "Matthew, here."

"Matt, this is James. I just finished my call with Felderman in New York. He's ready to move on this now. How soon do you want it to happen?"

"Yesterday."

A pleasant deep rumble of laughter came over the speakers. "In your dreams, but let me see what I can do. Will you be back in the office soon?"

"Give me an hour. Make that an hour and a half."

"Will do."

The phone disconnected.

"Sorry about that." Mr. Business glanced at me, then back on the road.

"That's okay. I don't need to be entertained. I'm just glad to have a ride." My stomach took that moment to rumble.

"And food."

"I didn't take time to eat breakfast this morning and as you just heard, I'm starved."

He pushed something on the steering wheel.

"Give a command." The woman-voice computer startled me.

"Call LuWing Restaurant." He gave me a quick look. "You do like Chinese food, don't you?"

"Yes, I love it."

"Calling LuWing Restaurant Business." Again the computer voice.

The phone rang over the speaker again. Someone answered, and Mr. Take-Charge ordered several items to go, with extra fortune cookies, then disconnected.

My stomach growled in anticipation.

"Is your office in Waxahachie?"

"Yes, one of them. You don't mind dropping me off there, do you?"

He has more than one office? None of my business. "Of course not, it's the least I can do."

Minutes later, the car swung into the parking lot of an outrageously expensive Chinese restaurant, the kind I've only dreamt of entering. He put the gear in park, opened the door, but before shutting it, he leaned down. "Chopsticks or fork?"

"Chopsticks."

"I'll see if I can get some wet cloths too."

When I looked questioningly at him, he laughed and gestured in my direction. "You've got a little dirt on you. I thought you might want to wash some of it off before you eat."

Humiliated, I offered a weak, "Thanks."

He chuckled, sprinted to the restaurant door, and then out of sight.

Why was Mr. CEO giving me his personal attention. Was he worried I would file a lawsuit?

Chapter 7

With the few minutes it would take before my companion would be back with the food, I thought it best to look at the damage he had done. Hopefully, I could clean some of the muck off of my face and hands.

One glance in the visor mirror had me cringing. I looked like a child who had been out playing in the mud. Opening my purse, I dug around inside until I came up with a pink package of Wet Ones.

Using the wipes, I cleaned my hands, my face, and some of the blood out of my hair, which took some effort to remove the now dry gook that seemed to act more like black glue.

When I finished that task, I turned my attention to the dirt on my clothes, but found they were beyond redemption and I was running out of wipes.

Finding my comb, I ran it through my hair. I pulled debris and other suspect objects from the congealed dirty blonde strands that were stuck together and resisting my efforts. Somehow I succeeded in freeing most of the filthy stuff. I secured my hair at the back with a clip, and though still a little worse for wear, I felt a bit more presentable.

From my peripheral, I caught Mr. Gorgeous coming out of the restaurant. I shoved the soiled wipes under my seat, stashed my purse on the floor board, and then waited, hands in lap. To say I was a little disconcerted allowing a virtual stranger to buy my lunch, even if he was a rich one, was putting it mildly. In a way, he owed me. He hit Agnes, I lost my job—Stewey's fault not his—and then he splashed filth all over me, but …

Oh, well, too late now.

He opened my door, handed me the sacks, a damp, white industrial cloth, and then walked around and slid into the drivers' seat. My stomach rumbled again at the smell of food.

"Since I haven't had lunch either, I thought we could have a picnic before you drop me off at my office. There's a little park right around the corner."

I wanted to send up a protest and tell him *no*, but thought it might sound mean-spirited since he bought the food.

"Thanks, but … if you don't have time, I can wait to eat until I get home."

"And have you keel over? I don't think so." He gave me a quick glance that turned into surprise, then pleasure. "Except for the clothes, which I believe I owe you a whole new outfit, you clean up pretty well. How'd you do it? Lick and spit?" He laughed.

"*Yuck!* No. Had some Wet Ones in my purse." I lowered my gaze and feigned interest in the sacks on my lap, my face blazing. I didn't want to think what pleasing him did to my emotions.

He turned into a drive and found a place in the shade to park. When he came around to open my door, my brain went into overdrive.

This isn't a date. It's lunch. Save it for your novel.

My heart wouldn't listen. The silly thing swelled as every nerve stood alert, anticipating his touch, then shriveled to the size of a pea when Mr. Hands-Off didn't touch me. Instead, he took the sacks and then walked over to a picnic table leaving me to trail behind.

You're acting like a silly schoolgirl or one of the heroines in your novels. This is a platonic lunch. A man being thoughtful, nothing more. No expectations. No attraction. Nothing—period!

The park, with a small lake and flowering bushes throughout, was deserted except for a sprinkling of people. Sprawled on a park bench a little distance away, a man with a newspaper over his face seemed out for the count. A mother and two children was in the playground—the woman swinging the little girl, while the boy climbed to the top of the slide.

"This looks like a nice shady spot. What do you think? Will this do?"

"Yes." *Is that all you can say? Yes? Think of something—questions to ask, comments on the park, be entertaining, not a bump on a pickle.*

I looked around, stumbled, and would have landed on my face if Mr. Johnny-On-The-Spot hadn't caught me and led me to the table.

You don't have to be that entertaining.

One by one, he tore the sacks down the middle, spreading them open for placemats, one for each of us.

"Your utensils."

He held out a pair of black, plastic chopsticks, placed a bowl in front of me, and then proceeded to open six carry-out Chinese boxes full of food and two small containers of sauce, one sweet and sour, the other some type of soy sauce mixture. He set them in the middle, between us. Next came two tall cups of steaming hot tea.

Scraping a little out of each box into my bowl, he then filled his before motioning with his chopsticks. "Dig in."

The smell floated in the air. My mouth watered, aching for food as my stomach tightened with eagerness as I did as instructed. I dug in. Neither of us talked while we shoveled in food—he a starving billionaire, me a starving down-on-my-luck, out-of-work gal.

In my novels I would have described this lunch quite differently.

> *The birds sang as the light breeze blew across*
> *the fresh mown grass. The echo of children*
> *playing drifted on the wind. Lizzie, filled with*
> *excitement, gazed into Matt's—*

I yanked myself out of the daydream and back into the here and now. This wasn't a romantic get-away for two, nor was I stealing an hour with someone I loved. This was lunch with Mr. Exec who had no designs on my person, or even liked me, or I him.

I lowered my gaze and continued to eat until my bowl was practically empty and my stomach completely full.

Stuffed and fully aware of the person across from me, I hoped, *no,* prayed, he couldn't discern my thoughts. I pushed my bowl back and sipped on my tea.

It was a pleasure watching Mr. Manners—chopstick to food, food to mouth, and back again. The companionable silence seeped into my soul, and the dream of one day finding Mr. Right and enjoying a picnic with *him,* like now, made my heart long for the day.

"Are you going to eat that?" He motioned to the chicken in my bowl among some noodles.

"No. Do you want it?"

"Can't let LuWing's food go to waste." He stretched his arm over the table, intently watching me.

"By all means, be my guest." I shoved my bowl toward him.

Lizzie took her chopstick and speared the chunk of succulent chicken dripping with citrus honey sauce. She moved the piece toward Matt as he opened his mouth. He closed his lips around the chopstick drawing the meat from the utensil. His tongue slipped out and licked a drop of nectar from his lips. He leaned closer, offering—

"Would you like one?"

Snapped back to reality, the hero of my romance novel sat in front of me. Mr. Matthew Thomas Ainsley the Third had the same face, same strong jaw, same magnetic appeal and ... I called him Matt. What was the matter with me?

The man of my daydream stared strangely at me, not like a lover, but more like I had sauce running down my chin or a pesky, tiny seed between my teeth.

Picking up my napkin, I wiped. The paper came back clean—no sauce, no trace of meat, nothing. Even swiping my tongue across my teeth, I felt sure no spinach was there either. However, his continued gaze made me feel uncomfortable, causing my insides to be all tingly-like.

"Would I like one what?"

"A cookie." He shook the small sack in front of my face.

When I realized he was offering me a fortune cookie, I felt foolish. Awkwardness settled in. Self-consciously, I reached inside the bag.

"I love these things. Have since I was a little girl."

I ripped the plastic, shook the cookie out into my palm before breaking it open. After eating a portion of the sweet crunchy goodness, I unfurled the small rectangular paper. Thankfully, I had the presence of mind not to gasp.

Hearing a rumble of laughter, my eyes jerked to Mr. Perfect, thinking he must know what my fortune said. However, he held one of the little papers between his fingers.

"You will meet someone that will bring you happiness." He laughed. "Could it be you?" Mr. Thinks-He's-Funny had the nerve to laugh again.

I stared back at him speechless then gathered my wits about me. "I wouldn't take much stock in these silly things." I waved my fortune, crumpled it in my hand along with the wrapper, then threw both into the bag with the other unopened half dozen or so cookies.

Mr. Sauvé dug inside the bag. "You're not getting off that easy. Let's see what your fortune says." He pulled out the fortune. *"Love and happiness is before you."* He cleared his throat and without a look in my direction dug into the bag and pulled out two more cookies.

"Shall we try this again?"

Our eyes collided.

My heart slammed against my chest. I prayed he couldn't read my thoughts. As if by rote, I took the offered treat, ripped the plastic open, then broke the cookie in half. That's when I pulled my gaze from his and read.

Again, I crumpled the paper in my hand ready to throw it in the bag. "These are laughable and too preposterous to believe. They sound like a silly horoscope. But they're fun to read."

"No, you don't. Let me see it." He held out his hand.

I dropped the crumpled slip into his palm.

"A mysterious stranger will change your life. Well, I'm certainly not mysterious. You think it could be that man over there under the newspaper?" He plopped a piece of a cookie in his mouth.

As if by magic, the man under the newspaper stirred, shoved the paper back, and sat up looking around. His eyes landed on the two of us, he heaved forward to his feet and staggered in our direction.

I stood and began to gather the empty containers and the remnants of our meal, ready to be done with fortunes that sounded more like fairytales.

"Aren't you remotely interested in my fortune?"

"Read on." I waved my hand in acceptance, then dumped the first load into the trash can.

"*You're life will change for the better.* Now what do you think that could mean?"

"Maybe your next merger will bring you billions instead of millions." I moved to the garbage can and dumped the last of the cartons inside, feeling a bit out of sorts for being so rude.

"I don't think that would change my life for the better. Just increase my work load and responsibilities."

"Oh, *poor* you. You're so unfortunate to have such huge worries. Now me? I can be carefree, because I don't have the kind of money woes you do."

"But, do you like your work?"

That stopped me in my tracks. I turned to face him and didn't know what to answer. I decided a partial truth would work best.

"I enjoy helping people. Hadley's wasn't my first choice for work. In fact, I took the job to keep the wolves from my door. When I got my degree, no one was hiring. Thus, Hadley's."

He cocked his head to the side and studied me. "What are you, a late bloomer?"

The man sure knew what buttons to push. My fists on my hips, I bit out, "Some people don't have education handed to them on a silver platter. Unlike you, Mr. Ainsley, I had to work while getting my degree. Shouldn't we leave now? Won't you miss an acquisition or something?"

"Hey, Gertie, is that you?"

I turned to look at the park bench vagrant careening down the sidewalk in our direction.

"Yah, that is you." The man wobbled like a drunken clown in the wind. Puffy, baggy skin framed blood-shot eyes. Nasty, matted grey hair laid claim to his face.

If this had been one of my books, I would have written *demon rum had taken his soul, leaving a wasted shell behind*. But this wasn't one of my novels. This was real life, and the man was calling me Gertie.

"I'm afraid you're mistaken. I'm not Gertie." The foul stench of alcohol and unwashed body drifted on the wind causing the Moo Goo Gai Pan to swim upward in my stomach. I backed up a few feet, unsure if the man was going to drag me off, or plant a big sloppy kiss on my lips.

"Sure you are." He wobbled a couple of steps closer.

I backed up a couple of steps farther.

"Don't you remember me? I'm Alfie. I'd know your pretty face anywhere. Yous and me we were like"—He held up crossed fingers, then listed to one side, almost falling—"that."

Mr. I'll-Protect-You stepped in front of me. "Alfie, is it?"

The man nodded and swayed again.

"Well, Alfie, I'm afraid you're mistaken. This is my friend and I happen to know for a fact she's not Gertie."

"Well, I'll be a woodpecker's uncle. I would have sworn she was my Gertie. Ya sure?" He peered at me again.

"Quite sure. You're wrong. How about some Chinese fortune cookies?" Mr. Take-Charge handed over the bag of the remaining cookies.

Apparently satisfied with the deal and that I wasn't his Gertie, he took the sack and ambled back to the bench he'd vacated earlier.

"Thanks." I motioned back at the park at large.

"No problem, *Gertie*."

A laugh sputtered from my mouth, and Mr. Smiles joined in. His smooth laughter caused my stomach to do a quivery flip-flop.

He looked into my eyes and something sparked. A firefly at midday? *Oh, yeah.* I wished it had been, but it wasn't. It had everything to do with him.

For several seconds, I felt uncomfortable with Mr. Pretty-Eyes' gaze searching my face. I wanted to reach up and smooth my hair, or run my tongue over my teeth to make sure I didn't have one of those pesky little sesame seeds stuck in the crack. I refrained and headed for the car.

Jerked to a stop by a vice gripe on my upper arm, Mr. Woman-Handler turned me around to face him.

His face contrite. "I'm sorry."

I waved back at the man on the bench. "That wasn't your fault."

"No, not him. I'm sorry about the *late bloomer* crack. I didn't mean anything by it, just curious, that's all."

Late bloomer? Oh yeah, that crack about my education. "Forget it. It didn't bother me."

His knuckle lifted my chin so he could gaze into my face. He was too close, too appealing, too, too, too male. And at this particular moment I was too vulnerable. My hormones kicked into overdrive. I wanted to back away and run, but my feet were glued in place.

"Forgive me, please?"

The breath from his words fanned my face. His eyes began to pull me. Unable to resist whatever he was offering, I leaned toward him desiring something more— human touch, sympathy, love? Not sure.

I snapped out of whatever trance he'd woven around me, took two steps back, and fortunately, the distance cleared my head.

Surely, the heat had addled my brain. Yet, I couldn't call the mild temperatures we were experiencing heat. Maybe there was something in the yucky muck he splashed on me earlier that was causing me to act out of character.

"I accept your apology. Now shall we go?"

After giving me a puzzled look, he gestured toward the car. "Certainly."

We walked in silence, entered the car in silence, and except for the soft music hanging somewhere in the background, we rode in silence.

I wanted to kick myself for allowing Mr. Man-of-Every-Woman's-Dreams to see how susceptible I had become to his alluring charms. I had nearly fallen into his arms. Mortified at my stupidity and romantic tendencies, I vowed to be mildly cordial when we stopped at his office.

A couple of times, he took quick, little assessments of me out of the corner of his eye. I squirmed, praying we didn't have much farther before I could deposit him at his office and be on my way home.

We rolled up to the curb outside of the Morgan Building. The three-story structure was one of many built around the Waxahachie town square surrounding the striking red stoned Romanesque courthouse. My gaze traveled upward over the beautifully restored Greek revival county seat, particularly pleasing to the eye.

I thought of the sad story of crossed lovers associated with the architect of the courthouse. If the tale were true, he at least got his revenge with the ugly gargoyles at the corners, depicting his spurned love.

Looking at the Morgan building, I figured my rescuer's office window would be the one overlooking the square. The clearing of his throat drew my attention back to my companion.

"This is the place." He looked out the window, then back at me. "I enjoyed the picnic. Sorry about soiling your clothes. Send me the bill for cleaning, and if they can't be cleaned, I'll send money for a new outfit."

"Oh, don't worry about these old things. They were ready for the rag bag anyway." Now why was I lying like a sinner on judgment day? Mr. Richie-Rich seemed to pull the worst out of me. My clothes were last year's Christmas gift from me to me.

Once again, an awkward silence fell over the car.

"Keep the car until they're finished with your VW."

"What's the name of the agency so I can return the car?"

"No agency. This one belongs to the company."

Shaking my head, I said, "I can't use your car."

He smiled. "Don't worry about it. It's one out of our fleet and hardly ever used, so it won't be missed. You have my card. Give me a call when you no longer need the vehicle. I'll send someone around to pick it up."

"Are you sure?" I didn't want to be an inconvenience, even though he'd inconvenienced me.

"Yes."

"All right then. Thank you for lunch." Ill at ease, I opened my door, slid out to walk around to the driver's side where Mr. Manners stood waiting, door open.

"Remember, no rush on the car."

He waited until I was in the driver's seat and buckled before he bent down to my level.

"I wouldn't mind lunch or dinner again sometime. I enjoyed your company. You're cute even if I've only seen you in the worst of light." He tweaked my nose with his bent knuckle.

Before I could react and give him a piece of my mind, he shut the door. When he strolled to the entrance, he stopped, waved goodbye wearing a sunny grin, then was gone.

Cute? Just what does that mean? Like a kitten? A little puppy dog? What guy calls a woman cute?

"Well, Mr. Matthew Thomas Ainsley the Third, even if you are one of the most eligible bachelors in Texas, you are one puzzling guy.

"It's a shame we didn't come from the same world. As it is, I wouldn't fit into yours, and you certainly wouldn't fit into mine."

Chapter 8

"Sally, what does a gal do when she's been fired because of some no-good lowlife?" I sniffled, hardly able to breath.

"And, please, don't tell me get out and look for a job, which I would have done if I hadn't been sick as a dog with the flu. And don't tell me to put my résumé out on all those *for hire* jobs on the Internet. I did. I learned too late it's absolutely the wrong thing to do!"

"Oh, no. Surely you didn't." On the other end of the phone Sally Carlson, one of my closest and dearest friends since seventh grade, had a good laugh at my expense.

"Well, how was I to know all the perverts, sickos, weirdoes, and get-rich-schemers would be out there lurking on the Internet. They were ready and waiting to snap up my résumé with all my pertinent information. They all say they have just the right job for me. And guess what. All they need is a few hundred dollars for a set up fee and my social security number. *Yeah, right.*"

"Tiffany, you didn't did you—give them your social number?"

Her words were strangled and clearly aghast at the thought I would be so foolish.

"No, thankfully. Though sick and nearly dying—"

"You had the flu."

"Give me a little sympathy here, please."

"No, really, I'm so sorry you're sick." Sally chuckled.

"Yeah, yeah. You're sincerity is *so* touching. Anyway, like I was saying, I wasn't at my best when I applied for those online services. At least, I had enough presence of mind to know better than to give them by social or bank account numbers."

I made a disgusting sound clearing my throat before continuing.

"All they wanted to do was fleece me of what I have left in my bank account. Which happens to be a big, fat, zero, nada, as in nothing left after I paid my rent. Of course, discounting the three hundred bucks from Mr. Generosity, which I wouldn't dare touch.

"I'm surprised I didn't get a personal invitation to join the loser's club. That's just pure wrong."

Sally's laughter filled the phone again. "I know what you mean. Don't you just hate it when you get those scam and bogus emails all the time? I wish someone could put a stop to them."

"Yeah, I hear you. The nastiest offenders are the porn industry and Viagra emails. Who needs it? Not me."

"Speaking of Mr. Most-Eligible—"

"I wasn't. I didn't mention his name."

"—have you heard from him since your picnic lunch."

"What am I a piece of cheese? You're not listening. I said I was through talking about him."

I'll never know why I didn't I keep my big mouth shut instead of spilling my guts to my friend. Now I had to face the incessant questions.

"Well, have you?"

"No. And I doubt I will. And like I told you earlier, it wasn't a date. He caused the wreck, splashed and destroyed my clothes, and felt guilty enough to buy my lunch. That's it. End of story."

"I'm not so sure. If he wasn't interested, why would a dude like him sit across from the stinkin' mess you described. He would have been quick to be done with you, not buy you lunch. And as a high level exec, why wouldn't one of his minions deliver the car—tell me that, will ya?"

"At this particular moment, I don't know and don't care. And I don't wish to hash over the embarrassing details again." All she could think about since dropping Mr. Perfect off was how he was *sooo* Mr. Right with minor flaws, but not for her, which she wouldn't mention to Sally.

"Tiff, I'm sorry. I know you don't feel good. If I didn't live so far, I would come nurse you back to health."

I grabbed the last tissue from the box, groaned, and then blew gunk into the thin sheets.

"Do you need money? I could spare a couple hundred, or maybe a little more."

"Not yet. But thanks."

"What are you gonna do about a job? Food?"

Worry myself sick. "That's just it. I have a viable lead, or at least I think I do. Someone from—" I leaned over, snatched the slip of paper from the floor and almost fell off the sofa, righting myself at the last moment. "—MTA Amalgamated, or some such thing, called yesterday morning. I have an interview tomorrow at ten. I just hope it's legit. I have no clue how they got my name and number."

"But will you feel like going?" Sally hit the problem square on the head.

"I hope so. Some chicken noodle soup should get me up and running. If not, mom's recipe of hot lemons with honey should do the trick."

"You will be careful won't you?"

"Yes, I'll be careful, *Mother*." I blew my nose again with the same tissue then added it to the others overflowing the small trashcan beside the couch.

"I'm only acting the Mother Hen because I worry about you. What about your car? Did you get it back yet?"

"No, it's not done, thank heavens. I've been too sick to deal with Agnes anyway or to even think about getting the loaner back to Mr. High-Roller."

"Poor thing. I know you think of that car as practically human." Sally gave another snort of laughter. "What kind of job will you be interviewing for?"

"That's just it. I don't remember. Some company needs the particular skills that I just happen to have. For the life of me, I can't remember what those skills were. I was too out of it when they called. I hope it's not some psycho with a modeling company for pin-up of the year."

"The psycho with a nefarious plan—" Sally let loose a wicked laugh. "—like the character in your book that wants Judith for his own? *Oooo.* Think about it. He could be a Dr. Jekyll and Mr. Hyde who is—"

"Cut it out, Sally. I'm too sick for this." I wanted to wring her neck, and if she were closer than three hundred miles away in San Antonio, I would have. "That's not funny. Those things don't only happen in movies, you know. Stranger things have occurred. But, this could be a *real* job, and I *could* be offered a *real* position."

"You think?"

"No. But I can hope." Knowing my friend like I did, I could almost hear the wheels turning inside Sally's head.

"Wouldn't it be great if you got the job and you found Mr. Right? And only after two weeks out of work. *Wow!* That would be some kind of record or something. Maybe, this once, God will smile down on you—not that He hasn't been all along. But you know what I mean."

"Yeah. And maybe the tide has turned and is going to drag me out to sea to drown." I let loose a gusty sigh. "Sorry. I think this flu bug is doing a number on my positive attitude—turning it into cruddy." A spasm of coughs started up, choking me. "I better let you go."

"Okay, but keep me posted on the interview. I'll be praying for you."

"I will. Thanks. Later."

Placing my cell phone on the edge of the coffee table, I scooted down on the coach cushions and pulled the throw around my neck.

How in the world would I disguise my stuffy, swollen, red nose for the interview tomorrow? I just hoped and prayed I wouldn't wheeze then sneeze all over the interviewer—if this was an actual, for real, meeting. With my luck—what were the odds?

Chapter 9

Dressed in my one and only navy suit, white blouse, and sensible pumps, since I was still a bit shaky on my legs, I walked inside the building, praying for a favorable outcome to the interview. Fortunately this morning, I woke up less stuffy and wheezy sounding. Maybe things were turning around for me.

The reception area, tastefully done, but not expensively so, gave no hint of what type of company or job I had applied for.

"May I help you?" The young woman behind the desk had a computer and a few things office-wise. Thinner than me, brunette wavy hair, with a pleasant smile, she appeared to be about my age.

So far so good.

"Hi, I'm Tiffany Gates." I glanced down at the note in my hand "I'm here for a ten o'clock with Katherine Owens."

"I'll let Ms. Owens know you have arrived. Please have a seat."

"Thank you."

I ambled over to a dark blue utilitarian upholstered chair, one of several around the room, picked up a magazine on the end table, then sat down thumbing through the pages. Since the front office looked like a honest-to-goodness business, or they were very good at a con, my mind settled down, hoping for the best.

When the woman got off the telephone, I asked, "Have there been many other interviewees for this position?"

She studied me, smiled, and then said, "No. You're the first."

My radar kicked in. "I guess I'll have the jump on all the other candidates. I assume you've had a lot of calls for the position."

A reserved look this time. "No."

Was this a con? Something didn't quite add up here, but in for a penny and hopefully out with a pound. I worried my bottom lip with my teeth.

A woman in her early fifties, brown hair pulled back at the base of her neck in a knot, walked toward me. Her stylish sleek suit shouted Niemen Marcus, and with each step in my direction. The red soles as her shoes peeked up at me whispered Christian Louboutins.

I may not wear quality but I do know expensive when I see it. A girl can dream, can't she?

Within a split second, her direct gaze cataloged my JC Penney's suit special, sensible pumps, and my no brand named bag, not to mention my red nose that I was unable to completely disguise.

You called for this interview, Lady. This is what you get. Me.

"Ms. Gates, so nice to meet you at last." She held out her hand.

At last? What did she mean by that?

"Nice to meet you also." I stood, giving my best smile, knowing I needed the job, yet, unwilling to sell my soul.

Her handshake was firm and soft to the touch. So far, so good. She doesn't look like a rip-off artist, but then, what exactly did a rip-off artist look like? *Beats me.*

"I'm Katherine Owens. Follow me, please."

Traipsing along behind Ms. Best-Dressed-CEO, I noticed there were several offices, doors standing open, unoccupied but with normal office paraphernalia scattered on the shelves and desks. So far so good, but where were the employees? On break? All of them at the same time? Not likely.

We entered the last office at the end of the hall. Just as she had cataloged my clothes earlier, I did the same to her office.

A large, rather richly furnished room with paintings on the walls, family photos on the book shelves, a Victorian desk setting at a angle with a supple leather executive chair—all trappings of an executive. Maybe the interview was on the up and up. Realizing I had allowed Sally's words to affect me, I shoved them from mind and relaxed.

"Have a seat, please." She motioned to one of the two chairs sitting at an angle in a corner of the room. She sat across from me instead of choosing her executive chair behind the desk. Picking up a writing tablet, she gave me a thorough look, then smiled.

"Tell me a little about yourself, Tiffany."

My suspicion antenna went up, feelers testing the air.

I handed her my well-executed résumé and then obliged her by proudly rattling off my qualifications, but nothing more. I decided to give her as little of my personal information as possible.

"Are you married?"

"No.

"Have children?"

Her line of questioning was a bit disconcerting. Isn't there some kind of government regulation about asking personal questions?

"No—do you?" I smiled prettily.

At first, she gave me a startled look before her gaze turned into ... *admiration?* Whatever the look, it came with a Cheshire grin, as though I had caught her in some kind of game. Yet, I was unsure what her true motive could be.

"Yes. Two. A daughter, who has given me two of the most amazing and enchanting grandchildren on the face of the earth with another one on the way." She hiked her nose as if the subject was repugnant. "And a son, who isn't married and works too hard at his job and wants to stay that way—single that is."

She pursed her lips and gave me a speculative gaze.

"My hopes for him are that the first will be remedied soon, and the later will be remedied once he's married— giving me more grandchildren. In fact, I'm hopeful his future wife will show him how to slow down and enjoy life. You don't have an aversion to children, do you?"

"No. I love children." Why did I answer? That question was way out of line. I wasn't being hired as a nanny.

"Wonderful." She wrote something on the pad of paper, her smile evident.

Her penchant for strange questions was baffling. I couldn't begin to fathom the motive behind her line of questioning.

"How would you rate yourself with relationships?"

"What type? Business?" I didn't know what she was fishing for, but there it was again—a little glint in her eyes.

My suspicion barometer went inching up several centimeters.

"Start with business. How do you handle difficult situations and challenging people. And then tell me about a few of your interpersonal relationships."

My barometer blew out the top.

Her personal questions were unethical and just plain wrong. Definitely none of her business. I knew, and so did she, questions like these were not reasonable nor within the scope of the Rico Act or Workman's Act, or whatever act encompassed the fair hiring practices. However, I clamped a lid on my temper and suspicious nature. I needed this job.

I gave her a quick rundown of how I handled myself around business associates and sticky situations. However, I decided to nix the part about the Hands-On Stewey incident and my firing by Old Man Hadley. I wasn't hiding anything, because if she checked my references, which she was bound to do, she'd learn what happened at Hadley's anyway. That is, unless they kept a lid on Stewey's grabby hands for fear of lawsuit.

Once I had thoroughly exhausted what I thought pertinent as to my personal relationships and lack of family without getting too personal, I stopped and waited on the next volley of questions.

"You don't have any family?" I heard the empathy in her voice.

I found her compassion, if that's what it was, quite soothing and let down my guard.

"No. I am an only child from a small and almost nonexistent family. My mother and grandmother were taken from me in a tragic car accident ten years ago, and the few relatives I have left are too distant to mention." I sat waiting for her to proceed.

"I didn't hear you mention anything about a special friend." She raised her brows.

Mine rose in equal height and manner. "I didn't mention one."

"Well, do you?" She pierced me with her gaze.

"Do I what?" I threw a piercing gaze right back at her, adding a challenging squint to mine.

"Have one—boyfriend, fiancé, intended, live-in?"

This woman, without a doubt, was without scruples. Her line of questioning bordered upon the obscene and ridiculous. Not to mention Ms. Owens was treading on thin eggshells or ice or whatever you tread on when you're way in over your head and about to sink to the bottom and drown.

If I were anyone else, her designer suit would be sued right off her back, along with her expensive Louboutins.

What kind of person does she take me for anyway?

"No. No. No. And definitely, *no*."

Did I just answer her ridiculous questions? It appears I will sell my soul for this job.

I couldn't be sure, but I thought I heard her mumble under her breath, "Good."

She offered up a serene smile. "If you want the job, Ms. Gate, it's yours. You're hired."

My gasp shocked even me. "I'm hired? Just like that?" I snapped my fingers.

Shut up, Tiffany. You need this job, whatever it is.

Taking another breath, I asked, "You don't want to read my résumé? Get in touch with my references? Make sure I am who I say I am?"

Why was I jeopardizing the only legitimate job offer I'd had since my firing from Hadley's? Or since getting my degree?

Be quiet before she withdraws her offer and you're out in the cold.

"Yes, you're hired. And as for your résumé, I'll look it over, but I won't need to check your references. I like what I see, and I'm willing to take you at face value. You will find I am a person that makes snap decisions. And you will do. Yes, you'll do quite nicely." Again with the disturbing look as if she were analyzing me to see if I would fit into her nefarious plans.

"I would like you to start tomorrow. However, if that doesn't work with your schedule, Monday will do." Her eyes, pale bluish-green, watched me, her gaze never faltering.

My mind raced around in circles. Thoughts and questions ran amok inside my brain. I wanted to jump up and victory-punch the air.

I controlled the impulse, only to notice a sporadic gig had taken over my right leg. With much difficulty, I put a stop to the unrestrained bouncing. I prayed Ms. Owens hadn't noticed my nervous oddity.

By the controlled mirth on her face, she had.

There was something important I knew I should ask, but for the life of me, I couldn't think what.

Money—wages are important. What kind of a job will I be doing, might be nice.

"Ah, ah salary. I mean, is the job full time, hourly or salary. Eight to five? What will I be doing ... *exactly*? Nothing illegal, I hope." I gave a quasi smile.

Ms. Owens' emitted a soft chuckle. "No, Ms. Gates. Nothing illegal, I assure you."

Then she did it again. She gave me a look that seemed to be digging deep inside me searching for my flaws. For certain, my many shortcomings would be known soon enough.

Things were moving *way* too fast. I wasn't sure if the position would be a blessing or a curse. But at this moment, whatever the job, if within the confines of honesty, decency, and integrity, it would solve my problems. Surely, the wage would be more than minimum ... wouldn't it?

"Your title is Executive Liaison Specialist. You will work directly for the Chairman and CEO of MTA Amalgamated, and also work some with me. You do use a computer, don't you?"

And she's just now asking?

"Yes, of course. My typing speed is 95 words per minute, which is reasonably fast."

A grin tugged at Ms. Owens' lips.

"But won't the chairman want to meet me before I'm hired. What if our personalities clash?"

"There are very few personalities that don't clash with our chairman, especially in the boardroom. However, I believe you will work out splendidly. You did say you could handle difficult people and difficult situations, did you not?"

She was putting me on the spot. I felt a tingling in my armpits. In my present state, I prayed my nervousness wouldn't reveal itself by large underarm, blotchy wet spots on my suit coat.

"I feel I'm rather good at smoothing ruffled feathers—"

"Great. You accept the position." Not a question, a statement.

"Well, I—"

"The job comes with health and dental care, zero co-pay, company stock after the first six months, twelve paid holidays, and a three-week vacation—four after two years. There'll be some travel. You will accompany the CEO when needed. You are willing to travel, aren't you? All expenses paid."

The last she said smoothly, sealing the deal like a baker frosting a cake.

"Yes. I don't mind traveling." There went my leg again. I locked it behind the other one to ensure the thing kept still.

"Good. You'll have use of a company car, your own private office—connected to the chairman's, of course— and you're yearly salary will begin at $75,000.00 per year, with a raise in six months if you continue in your job."

I sucked in air and then choked on the spittle, resulting in a round of coughing spasms. Fearing I hadn't heard her correctly, but too scared to ask her to repeat the obscene sum for fear she'd retract her offer—I answered with a weak, "Yes, I'll take the job. But I'd rather start Monday."

I coughed some more, praying she wouldn't reconsider.

The old man could be an ogre with horns for all I cared. He wasn't about to run me off, not at that salary and company benefits. Just so long as he doesn't get the idea I'm one of his fringe benefit.

Chapter 10

"For the life of me, I still don't know what took place in that interview last Thursday. I just hope the job is an honest one and something I can live with in good conscience." My mind worried the problem at the speed of Mrs. MacIntosh's knitting needles.

With each clickety-clack, the pointed sticks consumed the pink fuzz, spitting out perfect, even rows of knitted afghan. She sent me a cherub smile, barely lifting her eyes from the task.

"Now, Tiffany, dear, I wouldn't worry your pretty little head one bit over how the job came to you. I feel sure it'll be a good position. And don't you worry about that old ogre either. Why, the good Lord is watching out for you, that's all there is to say on the matter. And as my dear Edgar would say, Lord rest his soul, *God helps them that gets outta the way.* You'll see."

To imagine what she meant would take more time and energy than I had to give to the matter. Mrs. Mac's line of thinking didn't always make sense, but she was a sweetheart and a second grandmother to me.

"I don't think the ogre will be that bad. Besides Stewey Hadley and his grandfather, I normally get along quite well with people, older men in particular."

"I know you do, dear. I've often said how my Edgar would have loved you if he hadn't gone on to his great reward. But that Stewey, now, he's a rotten apple right down to the core. That Grandpa of his should have taken a switch to his backside … well, on second thought, I don't think a switch would have took."

"I think you're right." I pulled the edges of my cardigan up tight around me and crossed my arms over my stomach, the worry still gnawing at my insides.

"Yes, and you've been rewarded with a better job. One you're gonna love. What soul in their right mind wouldn't want to please you? You just wait and see. The sun will shine on your parade, and you can take that to the bank." She nodded, pushed her foot on the floor, sending her rocker back and forth to the rhythm of her needles.

This time I thought I knew exactly what she meant and hoped she was right. "The CEO's probably a little old man that won't let loose of the reins until he's in the grave. The best I can hope for is that he's not too terribly set in his ways. But if he is, I'll manage."

"I'm sure you will, dear. You'll soon set the old codger straight, no doubt about it."

I almost laughed, but didn't want to hurt Mrs. Mac's feelings.

"Them that does well, gets well and often. And you do." Her curly white head bobbled up and down.

Smiling, I wondered how thoughts could get so jumbled up in one's brain. There was no denying, my landlady was special.

"Thank you, Mrs. Mac. I don't know what I would do without you to cheer me on." I rose from the chair, then gave her a peck on the cheek. "I'd better be heading upstairs. I have a lot to do to get around for tomorrow."

"Oh, I do understand." She rocked some more, the needles clackety-clacking. "But would you mind reading me just a page or two of that wonderful book of yours? I really would love to know how Lord Roth and Lady Judith are coming along."

How could I resist such an avid fan? "Only a few pages, then I must leave."

"Thank you, dear. I always look forward to our little reading times. I hope Lady Judith won't succumb to that awful Lord Sebastian's evil ways. Let me tell ya, he's one that certainly needs a paddle laid to his backside. Come to think of it, a paddle to the head might do more good."

I laughed and opened my computer. As soon as my laptop had gone through its paces, I found the spot where I'd left off the last time I'd read to Mrs. Mac. "I think you can rest assured, Lady Judith won't succumb to Lord Sebastian."

A growl filled the air as the red wine trickled out Lord Sebastian's mouth, down his chin, and onto the front of his garment. His anger erupted. His hand whipped out and latched onto Judith's arm punishingly. He drew back and slapped her across the face, the sound reverberating around the room.

Judith's head reeled with pain. Stinging heat filled her cheek as nettles pricked the skin from the blow. She nearly swooned as his fingers dug into the flesh on her arm, pulling her close to his face. His foul breath, sickened Judith and the babe in her womb lurched. She put a protecting hand to her belly, straining against Sebastian's hold.

"Let go of me. You have no right to lay a hand on me. And if Rolf finds out you've touched me in this manner, he'll kill you."

"Rolf." The name came out slurred but filled with more hatred than she had ever imagined him capable. The veins in his neck bulged and pumped, infusing his face with anger. A hideous laugh sounded as Sebastian's bilious nose came within a mere whisper of Judith's.

She struggled, straining against his hold but to no avail. His arm snaked around her and fastened her close within his embrace.

"My brother will know nothing of what we do here this night nor the times to come. When I wish to have you, I will. Only after I've tired of you, will I let Rolf know what I've done. I'll sling it in his face and tell him about his beautiful, faithless wife. When I've finished, he'll know you are no different than all the other strumpets in the village."

He pulled at Judith's sleeve, rending it from her bodice, tearing lace and trim as her screams were ignored. She reached up with her free hand and clawed a path across Sebastian's eyelid down to his chin, leaving behind a path of blood oozing from torn, jagged flesh.

His arms slipped away, hands covering the tear, as a bellow of rage filled the castle. Furious, he used the back of his hand across Judith's face, felling her to the floor, rendering her shaken and dazed.

"You shrew. I'll kill you for that."

"Oh, my. I fear for Lady Judith's safety." Mrs. Mac's worried eyes snapped. "Please tell me you won't let anything happen to her or the baby she's carrying. I just couldn't stand it if she were to die." Her hand covered her throat nervously, her needles silent in her lap.

"I can assure you, she won't die."

"Oh, thank the Lord." She picked up her knitting and the *clackety-clack* began again.

I lowered the lid to my laptop and smiled at Mrs. Mac's concern. "I'll read to you again tomorrow night. But right now I must get around for tomorrow.

Mrs. Mac shook her head. "I understand. But I sure hope you give that dreadful Sebastian the come-uppens he deserves. No man should hit a woman. He's a despicable person. And there's no doubt in my mind where he'll end up when he dies ... unless he changes his ways, of course."

A small bubble of laughter rose in my throat. I could always count on Mrs. Mac to cheer me.

"I'll come by after work tomorrow and tell you all about the job. How does that sound?"

Her faded blue eyes peered up at me over her spectacles, knitting needles quiet and in her lap again. "I would love that, my dear. In fact, I'll bake a cake to celebrate your first day with the ogre."

"I'd like that. And if I pick up pizza on the way home, would you share it with me?" It warmed my heart that for once I was able to afford to treat my dear friend.

Her face lit up like a child who had just found a hidden present under the bed. Her happiness was sweeter than a new-born babe's. "Yes, I would love that above all."

"Then tomorrow it is. Look for me around six, six-thirty."

"Oh, I will, dear. I remember my Edgar often saying, *we don't know what tomorrow may bring,* but I'm a thinkin' tomorrow it'll be pizza."

"Yes, Mrs. Mac, I believe you're right."

Chapter 11

I glanced at my second best suit hanging from the extension rod on the closet door, a black, thin pinstripe, with a cream shell to wear beneath. They were clean, pressed, and ready for tomorrow morning.

Lunch—a PB&J and an apple were in the flowered lunch bag I bought on sale at Hadley's last year.

Monday morning—less than nine hours away.

The next step in my journey to becoming financially solvent. In less than a month, I would be able to pay back, with interest, Mr. Matthew Thomas Ainsley the Third, which would be a load off my mind.

Up to this point, I had only used one of the hundred dollars for some minor groceries. The other two were safely tucked beneath the loose floorboard in the closet. The last place a thief would look.

With the evening ahead of me, I opened my laptop, turned on my computer, pulled up *Surrender at Dusk*, and scrolled down to my last entry.

I read. I waited. I read some more. I waited some more. Inspiration didn't come.

For the first time, I couldn't wrap my mind around the story of Lord Rolf and Lady Judith. It just wasn't there.

An author's most fiendish nightmare had taken over—*writer's block!*

The white page on the computer screen swirled into serene, pale green eyes, a miniscule dimple in the right cheek, two full kissable lips, and an errant light brown curl falling softly over one eye of Mr. Perfect personified—Matthew Thomas Ainsley the Third. He seemed to jump off the page and into my small living-dining-sleeping room.

I blinked, then rubbed my eyes, but his image was still embedded in my mind. No matter how hard I tried to rid his face from in front of me, his presence seemed bigger than life, crowding me out of my little efficiency apartment with a mocking, teasing smile.

I'm going nuts. Pure plain and simple. I'm going stark raving mad over a man who hasn't given me so much as one ounce of thought since the day I dropped him off at his office.

Why, after all these years of brushing off eligible men's advances, did the only totally impracticable, unrealistic guy seem to be the one my heart desired? Probably having no date for over a year had landed me in this unsettling predicament.

I moved to the stove and turned on the flame under the teakettle continuing to worry the problem of Mr. Big-Shot. Hearing the high-pitched shrill, I grabbed a cup, filled it with steaming hot water, and then stood aimlessly dunking the tea bag up and down.

Thoughts ran roughshod through my befuddled brain as I added sugar and cream before watching it dissolve with a swirl of my spoon.

Why wasn't it as simple to dissolve Mr. Richie-Rich from my subconscious? After another swift stir, hoping to banish the man completely from my mind, I ambled back to my computer.

Miracle of miracles. No face. No image. And no story … *yet*.

A yawn overtook me. I should have been in bed an hour ago. Morning would come too soon.

After shutting out the light, I pulled back the covers, slid in and nestled my head into the pillow. The quiet sounds of my little upstairs efficiency apartment settled around me. My last thoughts were of knights, maidens, and ogres.

I slapped at the offending buzz, only to realize the noise was my alarm. Shooting up out of bed, I stretched. Somehow, even after a night of tossing and turning and worrying, I slept, which amazed me. I breathed in and found no signs of stuffy nose or cough, which amazed me further.

One look in the mirror told me I would have to apply concealer to cover the dark circles under my eyes though. Looking haggard on the first day of my new job wouldn't be conducive for making a good impression on the ogre.

The whole dressing thing took me less than an hour. After giving a final onceover in the full-length mirror on my closet door, I grabbed my purse and my other things before heading out the door.

Mrs. Mac stood at the base of the stairwell. "So glad I caught you, Tiffany." She gave me a thorough inspection. "My, don't you look pretty, and so business-like too. She held out a container wrapped with cloth tied with a red ribbon. I made up a basket for your office, dear."

When I went to peek inside, her hand stopped me.

"No dear, you must wait until you are at the office before opening the gift. It'll bring the comforts of home to you, especially after you meet the old ogre." She beamed at me, her beautiful, wrinkled face so endearing.

"I promise I won't snoop. And thank you for the gift. I love surprises. I've gotta run. See you tonight. And don't forget I'm bringing pizza home."

"Don't you worry. I would never forget pizza, especially with extra pepperoni."

Bending down I gave Mrs. Mac a peck on the cheek. "Later …"

"Remember dear, don't walk under any ladders. And if a black cat crosses your path go around the block. If you spill any salt, make sure you throw a pinch over your left shoulder, or is it your right, no I think it's left? Oh, well, do both shoulders, that way you're sure to be covered. No need to begin the day with bad fortune. But don't you worry—you'll do just fine."

A chuckle escaped, so glad I could always count on Mrs. Mac to lift my spirits.

"Thanks. I'll do my best. I'll see you tonight."

Excited, but with some trepidation, I headed for my job at the MTA headquarters in Dallas. It would have been nicer to work at the Waxahachie office where I interviewed. However, the salary would compensate for any deficit in the cost of gas and time.

The closer I got to my destination, the more nervous I became. My palms sweaty, my stomach balled into a tight knot, I played mental games to bring calm. Surely, after the initial meeting, I would be fine, but until then …

Oh. I just hope I don't get sick. Wouldn't that be a pretty sight puking all over the floor in front of my new boss?"

Upon my approach, the tall, golden, glass building gleamed like a jewel in the morning sun. I hoped it was a sign things were on the upward rise. However, after driving up and down the rows of filled spaces, I soon realized a reasonably close parking spot wasn't to be had.

Finally, my perseverance paid off. I found one out in the back forty.

I gathered my things and began my hike toward the building. *Heels ... a bad idea.* I should have worn my tennies and changed into my dress shoes once inside. *A definite tomorrow.*

While hurrying at a fast clip for pumps, I glanced around at the MTA grounds. Where I had anticipated typical concrete structure with minimal shrubs, MTA was an all glass building surrounded by grass groomed to perfection, trees, benches, and winding walkways edged by flowering beds. The perfume of spring flowers in full bloom infused the air and took my mind off my first-day jitters.

As I moved through the revolving doors, I wondered if one could become stuck in between. Who would they call to the rescue, the fire department?

I chuckled, my thoughts too silly to imagine. To my disappointment, my humor didn't last long. I stepped out into the huge lobby feeling lost and out of my element. My heartbeat doubled. My breath came in short, quick spurts. I was in the throes of hyperventilating.

I forced my steps to slow to a sedate stroll and to breath slow and deep. My heels clip-clopped across the marble floor until I stopped in front of the roster, searching for Ms. Owens' name. That's when I saw that MTA Amalgamated occupied the whole building. I was working for the CEO—*whew*. I just prayed I'd be up to the task.

I'm competent, smart, and a quick learner. The ogre will love me. The scene with Hands-On Stewey at Hadley's flashed before my eyes. *Well not like that, or at least I hope not.*

After shifting everything in my arms, I gave a quick perusal down the list for 'O' names. Katherine Owens was on the thirteenth floor, but no suite number.

Thirteen. What would Mrs. Mac think about that? Apparently, not everyone was superstitious. I for one was not. And the owner of the building apparently wasn't either.

Chalk it up to first day jitters or meeting the old ogre for the first time, the *bomp-bomp* of my heart sped up. I knew if anyone had been within earshot, they could have heard the loud thumping against my chest.

My attention drawn by a ding, I raced to the elevator, stepped over the threshold, and heard a crack and then a splintering as the heel to my shoe gave way. My heart sank to the pit of my stomach. My face turned twenty-five shades of red as I listed three inches shorter to the left. The elevator full of people watched my humiliation.

The stares of all ten or more men and women followed me as I bent over to retrieve my broken heel from the crevice. The door bumped my hip with a powerful wallop. The door was doing its best to smash me in half. Before I could retrieve my broken heel from the crack, the loud obnoxious elevator buzzer blared in my ears.

Grabbing hold, I yanked the offending heel out of the crack. I backed into the elevator so the doors could shut and the noise would stop. I heard words of sympathy and a few *uh-ohs* as the door closed on my little saga.

I stood in humiliation, without a clue what I would do for shoes. I didn't have time to race the thirty miles back to my little efficiency, nor was I prepared for such an event.

"Do you have another pair at your desk?" The question came from a matronly woman in the corner with her fingers, arms, and neck weighted down by expensive jewelry. Her white hair, in a fashionable angular cut, framed her face, giving her an air of sophistication. She arched her brow and gave a disdainful look at the homemade basket in my hand.

The basket might not be Neiman Marcus quality, but it was made with more love than anything bought in that pricey store.

"No, this is my first day." I offered a tentative smile. "I don't have a desk, I mean I don't know where my desk will be yet." I sounded wretched.

I hobbled-scooted to the elevator wall, praying to squeeze into a tiny space at the back. My best hope was to fade into the rich wood paneling, which I knew would be impossible.

"Oh, that's too bad." Mrs. Bejeweled scrutinized me from top to bottom. Her gaze stopped on my cloth-wrapped package again.

Several commiserate groans and a couple of under-the-breath chuckles came from various people in our small confines. A ding, the doors opened, and then a few people got off. One gentleman was kind enough to wish me a better start to the rest of my first day.

"Thank you." The two words sounded weak and forlorn.

I emitted a small moan, wishing I could go home, get back in bed, and start my day all over again. I tucked my head, my mind feverously working on what I would do about my shoes.

"What size do you wear?"

The older woman's faded eyes looked familiar, even something about her face threw me a little off kilter. But then, it could have been my lopsided stance. "Pardon?"

"Your shoe size, dear—what size?"

"Size seven and a half." The heat rose in my cheeks as I gave a less than heartfelt smile. "Maybe if I could break off the other heel ... I'd be on a more even plain. What do you think?"

The bell dinged for the eleventh floor. Number thirteen loomed ahead.

"This is my floor. Come with me." Mrs. Well-To-Do stepped off, paused, then looked back at me. "Unless you'd rather walk around one leg shorter than the other."

Mrs. No-Nonsense sailed down the hall. Her commanding voice floated back to me. "I believe I have a solution to your problem. Come along. Quit dithering."

I followed her like a little lost puppy dog. My uneven gait more like a camel's.

"By the way, I'm Lucy Bell." As if she knew I had followed.

'Hi. I'm Tiffany Gates."

We rounded a corner, then entered a beautifully decorated reception area, all in pale purples and pinks. Instead of stopping behind the empty receptionist desk as I thought she would, Lucy Bell entered into a nicely furnished office in much the same tones as the outer room.

"This is my office. Have a seat." She flourished her bejeweled hand like a queen.

Demoralized, I yanked myself back to reality and set everything in my hands on the floor before sinking into one of the purple plaid, overstuffed chairs. Realization hit. This woman had to be some sort of an executive of the corporation to have her own secretary and such a huge office.

Lucy Bell walked around behind a beautiful burl wood Queen Anne desk, pulled out a drawer, and then held out a pair of black orthopedic-looking old lady's shoes.

At first I looked at the shoes stunned. When I noticed she meant for me to take them, I graciously accepted her shoes. I wouldn't allow my pride to take away the ray of sunshine in her act of kindness. At least I wouldn't walk as if one leg was three inches shorter than the other.

"These are size nine and a half, but I think they'll work better than being lopsided all day." She smiled one of those little *don't crack your face* smiles.

"Are you sure?" I gazed at the shoes wondering if I could break off my other heel. Then I'd be walking around with my toes pointing skyward all day, which would probably look worse.

"Certainly. You can return them tomorrow. I won't need them. I keep them here"—she flourished her hand again—"just in case."

In case what? Someone like me breaks a heel? She feels like dressing down? What?

After another dubious look at the answer to my dilemma, I slipped off my one shoe.

So what if they do look like black boats ready to launch. I only need them until I buy another pair of shoes at lunchtime.

Pushing aside my fashion scruples, I slid into the black utilitarian shoes, wiggled my toes in the hideous looking boats. *Roomy.* So much so, my feet could swim around inside even after I tied the laces up as tight as I could get them.

With a prayer the battleships would stay on my feet and that I wouldn't meet anyone before lunch, I stood and took a baby step.

Confirmed, I'll be taking my life into my own hands just trying to walk.

I slid my purse strap over my arm, placed my shoes and broken heel into my tote bag, and then took awkward, shuffling steps.

"Thank you, Ms. Bell. I'll return the shoes to you after lunch. I'll go out shopping for new shoes during lunch. I should run or I'll be late."

"What department do you work for?"

"I'm the new Executive Liaison Specialist. I work for Ms. Owens and the CEO."

Surprise raced across her face followed by derision. She looked down her long aristocratic nose. "Well, good luck with that. You're going to need it."

My heart gave a lurch, then jumped up into my throat. *Whatever did she mean by that?*

Chapter 12

To maneuver in the huge boats on my feet, *impossible*. Between Lucy Bell's office and the elevator, the borrowed shoes had flown off my feet too many times to count.

Exhausted by fighting a losing battle, but happy to see my destination close at hand, I shuffled off the elevator into the open reception area on the thirteenth floor.

Exuding a modicum of confidence in my ability to navigate the remaining short distance without calamity, I took the first, second, and even the third step without mishap. Seeing a young woman gazing at the computer screen, I rushed forward hoping to approach without her noticing my fashion faux pas.

The fifth step shot my theory all to pieces. A black missile flew through the air and hit its mark—landing smack-dab in the middle of the desk.

The young woman let loose a *yelp,* turned a brilliant shade of pink, looking around for the culprit. Her gaze landed on the black boat sitting smartly among her papers, and then turned on me.

As if the shoe were contaminated, with index finger and thumb, her pinky stuck high in the air, she held out the offending object toward me.

"I believe this must belong to you." She sent a scathing look in my direction.

Weary of fighting the shoes, and my humiliation skyrocketing off the chart, I shifted my smart-looking, if not rather stylish, tote bag onto my left arm along with Mrs. Mac's gift.

Stretching across her desk, I grabbed the dangling, misplaced shoe from her fingers. Then with a nonplussed air, I smiled serenely at the woman as though I always entered a room in that manner.

Trying for an authoritative tone, I said, "I'm Tiffany Gates. I'm here to see Ms. Owens."

The squeaky sound in my voice fell short of my original goal. Nonetheless, with a continued blasé approach, I proceeded as though my borrowed shoe hadn't just attacked her desk.

Hey! A couple more feet and the missile would have taken her out instead. That could have been far more humiliating.

She stared at me with a dubious, if not incredulous look. And then, as though flying shoes were the everyday norm gave me a much practiced arrogant tilt of her head.

"If you'll take a seat, I'll tell Ms. Owens you're here."

Her bland, nasally tone didn't leave me wondering what she thought of me or my choice shoes.

I refrained from asking where she would like me to take the chair. She wouldn't understand my sense of humor and would probably label me a nutcase, if she hadn't already.

Slowly, I ambled to a chair by the window not wanting another mishap.

My gaze was captured by the purple flowers thirteen floors below. They outlined the bushes spelling out MTA. I wondered just how long it took a gardener to train the plants to grow like that.

My mind conjured up tiny men working around the clock like little busy bees clipping and trimming until they achieved the right balance and look.

I must be going wacko.

"Ms. Gates."

Turning from the window, I greeted Ms. Owens with what I hoped was a bright, no nonsense, business smile with nothing whatsoever wrong with my appearance. Quick as a blink, I realized my disheveled and dowdy appearance had been stamped indelibly upon her mind.

Her face went from friendly to shock then back to semi-cordial by the time her gaze had taken in the full gamut of my attire—little cloth basket, black and green tote bag, and … black boats.

She was good.

The woman didn't so much as blink or miss a beat. I envisioned the thoughts running through her mind—*can I fire her now or wait until later?*

So much for first impressions, in her case, second.

Maybe one day I'll laugh over this inauspicious first day of mine, but at the moment, I'd like nothing better than a big hole to jump in and dirt to cover me so I could just roll up and die.

"You're on time."

Thankfully she didn't add *at least*.

Mortified, I nodded.

"If you'll follow me, I'll show you to your office and explain some of your duties, which, of course, once the CEO arrives he will give you further instructions."

She turned, sashayed her expensively clad hips down the hall, leaving me to follow in her wake. My face matched the winking red bottoms of Ms. Owen's Louboutin shoes.

Flip-flap, squidge, flip-flap, squidge echoed and bounced off the walls. From this day forth, my face would probably be a permanent shade of bright pink.

Thinking chatter might drown out the obnoxious sound of the shoes slip-slapping the bottom of my feet, I said, "I love the offices, and the grounds are spectacular."

"Why, thank you. We moved into this building five years ago, shortly after my husband's tragic death."

Flip-flap, squidge, flip-flap, squidge.

"I'm so sorry for your loss."

Flip-flap, squidge, flip-flap, squidge.

"Thank you, but don't be." She waived her hand like someone shooing flies. "I warned him not to take the leap, but he did anyway. It's his fault. And I'll never forgive him."

Speechless, my mind jumped to all kinds of conclusions.

Had he killed himself by diving off the building? Leaping out of an airplane? Jumping in front of a bus? Under a train? What?

"Here we are."

She opened a door to an office with a window view of the city of downtown Dallas in the distance. The office, my office, was much larger than I had expected.

"There are two manuals on the desk." Ms. Owens motioned to the leather, loose-leaf notebooks. One was the size of a thin book, the other three inches thick.

"One is all about MTA, Amalgamated. I suggest you familiarize yourself with the different companies and subsidiaries. The other book outlines company procedures, your duties, and what is expected of you.

"Although I've noticed you have worn some *very* practical shoes, even if they seem to be a trifle big, we'll save the tour of MTA until later this afternoon, or maybe tomorrow." She moved toward the door.

"Oh, these aren't my—"

"If you need anything, just dial zero. Kathy, our administrative assistant, will be able to assist you with whatever you need." Her hand on the doorknob, she turned and gave me an odd look. "I'll be back around ten o'clock to take you to the board meeting."

She gave me a smile that didn't quite reach her eyes. With one final inspection of me, the basket, my shoes, she turned and walked out the door, shutting it softly behind her.

My spirit plummeted, causing my stomach to twist into a knot. I cringed to think I would have to attend a board meeting in my borrowed orthopedics.

Knowing I had a long way to go before my humiliation would be complete, I slowly inhaled and wondered what next?

Slipping out of the boats, I shoved them aside and then sat my basket, tote bag, and purse on the desktop. Standing before the large plate glass window in my stalking feet, my embarrassment of moments before lifted. I punched the air with my fist.

"*Yes*. Welcome, Tiffany Ann Gates, to the corporate world of MTA Amalgamated—even if the first day has been less than a stellar beginning."

A chuckle erupted reminding me I still had a small amount of humor left.

After checking the view, I sat down in front of my desk, opened each drawer and found some of them empty and others holding necessary office supplies. I stowed my personal belongings away in one of the bottom drawers.

After gazing longingly at my ruined Candies, I dumped the shoes unceremoniously in the trash.

I opened the laptop, pressed the button waiting for the little tune to sound. MTA logo appeared before all the icons popped onto the screen. Thrilled to be among the working class once again and in the capacity of my degreed profession, I shot my arms into the air, twirled a couple of times in my desk chair, feeling exhilarated and charged in my bare feet.

I ignored the little heckler that kept trying to burst my bubble with thoughts of impending doom. Surely, I had gotten over the worst of my day. What more could go wrong?

A lot!

Chapter 13

After working my way through half of the large manual, I glanced up to rest my eyes and noticed the forgotten gift from Mrs. Mac sitting to one side of the desktop. Needing a break, I untied the red ribbon.

Inside, was a beautiful china teacup and saucer with a silver spoon. I recognized the pieces were a part of Mrs. Mac's favorite tea service. Also in the basket was a tin of Lady Gray tea and a crystal decanter of chocolates.

I opened the lid. Immediately the aroma had my taste buds watering. Unable to resist, I plopped one piece in my mouth and savored the smooth, velvety goodness.

The chocolate melted in my mouth as I thought about nothing except the pure pleasure of the moment and Mrs. Mac's thoughtfulness.

No mishaps. No broken heel. No disappointed bosses. All was well with the world.

Thank God for my dear, sweet landlady. She must have known somehow I would need one sane moment of pleasure in my first day.

I glanced at her unique presents scattered across my desk. Though zany and sometimes disjointed in thought and deed, Mrs. Mac was without a doubt a treasure, and I loved her dearly.

Reaching into the basket, I pulled out a red and white checkered cloth held together by the same type ribbon. I released the silk tie and the material fell away. Staring up at me was one of Mrs. Mac's most prized possessions—none other than her late husband Edgar.

I recognized the photo as the very same one that normally adorned the top of Mrs. Mac's television.

Edgar's stern eyes stared back at me through heavy, black, horn-rimmed glasses with the zeal of a firing squad. His thick, Hitler moustache framed unyielding straight lips. Bits of balding pate glistened through the crisscross comb-over with the plastered strands ending at the top of his right cauliflower earlobe.

Laughing, I set the frame on the edge of the desk. I moved back then laughed some more while wiping moisture from my eyes. True to Mrs. Mac's prediction, Edgar brought a lift to my spirits and did seem to bring the comforts from home to my office.

My hands on my hips, I asked, "What am I to do with you, Edgar? You certainly can't stay here. But then again, you could act as guard dog. One look at your surly countenance would frighten any would be harbinger of doom away."

I scooted Edgar from one corner to the next, then decided he was one prized possession I couldn't keep, even if he did bring a little savoir-faire with a bit of gloom to the room. I'd have to give him back to Mrs. Mac. I smiled. For the time being, he'd stay on the corner of my desk.

Aware the dreaded board meeting loomed ahead, I picked up the procedures manual to read. As I panned through the pages, acid bubbled in my stomach. The more I thought of meeting everyone wearing the black monstrosities, the more I wanted to run and hide.

Setting the manual down, I dragged the trashcan over to my chair, dug out my heels, giving a thorough inspection to the broken one.

What could be worse—skyward pointed toes or missiles and torpedoes annihilating the board members?

Decision made, I picked up the healthy shoe and did my best to pry the heel from the sole. After several repeated mishaps—face down in the carpet, almost toppling over in my chair, hitting my fingers a time or two—the little four-incher came off in my hand as my elbow nearly felled the lamp on the credenza.

Slipping my feet into the sky-slopped shoes, I wobbled around the room testing my ability to walk in what remained of the leftovers.

My toes, of course, pointed skyward but not as badly as originally suspected. However, what I'd failed to realize, the back part was rounded where the heel had once been. Walking brought about a slight rolling gait to my stride. After practicing back and forth, a fit of giggles, and finally regaining my composure, I learned to walk like a rather stiff-legged Barbie without twisting my ankles.

Seeing the time, I pulled out a legal pad, picked up two pens, just in case one of them stopped working—the way my morning was going, it was bound to happen—then took a quick look at my reflection in the window.

A knock sounded and the door opened. A man about my age, dark brown hair with two deep dimples, gave me one of the most adorable smiles I had seen in years. He reminded me of the brother I always wanted but never had.

"Hi, I'm James Foster. Her majesty sent me to drag you to the board room."

Seeing my puzzled look, his smile grew bigger, if that were possible.

"Katherine Owens—you'll learn soon enough. Everyone is waiting to meet you. I've gotta say, you've caused quite a stir among the employees and board members."

He looked down at my feet and laughed outright at my expense. "You're shoes? They are quite *umm* ..."

"Unusual? Strange? Or maybe atrocious? I have more adjectives if those won't suffice."

"No I think those work quite nicely." He gave me a quirky grin.

"I know. They're horrible. I broke a heel first thing this morning in the elevator. Then I broke off the other one so I'd have something to wear besides two black boats."

"Black boats?"

He was looking at me as if I had loose screws giggling around in my head.

"Shoes really. A Ms. Lucy Bell was in the elevator when I broke my heel, and she offered to help. Loaned me some rather large, black shoes that kept falling off my feet."

I gazed down, tipped back on my heels, toes turning skyward and almost went over backwards. I grabbed the corner of the desk to steady myself. "These at least fit, even if they do look rather peculiar."

"Ahh. You've met the dragon then."

Again his infectious laugh made me smile. "The Dragon?"

"Lucy Bell." He looked down at his Rolex. "I need to get you to the board room pronto. You ready?"

"Yes. But please take it slow. I've just learned to walk all over again. And it wouldn't be a pretty sight seeing me sprawled all over the floor or on the conference table."

He gave a generous laugh to which I joined in. His dark brown eyes crackled with humor, and I knew we were instant friends.

"For you, I'll take it slow and easy. Can't have you arriving worse for wear. Those old codgers can just have a hissy fit. It'll be worth it. And I want to observe their faces when they see what I've finally brought to the table."

His laughter rang out and my cheeks flamed again.

I could have been mistaken about that friendship. Time will tell.

James led me down a hallway, made several turns, then as my feet were beginning to get sore from walking off kilter, he stopped in front of two huge doors.

"You ready to meet the lions in their den?"

"Surely, they can't be that bad—could they?"

"Keep a stiff upper lip. Don't let anything they say throw you. And remember, they're people just like you. They put their drawers on one leg at a time."

James' deep rumble of laughter warmed my insides.

"They all think they run the show, but you'll soon find out there's only one person that runs this place. When he speaks, others jump to make it happen."

He gave me a bow worthy of a court jester, opened both doors with a dramatic push, and then with a grand gesture ushered me into the room. In a voice a little less than a stage whisper he said, "Move those pointy shoes, my dear. And smile—you're taking center stage."

Center stage? Whatever could he mean center stage?

I gave him a quizzical look and received a wink. That's when I realized there was a decided difference in the temperature of the room.

The rumble of voices settled and a disquieting hush filled the void. All eyes were on me. I felt like an actor walking on stage who didn't know her lines. As quickly as the silence came, whispers began around the huge table like a human wave at a ballgame. The only thing ... they didn't stand and then sit on cue.

My first inclination was to kick off my broken-down shoes and run. I would have too if my sidekick hadn't given me a nudge.

"Courage, sweetheart. Show 'em what you got."

James sounded like one of the old Humphrey Bogart movies Mom and Grams used to watch.

I stiffened my spin and squared my shoulders. Too nervous to take in the occupants of the room, my eyes skimmed over blurred heads and bodies as my wobbly shoes and knocking knees moved me forward. My palms sweaty, my body cold and clammy, I prayed my deodorant would hold up.

James steered me to a chair at the end of the table and pulled it out before sitting down next to me. My glance wandered down the long expanse of the conference table with five pairs of eagle-eyes on each side. I spied Ms. Owens sitting at the opposite end, next to the empty head seat.

I wondered if she would look up and acknowledge me. She kept her head down looking over a report. Ms. Lucy Bell smiled at me when I looked across the table. Or at least I thought it was a smile. It happened so quick-like, it was there and gone before I could decide.

A noise behind me brought about another stint of silence as someone entered the room. I didn't turn to look, not wanting to be obvious. The man sauntered past.

I caught a glimpse of his back and had a niggling suspicion that I knew him, but from where I didn't have a clue.

James tilted his head in my direction. "Hold on to your seat. This could get rocky." Then he laughed quietly under his breath. "Don't forget, I'm here to give you moral support." He crossed his fingers down by his side. "But let's hope you won't need it."

I looked at him, my brows furrowed in question, but he just shook his head and nodded toward the other end of the table. Glancing to where he indicated, I almost choked on my own spit.

Still as handsome as ever and with an air of arrogance that only he could display naturally, stood none other than Matthew Thomas Ainsley the Third. I sucked in a breath, blinked my eyes to make sure I wasn't mistaken, then turned to my partner. Quietly I asked, "Who is he?"

"Matthew Ainsley."

"No, I know who he is. What is he doing here?"

"You don't know? This is worse than I thought." James bounced his brows up then down. "He's the owner and CEO of MTA Amalgamated … your boss."

Chapter 14

"Oh."

The single word whooshed out as if the breath had been knocked from my lungs, which was close to reality. I wanted to slide under the table, instantly disappear, be anywhere but here, but that wasn't going to happen.

Why me? Why this job? Why was I sitting in a boardroom with stuffy old people who knew I didn't belong here? Surely, this was someone's idea of a cruel, sick joke.

Mr. MTA Amalgamated, dressed similar to what he wore the day of our wreck—a black pen-stripe suit, white shirt, a red and black tie—still had the ability to take my breath away. He thumbed through the pages of a report sitting in front of him without looking up.

I scrambled, thinking of reasons for my being here. Quick on the up-take, I realized he must have had something to do with my hiring. Why else would I be here? Yet, he wasn't overly interested in me. If he were, he would have checked to see how I was doing after the car accident, but he hadn't. He must have found out I didn't have a job at Hadley's any longer and felt sorry for me. That had to be it.

"Good Morning, everyone." Mr. In-Control smiled as he glanced around the table. His gaze skimmed over me, stopped, and then did a quick reverse. He stopped again, this time, nailing me with his stare.

The smile gone, there wasn't a hint to his thoughts.

For those brief seconds our eyes collided, my heart slammed against my ribcage, fluttered, then almost stopped altogether. His brows knit together over his gorgeous eyes before he broke eye contact.

Mr. Befuddled tilted his head toward Ms. Owens and spoke a few terse words. Said woman looked down the table at me, smiled, and then said something to Mr. MTA.

After another short glance in my direction, Mr. CEO looked back at the report, straightening the folder. "We'll start this meeting with the first item on the agenda ..."

His voice, clear and concise, gave my heart a twinge. My leg began to bounce like it has a tendency to do when I'm upset or nervous. I was both. Plus a whole lot more—troubled, mystified, and just a little miffed that I sat in the middle of a big, fat beehive and didn't know why.

Unable to pay attention to what Mr. Big-Bucks had to say, I had the awful urge to stand up and shout, *Will someone please tell me why I'm here?* Fortunately, I had the good sense to hold my tongue.

After about an hour of what felt like sitting on hot coals, Mr. All-Business looked straight at me for the first time since he had begun the meeting.

"I believe everyone has noticed we have added a new member to our staff." He gestured in my direction. "Ms. Tiffany Gates. She is our new Executive Liaison Specialist. She'll head up and be directly responsible for MTA's face lift and new image. Welcome aboard, Ms. Gates."

Murmurs of welcome came from around the table.

Mr. I'm-In-Charge cut though the low hum. "Ms. Gates, I'd like to meet with you in my office in fifteen minutes."

He gave me a straight-forward business glance, neither friendly nor unfriendly, more like one more thing ticked off the agenda, then looked away.

"Yes, sir." *That sounded mousey.* Mr. MTA seemed to bring out the worst in me—weak and a pushover, or bold and on the attack. Just a shame it hadn't been bold.

He dismissed the meeting and didn't even look in my direction before an ardent conversation with Ms. Owens ensued.

I felt a tug on my chair, looked up and saw James' dimpled smile.

"I'll escort you back to your office. I'm sure you'll want to do whatever it is a woman does to fortify herself for the next volley. If we weren't at work I'd suggest a stiff drink, but, oh, well." He shrugged.

"Sorry, I don't drink unless it's ice tea or Coke. You wouldn't happen to have either one up your sleeve, would you?"

James' laughter drew several stares from the board members and a frown from the other end of the room.

"Follow me, I've got you covered."

My new friend led me out of the boardroom, down a maze of halls, and then into a better than average-looking lunch room—the executive lounge.

Instead of the usual large drink dispenser, utilitarian tables and chairs, and Formica countertop, this one had a sleek brushed stainless steel refrigerator and a granite-covered counter with an under-mounted sink. Plush leather chairs in little groupings of threes and fours were placed around glass-topped tables. And stains? I couldn't find even one on the super plush carpet.

Over the counter, sparkling MTA embossed glasses lined the clear see-through shelves. And MTA embossed napkins rested in a neat little swirling pattern next to the condiments for the cappuccino and single-cup coffee maker—no coffee standing in pots going stale here. Fresh fruit in bowls and pastries and cookies under a dome lid looked inviting. I had heard about executives lounges like this one, but never stepped inside one until now.

I stopped just inside the door, feeling a little like an interloper, and watched James walk to the fridge, open it wide, and then look back at me. "Name your poison. Tea, Coke, juice, or maybe some string cheese or fruit." He looked at me inquiringly.

"A Coke please. Nothing more."

"Sure thing."

As he went about getting the soft drink, I moved farther into the room and mustered enough courage to ask what had been at the forefront of my mind.

"James?"

"Mmm."

The small, square ice cubes clinked and the fizz of the soft drink being poured into the glass all seemed surreal. I prayed my future job wasn't about to burst like the thousands of tiny bubbles were doing in the glass he held out to me.

"What do you know about my being hired for this position?"

He gave a quick glance, then turned back to the business at hand. "Not much. Have a seat."

"That bad, huh?" I scrunched my brows together, not daring to sit down, knowing I might collapse and never get up. The knot of worry grew larger in the pit of my stomach as the seconds ticked off. I felt like I was in the big, fat middle of something, but I was the only one around this company that didn't know what that big, fat middle consisted of.

He avoided looking at me. "Depends. Some would say you're in a good position, especially if you play your cards right. Others might say you've been placed in a hornets' nest."

"Which means? Plain English, please." I watched him carefully for subterfuge.

"Both could be correct."

"What do you say?"

"I'd say you'll soon find out." He jerked his arm up and turned his wrist over to look at his watch. "In fact, you've got about five minutes before you will determine for yourself what it will be. Take a few fortifying drinks of your coke before I escort you to the Lion's Den."

I took a deep gulp and regretted my action. The carbonation stung and sizzled all the way down my throat, then settled in my jittery, empty stomach sending up a revolt.

"Have I been assigned to you as a special project to watch over?"

He's eyes sparkled. His dimples were even deeper than before. "I wish." He raised his brows and smiled. "But, no. Katherine told me to bring you to the board meeting and sit beside you, which I did. And I might add ... it was my pleasure. The rest"—he swung his arm wide indicating the room we stood in—"I did because I wanted to." Again, the boyish grin.

There was something about James I liked. He seemed unaffected by his surroundings and honest to a fault. I moved to set the glass on the counter.

"Here, let me fill it up." He poured the remainder of the can into the glass, the fizzle filling the silence. "Take it with you. You can nurse it while the inquisition is taking place."

We both laughed.

I heard the door open and without looking, my second sense told me who had entered the room.

"I hope I'm not intruding." The voice held a rigid, no-nonsense quality.

The chill started at the base of my neck, ran down my spine, and ended with a tingle that curled my toes even though they were already turned up. I couldn't deny the deep baritone voice had done a number on my overwrought senses. For some reason, Mr. Bossman disturbed me to no end.

"No. You're not intruding. Just getting *Tiff* a Coke before taking her to your office. I thought she deserved a little refreshment after that stuffy board meeting."

Not knowing why he used the childhood derivative of my name, I smiled, thinking it felt good to have at least one ally in this place. I wasn't discounting Ms. Lucy Bell, if, in fact, she actually could be thought as such.

I turned and looked into the enigmatic face of Mr. CEO and knew something wasn't sitting well with him. Unable to ascertain if it was me or James or the both of us, I somehow knew he didn't like finding us in the employee's lounge together. Or was it just me he found fault with?

"Don't trouble yourself. I'll show her the way." Mr. Exec's stern look didn't bode well.

"She's no trouble at all, Cuz. We were just leaving." James opened the door, stepped back to allow me to pass. "Shall we?"

Cuz! Now I knew ... I couldn't trust anyone in this firm, not even Lucy Bell.

"Jimmy ..." Mr. Commander's irritation was as plain as the grating on an emery board.

Not knowing whether to stay or go, I decided escape might be best. I slid through the opening and out into the hall, determined to find my way back on my own.

"Matty." James chuckled as he pulled the door shut.

I thought I heard Mr. Turbulent call out *James*, but apparently not, because James kept right on walking and started whistling.

When we were well away from the employee lounge and out of earshot, I uttered what had been burning on my tongue to ask.

"Did I hear correctly? Are you two related?"

"What makes you think that?" His deep dimples were in place again along with a glitter in his toffee colored eyes.

These two men were acting like little boys fighting over a toy. Apparently, I was that toy.

Gritting my teeth, I wished I could knock their heads together and make both of them behave. I wanted answers, not jokes, so I gave him a no-nonsense look.

"Yes. We're cousins. It's complicated."

"I can do complicated."

"All right. Try this on for size." He dimpled up again. "My mother is his grandfather's wife, who also happens to be his aunt and his mother's sister."

Grandfathers, mothers, sisters—"Mind running that by me again, but take it a little slower this time. No forget it. I'll never understand."

His laughter echoed through the halls. "Katherine is my aunt. Her sister is my mother, which makes us cousins. My mother had the audacity to marry Matt's grandfather on his dad's side, so that makes me his cousin and step-uncle, if that makes sense." He must have noticed my scrunched up nose and brows. "I told you it was complicated."

"Wait a minute." The light bulb was flashing at the speed of light inside my head and almost blinding me. "You mean to tell me Katherine Owens is Matt's—Mr. Ainsley's mother?"

"Give that woman a prize."

His voice sounded like a barker at a carnival.

"I can see you're not slow on the uptake, at least in some matters."

"Oh, you're so wrong there. Now things are more confusing than ever. Why would Ms. Owens and Mr. Ainsley have two different names?"

"Come on now. Put your thinking cap on." His eyes sparkled.

"She's remarried."

"Bingo." James touched his finger to the tip of his nose. "A couple of years after my Uncle Ainsley died, she married Carl Owens. Carl died during a parachuting accident." He stopped to open my office the door.

"There's a lot more to explain about the family tree, but that's for another time. Duty calls. I have a long distance conference call I have to handle in five. But if I can help you in any way, my extension is 212. Maybe lunch?" He winked raising his brows.

"I brought my lunch." I wanted to soften the blow to this man who had been kind to me, even if it were in the line of duty. "Maybe another time. I have a lot of reading to do. And I need to go out and buy a pair of shoes during my lunch hour."

"All right. Catch you later."

Too much to think about with no time allowed.

The door had no sooner shut than I heard the connecting door between my office and the CEO's open. Without looking, I felt his presence and knew he stood in the doorway.

"Ms. Gates, would you step into my office, please?"

This can't be good. But what do I have to fear—they hired me, not the other way around. I'd like this job to last long enough to draw at least one pay check ... please, God.

"Yes, sir, I'll be right with you."

Nothing in life had prepared me for being the pawn in this game Mr. CEO and Ms. Executive Mom were playing. I knew for either to win, I would have to be sacrificed.

When I took this job, I had plans to last longer than a day, but it didn't seem likely now.

Chapter 15

After our first initial meeting, or as Mr. Trivial called it, *our little fender bender*, I had often wondered what his office would look like—the place where he did those mega buck deals I had read about.

I never envisioned a huge vintage model airplane hanging from the ceiling, nor pictures of all types of aircrafts on the walls, tastefully done I might add. Nor was I prepared for the shock of the nose and partial wing of an actual bi-plane protruding out of a portion of the wall and fifteen foot ceiling.

On the left wall was an actual full instrument panel pulled from a classic aviation aircraft, levers and dials intact. The temptation to pull and twist a few of the gadgets to see if they would move was hard to resist. However, I checked the impulse.

For seating there were aviator chairs mounted to a swivel base, upholstered with thick padding. And though I had flown only a couple of times, Mr. CEO's executive chair looked as though it came straight out of first class seating, the same ones I would pass on my way to the coach when I flew.

The only thing missing were the stewards with their little carts and the hum of the plane engines.

The cost of the decor for the room would have kept me quite comfortable for several years and then some.

This guy was certainly out of my league.

"Have a seat."

Mr. Exec sounded a little on edge, and of course, that led to an upheaval in my middle regions. If I had been on a more even plain to what was going on, I wouldn't have felt at such a disadvantage.

I moved into one of the aviator chairs, kept my feet firmly planted on the floor, folded my hands primly in my lap, and waited for what was to come next. Hopefully, not *... you're fired.*

"Ms. Gates, I'm not sure where to go or what to do from this point."

Quiet sure he meant keeping me at my job or letting me go, I kept silent.

"At times, my mother is quite the meddler into my affairs. But today she seems to have out done herself."

"I hope you don't think I had anything to do with—"

He held up his hand. "No, I know my mother well enough to believe you had little to do with your hiring. Did she even ask for your credentials?"

"Yes, and I made sure she had my résumé." I felt like a little girl talking with the principal. The only thing missing ... the stink of sweat and old food.

"I'll bet she didn't even ask if you had a degree, or even what that degree might be."

"No, sir."

"I thought not."

Swiveling his chair around to face the picture window, he reached out and spun the propeller of a small model airplane sitting on his credenza. He leaned his head against the back of his chair and released a loud breath.

The *zinnnng* from the propeller spinning spilled into the silence of the room. I didn't know whether to sit or leave quietly.

I decided the best course of action was to remain in my seat and pray he wouldn't tell me I didn't have a job any longer.

After several long excruciating moments of nothing except for the propeller slowing to a tick, tiiick, tiiiiick. I threw caution to the wind. "Mr. Ainsley—"

His head popped up off the backrest, and he turned toward me as though he'd forgotten I was still in the room.

"I have a double degree in marketing and business. Though I have never worked in the capacity of my degrees, if you will give me a chance, you will see I'm quite knowledgeable and capable of handling any task set before me. And I'm a quick study."

"I just bet you are." He cocked a brow.

His probing gaze seemed to dig deep inside me searching for ... what?

I almost lost my courage to go on, but decided keeping this job was tantamount to my keeping food on the table and a roof over my head. I wasn't giving up without a fight.

"From what I gathered at the board meeting, and if I understand your company's needs correctly, I have what you're looking for."

"Ohhh. And what exactly is that Ms. Gates?"

He gave me the once over which flustered me more than I thought possible.

I sucked in a quick breath and forged ahead, giving him a full rundown of all my finer business qualities and what I could do for his companies. During the long litany of what I would add to the MTA team, I wondered if anything I said was making sense or if it all sounded like a bunch of garbage.

When I finally ran out of steam and stopped, Mr. Sure-of-Himself smiled.

"Ahh, but Ms. Gates, you failed to mention the one and only quality my mother hired you for."

I racked my brain to remember what Ms. Owens and I had talked about as far as my qualifications, and couldn't remember one single thing she had mentioned.

"Besides being qualified for the job, I can't think of what that could be."

Mr. Smug acted as if he was on the verge of a deep belly laugh. "Oh, I'm quite sure she never mentioned the true reason she hired you."

"If you'll explain what it might be, I believe you will find I am capable and knowledgeable enough to do any job you may have. Or, if you'll allow me, I'd be willing to learn on my own time, if need be."

He looked tired, almost weary when he let out a breath.

"My wife."

Chapter 16

I gasped, cutting off all intake of air, strangling me. I coughed on my spittle, tried to catch my breath, then coughed some more.

Mr. All-Concerned looked amused at my shocked reaction.

I desperately need this job—but not to the extent of marrying the boss.

He's handsome enough to be sure, but I couldn't marry anyone except for love, not even if it cost me a job or money.

Astonished to learn I was the instrument of Ms. Owens' designs for her son, I didn't know whether to be offended or humiliated. I knew I should get up, collect the few things I had brought with me, and walk out.

My little efficiency, where life was normal was sounding better and better by each passing moment. That is, if a person can count normal as having the rent paid for twenty-five more days, but no money left to pay bills or to eat.

And then there was that little matter of the three hundred dollars I owed the man looking at me with calculating eyes. Did I just say *little matter?*

There was nothing small about three hundred dollars. It was *HUGE.*

"Is this some kind of sick joke?" I couldn't believe I was even talking to Mr. Arrogant. I moved to stand.

"No. I'm afraid it's not a joke." He shrugged. "Sick maybe, but no joke."

He waived me back in my chair, but I wasn't about to heed his command. I moved to leave.

"Ms. Gates, please be seated. Hear me out." He motioned again. "I believe my plan will benefit both of us."

I hesitated.

"I promise I'll explain everything, but first, please sit down."

I vacillated for a few seconds. Something in his eyes—pleading? regret?—had me sliding back into the aviator chair. However, this time I perched on the edge of the seat for a quick getaway.

"As we both know, we have been duped by my mother."

"What do you mean duped?" In the back of my mind, something pricked my subconscious. I ignored the nudge.

Why would Ms. Owens hire someone to marry her son? All Mr. CEO had to do was snap his fingers and a dozen young women would line up for the honor ... just not me.

"Allow me to explain." Irritation eked from his pores. "My sister is married. She's given my mother two sweet, rambunctious grandchildren, with another one due in about two months."

"Yes ... I believe she mentioned something about your sister and the grandchildren during my interview." That little niggling thought was back in my brain again. *Come to think of it, that wasn't all Mrs. Owens mentioned.*

An ironical grin rode Mr. Smug's lips as if he had insight to my thoughts. "She didn't bring me up during that interview, did she?" His eyes watched me like a hawk detecting a rat.

"She mentioned an unmarried son." My cheeks blazed.

"I thought so. But I'll wager she didn't mention her son's name."

Looking at him, I shook my head. How could I have been so gullible?

"I figured as much." Picking up a crystal paperweight with a miniature airplane suspended in the glass, Mr. CEO turned the cube in his hands, studying it, before setting it back down.

"What we have here, Ms. Gates, is a classic mother-gone-amuck. In this case, one Katherine Owens, who would do anything, including alienating her only son to get him married off."

This impossible situation was worse than sitting on a bed of hot coals. More like sliding down a banister turned into a razor blade. I fought the impulse to squirm at the vivid visual.

Knowing I was about to ask one very stupid question, I plunged in headfirst anyway. "Why me? Why not someone you already know?"

His eyes stared at me, knowing perfectly well I could see the broad stroke of the brush without him revealing the answer.

"Surely not." The words popped out breathy, barely audible.

His intense, light green eyes never left my face as I sat quietly allowing the whole treacherous reality to sink in.

"Why would she pick me as your would-be bride. Your mother doesn't even know me. You don't know me."

"Assumptions." His face turned a darker tan making his adorable eyes even more pronounced.

"About what? … No, don't answer that." Palms sweaty, I squeezed my hands together, refusing to wipe them on my skirt.

Why me, Lord? Why couldn't life be simple? All I wanted was a decent job. Work eight to five. Go home and write my novels with none of this drama unfurling before me.

My anger bubbled over at the very thought of these arrogant, rich people using me as a pawn, not caring how they were affecting my life. I stood, hands to my side, refusing to ball my fists.

"I'm sorry your mother has wasted my time and yours, Mr. Ainsley. I'm not looking for a husband. All I want is an honest job, to do a good day's work, and collect a decent wage. You can send my check for"—I looked at the clock in the instrument panel and calculated my time—"four hours and twenty-three minutes to the address in my file.

"I hope you and your mother find what you are both looking for. Have a nice life."

On shaky legs, I rushed toward the exit. My hand was on the door handle.

"Before you walk out of my office, you may want to hear what I have to offer. I'm not looking for a wife. But I do have a proposition for you. Please, hear me out."

Why was I vacillating? Why hadn't I walked out of Mr. Aero-Dynamic's office?

There was that little something in his voice that stopped me and made me turn to look at him.

"Tiffany—"

My eyes narrowed. He had never called me by my given name before, not even when we had our fender-bender.

He shrugged. "So be it, Ms. Gates. If you'll hear me out, I will make it worth your while. I think we can save your job, which I believe you need desperately, and at the same time, save the marriage noose from tightening around my neck."

Keeping my hand on the doorknob, I continued to stare at him.

"Please." He motioned at the chair.

I didn't move.

"Let me explain what I have in mind. Then if you disagree, you may leave, and I'll pay you one month's severance pay for your trouble. How does that sound?"

"Generous to a fault. But why would you?" Why was I waffling or even discussing the matter?

"You've been placed in an untenable position—a battle between my mother and me, for which I apologize. Unfortunately, you are the casualty." He turned palms up and shrugged.

"I took a few minutes to look over your résumé. Here's what I'm willing to offer.

"For the next three months, let's see what you can do with the position you've been hired—ah—been given as Executive Liaison Specialist. This is my way of making amends to you, and I believe, if you agree to my plan, it will also fix my meddling mother once and for all." He motioned again for me to sit down. "Please."

"This doesn't involve marriage, does it?" I gave him an obstinate look, hoping he knew I wouldn't play any games of husband and wife, touchy-feely, or any other type for that matter.

"No."

For the first time since I'd walked into the room, he smiled—a genuine honest-to-goodness, brilliant smile. It warmed my toes, not to mention my heart.

If what he proposed wasn't illegal or immoral, I could live with a three month-trial basis, within reason. Three months' salary was huge. Three months would give me time to look for another position, or prove my worth at MTA—if I wanted to stay.

With my frugal ways, the money could last me up to six months or better. What could it hurt to at least hear what he had to say?

Moving into the seat I had vacated a second time, I slid back and got comfortable. To my way of thinking, Mr. I've-Got-a-Proposition and Meddling-Mama owed me something at least for my inconvenience and for what they put me through. And with the one month's severance pay Mr. Big-Bucks was offering, I could listen.

"Just so long as we understand each other. I won't be anyone's victim. If it involves anything shady or immoral, I will be out that door faster than you can sneeze. And I won't look back regardless how good the pay." I cocked my brow for emphasis.

"I'm not here to play wife or house, or become the brunt of someone's sick joke. So if that's what you're suggesting, you might as well save your breath."

Giving me a half smile, he leaned forward, his elbows on the desk, cupping the crystal plane paperweight in his palms. For several seconds that seemed more like an eternity, Mr. MTA studied me.

I wanted to squirm, to leave, but I did neither. I was too curious how he would handle his mother's interfering ways. Call me plain foolish or even a little daft, but I couldn't have left if my life depended upon it—*which it might*.

"Please listen to all I have to say before you react. After hearing me out, the decision will be yours alone to make.

"Let me mention up front that you are a very attractive woman. However, rest assured, you're not my type. So you can take my word for it, I have no design on you as a woman of interest or a potential wife."

That sure smarted. Too homespun? Too plain? Too what? What do I care?

"Thank you, and I might add, you're not my type either."

I don't know what my type is, but without a doubt this one well-buffed, attractive, mega rich guy wasn't it.

"I didn't mean to offend."

"No offense taken. And the same to you. My words weren't meant as an insult."

He stared at me, no doubt, trying to take my measure.

Well, measure on, buddy. You'll never figure this woman out.

"The proposition I have to offer is two-fold. For the next three months I propose you work in the capacity you were hired, Executive Liaison Specialist, which could turn into long term if you are right for the position. Your main thrust will be to give MTA's image a new facelift, building a campaign, that sort of thing. I'll give you the direction we wish to head, then see what ideas you can work up to implement the plan."

"And?"

He looked at me questioningly.

"You said two-fold."

Mr. Let's-Make-a-Deal grinned as though he'd won the prize behind door one, two, *and* three, and at this very minute was about to strike the deal of his life.

"And … you will help get my mother off my back by agreeing to be my fiancée."

Chapter 17

Flabbergasted, I began the choking thing again. *I seem to have a problem with choking around Mr. I've-Got-A-Plan.*

After practically picking myself up off the floor, I asked, "You're what?"

My head reeled as my body jerked to attention.

This guy must be some kind of nutcase. Not just him, but his whole family has to be insane. First, I'm not his type, and now he's proposing? I'm in the Twilight Zone.

"My fiancée. You will—"

"I heard what you said and I know what a fiancée is. And didn't we just agree neither of us was attracted to the other ... at least not in that way?"

He laughed—not a funny *ha-ha* laugh, but a humor me laugh.

"All I'm suggesting is an engagement, say, in a month of two, not a marriage."

He held up his hand to stay me from another outburst.

"Hear me out. We'll date some, gradually working it into an engagement."

"Let me get this straight. I'm not your type, but you want to marry me?"

"No, Ms. Gates, I don't wish to marry you."

He gave me a look as if to say, *are you obtuse?*

"What I want is an engagement of convenience. A pretense for my mother's benefit. Hopefully, one that will affectively cause her to stop seeking out women for me to marry, of which, you seem to be her woman of choice at the moment."

"Why did she pick me? I've never met your mother before the day of my interview."

A disdainful smile appeared. "No, I'd wager the interview was the first time you had even heard of her."

"Then why me?"

"The only thing that comes to mind for her sneaky, maneuvering behavior is the car."

"The car?"

"Yes. She found out I loaned the company car to you after the accident. And from that she received the brilliant idea I was interested in you, which I'm not."

No call to be quite so ardent with your dislike. What's wrong with me anyway?

He was doing it again—a big number on my self-esteem. I shot back, "The feeling's mutual."

"Wonderful. Since we've established our shared lack of interest in each other, we can begin immediately by laying down the groundwork. Once that's done, we will begin dating and then become engaged."

"Wait just a minute. I haven't agreed to anything." I gave him another firm look, which didn't seem to faze him. "What makes you so sure that I'll take your offer?"

"You'll have a good job, a good salary, which I'll bump up another couple of thousand per month for the added expense of clothes, shoes, hair appointments, all of which you'll need." He gave me the onceover.

This man certainly knew how to make a woman feel less than attractive and confidant. Fortunately, he didn't

turn up his nose as if smelling something rotten, otherwise,
I would have walked out.

"I can afford to pay for my own—"

"Not the type of clothing you'll need." Again, he
looked me over like a man getting ready to purchase a prize
heifer.

"We'll be attending black tie events, and you'll need to
fit in, which will be expensive. Plus, if we are to pull this
off, everyone will expect the woman I'm dating to look a
certain way, not that you don't look … ah—" He scrunched
his brow. "—respectable, but—"

"You don't have to paint a picture. I get the message
just fine."

"I'm sure you do. You'll have a good job for however
long you want it, as long as you can do the work. And I'll
have peace for a year or two, whichever length of time
works for you."

"A year or two!" I almost shot up out the chair.

"At least a year, or my mother will just start looking
again, which doesn't work with my plans."

"What if you find the woman of your *dreams?* What
happens then? Or if I find a man I wish to marry. Aren't we
painting ourselves into a corner, as the saying goes?"

Glancing at the paperweight, he moved it to the left,
twisted it just so, then glanced back at me.

The solitary, lonely look in his eyes almost made me
feel sorry for the man. Handsome and wealthy far beyond
what I could ever imagine, if the news articles about him
were correct, this thirty-three year-old bachelor should at
least be entertaining marriage with some socialite or
woman of his choice. Instead, here he sat doing his best to
convince me to play pretend fiancée. What a pity

"Let's just say, for the time being, or for at least a few
more years, I have no such plans to marry. I wouldn't
remotely consider popping the question to any woman of

my acquaintance. Marriage is highly overrated anyway. So you see, you'll be doing me a service, while at the same time, you'll have a lucrative income."

"Who soured you on the state of holy matrimony?"

His hardened penetrating stare had me squirming.

"Ok, forget I asked. It's none of my business."

His face brightened. "To tell the truth, Ms. Gates, MTA is on the verge of something so totally diverse that I don't have time for such nonsense."

Nonsense? Was the man without feeling?

I studied him for a moment and found him to be completely serious, and seemingly honest. Business, at this point, was far more important to him than a life or a wife apparently. And since I didn't have anyone on the horizon, I could invest at least a year if it meant I could keep my job and … *if he didn't make any indecent moves or proposals.*

Giving him a pleasant smile, I said, "Unlike you, I would like to marry eventually when I find the right man. However, I don't have any such plans in the near future. Let's just say for argument's sake that you or I find someone we're interested in. What happens then?"

"If that occurs, then we break off the engagement. No harm. No foul. And your job would be secure since neither of us will be emotionally attached." He rubbed a hand over his eyes and huffed out an exhausted breath as he leaned back in his chair.

"I can't believe I'm being reduced to trickery all because my mother wants to preserve the Ainsley name."

I witnessed the first glint of disgusted anger from Mr. I'm-In-Control. This agreement was affecting him far worse than he let on.

He turned his chair to stare out the window.

I didn't know if he expected me to say something, or if I should stay or leave.

Mr. Boss-Man took a deep breath. "She believes there should be a little Matthew Thomas Ainsley the Fourth running around for posterity. Why? ... I have no idea. The laugh would certainly be on her if I were to marry and father all girls. Then what would she do?"

The chair swiveled back around, and I saw a drop-dead, gorgeous smile and sparkling green eyes, all anger gone. "I'll soon have nieces and nephews enough to fill this company." He shrugged. "Oh, later down the road, I might want to find a suitable woman for a wife and to have children, but as I mentioned, not anytime soon."

"No strings attached to this agreement you propose?" I couldn't believe that I was actually entertaining such a preposterous idea. *I've gone and lost my mind completely.*

"None whatsoever." His slight smile was filled with sadness.

"What if I decide I want out of this farce—deal, you won't stop me?"

"No. But I'd prefer you stick to the arrangement until the merger is complete and up and running well, which should be in six months. However, if not ..." He shrugged. "If your work is satisfactory when we announce the engagement is off, you may keep your job.

"We'll just say we found we weren't compatible, but wish to remain friends. No reason to lose a valuable employee when it comes to someone who is capable, which I hope you will be."

"How will you convince your mother we're an item?"

"I'll take you out to lunch at first, then eventually out to dinner, and when we've finally become a couple in everyone's mind, I'll take you to the family dinner on Sunday. That should do the trick. Fortunately, the family get together only happens once a month."

He looked thoughtful. "However, before you agree, let me say, after our engagement is announced, I will expect you to accompany me to all functions that will require a dinner partner. However, I decline as many functions as possible. And, I think you will find I'm not all that demanding.

"We'll go to a play or symphony from time to time and maybe a movie, just to set the stage. But don't expect me to have a lot of free time or start thinking of this as a real relationship. You're at my whim and not the other way around."

"Understood." I stared at him and wondered why, of all people, he would want me as his fake fiancée? Surely there were women who were more suitable and traveled in his circles. The reasons he'd given seemed flimsy at best, and less than what he wanted to reveal.

"If you need someone to partner you to an event, if I can't go, I'm sure James would be more than happy to oblige."

The last statement surprisingly sounded a tad sarcastic. He fiddled with his Mont Blanc, the little diamond on the tip of the cap caught the light and winked at me as if to say *you've done it now.*

"So let me get this straight. I work as liaison for MTA on a trial basis for three months and if all is well, I will continue as liaison and as your fiancée for an indefinite amount of time. Right?" *I could do this—I think.*

"The engagement is to be at least until this merger comes through and the new company is up and running smoothly. I don't want to have to fight off my mother when all of my energies need to be focused on business. It's absolutely crucial for me to have no distractions." He paused, as if weighing what to add. "And at the moment you fit the bill."

Wow! Thanks. No wonder you don't have a wife.

Not sure whether to feel insulted or thankful over his choice of words, my partially deflated ego went completely flat. I was undesirable and blasé … *how depressing.*

"I'd like the agreement, all of it, to be in writing." Did I actually say that?

"In writing?" He scrunched his brows over amused eyes.

"I don't believe I've asked for anything outlandish. Just a few ground rules … a mutual understanding of what and what not to expect. Also, if I'm going to play this little charade, I believe a contract for three months with one month's severance is absolutely necessary."

I couldn't believe I was giving Mr. CEO my demands, but there it was in plain English.

"Anything else?" He gave a short chuckle under his breath.

"Yes." I didn't know how to explain the huge monster lurking at the back of my mind, tearing up my peace.

Out with it Tiffany, you can do it.

"There will be no physical contact other than what is absolutely necessary in public for the credibility of our so-called relationship. And that will be at a minimum."

He chuckled outright this time. "Go on. I can tell there's something more rattling around in that brain of yours."

"Yes, there is." I paused, wondering if I had lost my mind completely.

"And?"

"If there is to be kissing involved to be convincing in our roll play, I want it brief, and not deep throat, tongue play—understand? Chalk it up to scruples." *What's left of them.*

There it was out in the open and my face was on fire. If my demands were a deal breaker, then so be it.

His display of delight in knowing I felt uncomfortable talking about amorous matters ticked me off. I shrugged this time, trying to look unaffected.

"What should I say if someone happens to mention we aren't – ah – overly affectionate?" By the glint in his eyes, he found all of this highly amusing.

For me, these rules meant the difference of doing the job or walking out.

"Tell them I don't like displays of public affection. Or, tell them what you please. But I'll not change my position on these points. Only proper touching and minimal kissing when necessary."

A smile tugged at his lips. "Maybe I could say you're frigid in—"

I saw red.

"If this is a game with you, then I think we're finished." I moved to stand.

"Ms. Gates—" He waved me back in my seat. Once again, he leaned forward and rested his elbows on the desk.

"I apologize. This isn't a game. I want to put a stop to my mother and her meddling interference." He took a breath. "Since we are soon to be an engaged couple, may I dispense with the formality and call you Tiffany, or maybe Tiff?"

Knowing calling me Tiff was linked to James' use of my name, and still ruffled over his choice of words, I answered, "Tiffany will do."

"Hmm." He watched me through narrowed eyes. "Tiffany then. Draw up the contract for hire agreement." He pulled a small quarter-size drive from his desk drawer and held it out to me. "Save it on this jump drive, not on your hard drive."

I was careful not to touch his fingers.

"Make sure you write down all your taboos so I don't transgress." The sparkle was back in those appealing eyes.

"I'll read it over and make any changes I think fit. Once we've settled on a satisfactory agreement, print it out. We'll sign two originals, one for you and one for me, to make it legally binding. How does that sound?"

"I'll get right to it." I started to stand.

"Not so fast. I have a couple of stipulations also."

"I'm listening."

"You are not to disclose any part of our agreement to anyone—family, friend, or media. If you do, you will forfeit the job and severance pay. If media gets wind of this farce, it could be grounds for a lawsuit."

"That's agreeable."

"I won't be made to look the fool. You won't be allowed to see other men while we are dating or engaged."

"I wouldn't think of it. And likewise you."

"Agreed." He stood, came around his desk, his hand extended. "I believe we understand each other. Welcome aboard." A smile lurked as his eyes strayed to my feet.

"By the way, unusual shoes. Trying to set a new trend?"

Chapter 18

I should have my head examined. What was I thinking?

This was all a big joke to Matthew Ainsley, nothing more. Oh, he needed me, but would he hold to the stipulations of our agreement? I didn't believe Mr. In-Charge ever had to bow to anyone's wishes until now.

At lunch, I bought shoes, glad to be free of the big, black boats. My afternoon was filled with the contract, while little gremlins had a heyday mocking me for my part in the charade.

When I handed him the agreement, Mr. All-Business read it and didn't change one word. He signed and dated both copies. I did the same. He handed me one, kept one, pocketed the thumb drive, then shook my hand as if this was an ordinary business transaction.

Come to think of it, it was.

His strong grip caused a tingle in my palm to rush up my arm and into my chest. I chalked it up to nerves and the anxiety of being weighed down with something I wasn't wholly comfortable with. However, I would follow through due to my signature on the line.

He congratulated me on becoming a partner in the venture to forestall his mother and welcomed me to MTA.

Surely I was doing a good deed if I could stop a meddling mother from pressuring an unwilling son into a marriage with divorce waiting in the wings.

"In the morning, we'll talk more about what I envision for the new merger. I'd like to see what kind of ideas you may have."

I nodded, left through the connecting door to my office, a little confused as to which merger he wanted to discuss—ours or the company's? Unfortunately, my rationalization of how this was a job just like any other—w*ell, not quite like any other*—flew out the window.

Not at all in a sycophantic mood, I left the office without saying goodnight to my soon-to-be pretend fiancé. All I wanted to do was to go home, crawl in bed, pull the covers over my head, and pray tomorrow would never come. I knew that was pure folly.

Before leaving, I called in the pizza order, snatched the photo of Edgar off my desk, glad this day was almost over. Thankfully, I didn't see my new boss/soon-to-be fiancée.

The oddity of the day, if one could be singled out above all the rest, I hadn't seen Ms. Owens since the board meeting. The answer to *why* left me a little disconcerted. Maybe she feared I'd give her a piece of my mind, or she figured her son had fired me. Her non-appearance was probably for the best. Otherwise, I might have broken the contract before the ink was even dry.

Pizza would have normally bolstered my sinking spirit, but tonight the smell permeating my car made me a little nauseous and wishing for a bath and bed.

I couldn't believe I had just signed a contract to begin dating and soon become engaged to one of the wealthiest men in Texas.

My hands shook. The oncoming cars blinded me with little dizzying zigzagged patterns of light dancing across the dash. Dark and light. So much like the feelings deep inside for the deception I was about to perpetrate along with Mr. Boss-Man.

Should I think of it as a betrayal or as a stop to Ms. Owens unwieldy efforts as matchmaker?

How would I ever play the role convincingly when a lie on my tongue played like a neon sign on my face? All I could do was give it my best shot and pray for a speedy exit out of the chaos.

Mrs. Mac must have been watching out the window. Before I could get up the steps, the door flew open. The angelic face of my sweet landlady appeared. I gave her a weak smile and fell into her warm bear hug while doing my best to balance the pizza and the paraphernalia from work.

Her hands relieved me of the pizza. "My dear, you look tired. Was the ogre that bad?"

"No." I smiled adding in as much sparkle as I could find. "First days are always tough. New place, learning a new job." I wasn't about to tell her what kind of job I was really hired for.

"I'm sure it is." She sniffed the box. "I was hoping you hadn't forgotten our dinner engagement. But here you are. And here's the pizza, which I might add, smells heavenly"

"I wouldn't forget such an important date." I wanted to forget this day had ever happened though.

Mrs. Mac took a deep sniff. "Ahh, the smell of a specialty pizza with extra pepperoni. It's divine. You did remember the extra pepperoni, didn't you, dear?"

"Just like you asked."

She ushered me inside, then gave me a gentle shove toward the staircase. "Now along with you. Go on upstairs and put on something comfortable. I'll have everything ready to eat when you come down. We'll talk over dinner, then you can go to bed. You look plum tuckered out."

"Thanks, Mrs. Mac. Do I look that bad?" I wanted to cry.

"Sweetie, you never look bad. It just appears you've had a full day. And it's no wonder. First day on the job jitters, learning everything new, which I feel sure you'll be good at." She shooed me with her free hand. "Go on now. The pizza's getting cold."

I put one foot before the other as I dragged myself upstairs.

Once I changed into my warm-ups and splashed cold water on my face, I felt a little better. Upon my return to Mrs. Mac's, I placed her prized possession safely back on the top of the TV.

When she saw what I had done, she seemed particularly pleased, especially after I explained she needed Edgar more than I did. Her smile made everything seem a little brighter with the world.

We ate our pizza between snippets of Mrs. Mac's chatter and with an occasional nod from me. The ebb and flow of the one-sided conversation allowed my weary brain to relax.

She never once brought up the topic of my job, except to say, "Tomorrow evening, dear, you'll be more rested. You can tell me all about the job then, and you'll know more *the lay of the land.*"

"I'll do that. Tomorrow evening we'll have a nice sit-down chat."

After polishing off the last bite of my one slice of pizza, Mrs. Mac shooed me off. I took the gracious escape she offered, promising I'd give her the full scoop tomorrow.

I rushed up the stairs and went immediately to the bathroom to fill the tub. After sprinkling rose scented bubble bath into the stream, I slipped out of my clothes and slid into the deep, claw-foot tub of steaming hot water and foaming bubbles. I allowed the fragrance and warmth to wash away the memory of my ill-fated day.

My mind meandered through Lady Judith's dilemma.

Lord Sebastian, demented with revenge, pulled the dagger from his belt. He lifted it high above his head, ready to thrust. Spittle spewed from his mouth. His eyes glazed with hate.

"Since you didn't want me, Rolf won't have you either."

Judith cringed, circling her arms protectively around her belly and curled into a small ball on the floor where she had fallen, awaiting the fatal blow.

She heard a crash, a gasp, and then chards of pottery rained down around her. Releasing her garment, Sebastian fell against the table, then on top of her, pinning her beneath his motionless body. Judith felt someone touch her head and then her shoulder. She prayed it was friend not foe. Without strength to help or defend, Judith was relieved to see it was Rolf's elderly steward, Simon.

He shoved Sebastian, but the man wouldn't budge.

"Let me place my arm around your neck, Simon. I think I may be able to scoot out from beneath him with your assistance."

Simon did as Judith asked. Then both of them pulled her free from the unconscious man. She stood but almost crumpled when her leg gave way. The servant held her around the waist, allowing her to lean into him as he helped her cross the hall. She stumbled several times and would have fallen if not for Simon.

"Don't fret, milady. I've got ye. I'll hide ye away where the monster can't find ye until he be gone." He pulled her to the stairway, urging her

on, carrying most of Judith's weight. "Please, Lady Judith, move quickly. We must make the stairs before he wakens and kills us both."

She looked back at Sebastian's prone body and saw him beginning to stir. With Simon's help, she made the stairs, down the hall, and into the last chamber.

"There be a hidin' place. A cubby hole only me and the master knows." Simon pushed against a stone in the wall.

The scraping sound seemed loud in the quiet of the chamber as the wall moved back into a dark crevice. The cold, dank air woke her dulled senses as the smell of mildew filled her lungs. Judith looked at Simon with question.

"In here, milady." He motioned for her to follow. "It be dark and a mite smelly, but ye'll be safe until the master comes home."

She allowed Simon to lead her down a narrow path of steps, deep into the bowels of the castle with only the light coming from the hall.

"Here, milady, take this flint. Light this candle once I be gone." He placed both in her hands. "I must get back before he finds me missing and knows I helped you escape. If ye go on down a little ways further, ye'll find a chamber with a straw bed, not sure what condition it be in, but ye'll at least have a place to sit and rest until I can come get ye."

"Thank you, Simon. Go on back now. Before you return for me, make sure Sebastian has left the keep. Lord Rolf should be home on the morrow. I'll be fine until then." She had to be brave to save herself and her unborn babe.

The chill of the damp seeped through her dress, deep under her skin as the echo of Simon's retreating steps grew smaller and the shadows grew darker. She shivered, wondering where she could be. Why had Rolf never mentioned this place? She prayed he would be back soon and Sebastian wouldn't find her.

Knowing she didn't dare move without light, she tried to strike the flint, but her cold hands wouldn't cooperate. The thoughts of a misstep and plunging to her death didn't appeal to Judith.

Pulled out of my reverie by the cold creeping into my skin, I realized the water had turned lukewarm. My fingers and toes looked like shriveled up little prunes. Lady Judith would have to wait. I needed sleep if I were to face the lion in his den tomorrow.

As I slid beneath the cool sheets, I allowed the sounds of the house to lull me into a relaxed stupor.

The ringing of my cellphone caused a knee-jerk reaction. I yelped and snatched the culprit off my nightstand. Not recognizing the number, I hesitated to answer but decided curiosity would drive me nuts and I'd never get to sleep.

I cleared my throat. "Hello?"

"Don't bring your lunch tomorrow. We'll have a power lunch and discuss strategy."

Power lunch? "Excuse me, who is this?"

I knew perfectly well who was on the other end, but I wasn't about to allow Mr. Orders to get away with displaying despicable manners and a general lack of civility, regardless if time for him was money. He owed me respect.

"This is Matt, of course. Who else would be calling you at this hour?" He paused. "Do you often receive calls from men at night asking you to lunch?"

By the sound of his voice he was annoyed and a little uptight with her. She smiled. For once, she was glad to get under his skin.

"Oh, hi Mr. Ainsley. I can't say that I do. However, there have been a few—"

"Matt. The name is Matt. I thought we agreed upon first names. How will it look to others if you call me Mr. Ainsley?"

"Wouldn't it be a little too soon, me being new and all?"

"Not in the least. At the office everyone is informal. We all go by first names. Plus, I've already left hints that we've known each other for awhile."

"Already?" I didn't know what to think. This was going a little too fast for my comfort.

His deep, uninhibited chuckle did a number on me. "Yes. *Already.*"

A man of action, this one. He didn't let any hayseed grow under his feet. I'll never survive—what?—six months, a year, maybe two?

"I wouldn't consider two weeks with three face-to-face meetings as all that long of an acquaintance."

"No one is aware of how long we have known each other. So try to remember in the future to use my name ... Matt."

"All right, *Matt.* I think you mentioned something about lunch." I wanted him to ask me, not give me a command.

He released an irritated breath aware of the game I played.

"I hope you're not going to be difficult." A pause. "How's this?—*Tiffany*, if you're not busy, would you have lunch with me tomorrow? We can eat and talk over our strategy—Is that better?"

"Much. And no, I don't have other plans, *Matt,* I'd love to. What time?"

"Eleven o'clock. That way we'll beat the rush. I need to be back at one-thirty for a meeting. Will that work for you?"

I could tell he didn't like having to explain his actions to anyone, especially me. However, I delighted in forcing the issue. It gave me a feeling of power and some control, even if I knew I had neither.

"I believe that'll work fine with my schedule."

"Since I'm your boss, I know it will. I'll touch base with you in the morning."

The phone went silent. For a moment, I thought he'd gotten angry and hung up.

"And *Tiff*—"

"Yes?" I shook inside. This sound in his voice was one I hadn't heard before.

"Don't play your little woman games with me. I don't like it. I'm familiar with them all. I've had lessons from the best, and hon, you're out of your league. Pleasant dreams."

I heard what I thought sounded like a chuckle before the line went dead.

Did I touch a sore spot or what? And *pleasant dreams,* easy for him to say.

Any sleep that I might have laid claim to, he destroyed. And dreams, well ... he was one dream I would love to be rid of but knew that wouldn't happen any time soon.

Chapter 19

Today, I was prepared for every eventuality—a pair of shoes, a backup pair, and just about anything else I could conceivably think I might need was in my bag. I hefted the tote bag and winced at the weight. At least today, I had arrived early enough to get a parking space reasonably close.

Heading toward the building, I felt a jerk and the bag lifted from my hand. "What—" I turned to find Mr. Future-Fiancé by my side in a black pinstripe suit.

His hair looked like he'd just stepped out of the shower. A hint of spicy-woodies cologne drifted to my nose and caused me to take a deeper breath. He wore a delicious grin from ear to ear.

"Good morning, Tiffany." His smile turned to a frown. "What in the world are you carrying in this thing? Rocks? It weighs a ton."

"Good morning to you too, boss. And I can carry my own bag, thank you." I reached for it, but he held on tight.

"And claim workman's comp? I don't think so. And since we are already practically engaged"—he gave me a mischievous wink—"it's my duty to watch out for your welfare."

"Oh, give me a break. I don't buy that for a minute."

"Sleep well?" His brows lifted as if he knew I hadn't.

I glanced away for fear I'd color up and he'd see the truth. "Quite well. And you?"

"Ahh, now that is a puzzle. After I hung up, my blood was pumping and my imagination working, so much so, I couldn't sleep a wink. My mind reeled with ideas. I'll have to make it a rule not to call you before bedtime. But I did have some amazingly productive hours. I was able to work through the merger documents that you'll be working on. I've got some research I want you to do before lunch."

"Mornin', gorgeous." James jogged up to my other side and got in step with us. "My, my." His gaze ran the full distance over me. "You look good enough to eat, doesn't she Matty. *Mm-hm.*" Dimples in place and a sparkle in his cocoa eyes, James gave me an audacious wink—too identical to his cousin's for comfort.

"Act your age, Jimmy, and quit drooling all over Tiffany. Drooling isn't becoming of a grown man." Mr. In-Command reached around and shifted me to the outer side, placing himself between James and me.

"Hey, no fair." James maneuvered me back into the middle and grinned. "Don't you have important business waiting on you? Rush along inside, Cuz. I'll escort Tiffany to her office." He grinned down at me. "Would you like to get a cup of coffee first?"

"Enough, *Jimmy.*"

James snapped his heels, saluted, and said, "Aye-aye Captain." He glanced down at me. "Got lunch plans? If not, how 'bout having lunch with me."

"I've—"

"She'll be with me."

"Oh-ho. That's the way it is, is it?"

By James pestering, I could clearly see it was only a matter of time before Mr. Property-Owner's barometer rose to the top and burst. I didn't want to be around when that happened.

"It's a business lunch. We're discussing the merger and Tiffany's duties."

In more ways than one.

"Tiffany's duties. And just what might they be?"

"Enough James." The stern tone settled *cuz* down.

"Okay, okay, bro." James looked down at me. "Sorry you're not available today. Maybe tomorrow."

"She'll be busy tomorrow all day … with me."

My questioning stare crashed with his dark stormy gaze delving deep into mine. Matt meant to mark his claim, beginning with his cousin James.

"I'm taking you around to see MTA investment properties." Mr. All-Powerful ushered me into the revolving door. Once through, he took my elbow and steered me toward a private bank of elevators I hadn't noticed yesterday.

"I'll call you later, Tiff." James waived and ventured off toward the Starbucks in the far corner of the building, leaving me with Mr. Egotistical.

"Why were you so surly to James?"

His highhandedness put me off. I moved to the back of the little cube and noticed full-mirrored walls, plush carpet, and no buttons to push.

"Surly?" Mr. Highhanded held a plastic card in front of a scanner, his eyes locked with mine in the mirrored wall. The doors shut and the elevator immediately became too cramped.

"Oh, never mind. If you don't see how you were acting toward your own flesh and blood, then far be it from me to point it out." I tried to look elsewhere but it was impossible. Anywhere I looked, I saw Mr. Gorgeous-Specimen watching me.

"For this to work, Tiffany, even James will have to be convinced you and I are madly in love. And just now your performance was less than stellar. If I hadn't known better, I would have thought you were more interested in my cousin than me."

"My interest is purely professional."

"Humph."

The elevator made its speedy rise to the top, though not soon enough for me. A soft chime, the doors opened, and we were on the thirteenth floor staring at the empty reception area.

"Shall we?" Mr. Take-Charge motioned for me to move forward.

"I'm sorry I forgot that I was playing a role. I'll do better once I get used to the idea we have to deceive everyone we meet."

He placed his hand to the small of my back leading me forward. My legs wanted to protest as my insides warmed to his touch.

His mouth moved next to my ear. "Now you get the picture. But don't worry. No harm done. This is only your second day on the job."

Like ice water thrown in my face, that warm fuzzy feeling lifted. My legs were no longer rubber. They and my backbone became as stiff as steel.

Did he mean my actual job or my acting job? Whichever, weren't they one in the same?

He opened my office door, walked in and deposited the tote bag on the floor next to my desk. "You really should consider buying one of those rolling bags. You'll strain a muscle and be laid up and unable to work if you don't. I'll see you in my office in thirty minutes." He walked through the connecting door, shutting it behind him.

"Yes, sir." I wanted to click my heels and salute like James, but thought it would be rather churlish and might cost me my job.

You'll have to do something about your attitude if this is going to work.

I racked my brain for how I felt about my soon to be fiancé. Could I make myself act as if I loved him when we were together and around others? My heart told me it wouldn't be a hardship.

Mr. GQ was the stuff of every woman's dreams—appealing, ruggedly handsome, and intelligent. He could be funny and at times make me laugh. And thoughtful, even though he thinks the world revolves around him, which it pretty much does—*his* world at least.

But can I pull off this farce and make others believe that I fit into his world?

Fortunately, I possessed social graces—which fork to use, which direction to pass the bread, listen with interest—so I shouldn't embarrass him or myself in public. I'm clever, can converse and hold my own with the best of them, and in two languages if need be.

Though I may not come from money, neither am I a snob because of the lack of change in my pocket. And even if my little efficiency would no doubt fit in one tiny corner of Mr. Perfect's house, I wouldn't feel uncomfortable around the rich and famous.

On second thought, I should march right in there and tell him I quit. Give me my severance, and I'm out of here. Forget the severance. It would do me little good and would be gone like dust in the wind!

If only I didn't have a conscience that wanted it both ways. I couldn't leave Mr. Wonderful to fend for himself.

Please, oh, please, Lord, help me get through this and not be scorched in the process.

Chapter 20

"You're here." Katherine Owens stood in the opened doorway looking surprised and a little unsure what to do. She at least had the decency to look a tad bit embarrassed. "I didn't hear from Matthew yesterday and well …"

"Why? Was there something wrong? I was supposed to be here, wasn't I?" I did my best to act confused, and by all appearance pulled it off.

Katherine gave me a small drawn smile. "Oh, no, I mean yes, you are supposed to be here. It's just … Well sometimes-ah-with new employees, you know the pressures of a new job and what is expected can be a little overwhelming. And after meeting with Matthew yesterday, well … he can be a tad intimidating at times. But he doesn't mean to be. I wasn't sure if-ah-if you would think the job was-ah"—she looked about the room as if she were searching for inspiration to pop out of thin air—"too demanding." She smiled.

Her gaze roaming over the few things I had brought from home. "I can see you are settling in quite nicely."

I wasn't sure if she felt pleased I'd stuck around, or she'd changed her mind and wanted me gone.

"Yes. After Matthew and I talked, I knew I had found the perfect position. Of course, being a woman, you understand the nesting side of our nature. I brought a few personal things to make me feel more at home."

I thought the Matthew part added a nice touch and a little more personal. The double entendre on the nesting bit seemed to more than hit the mark also. Hopefully, I wasn't smearing it on too thick.

But, hey, may's well go for the whole bank-wad. No penny-ante game here.

I smiled one of my intimate buddy smiles.

"Would you like to have a seat, Kathryn?" I saw a slight stiffening before she relaxed. "You don't mind me calling you Kathryn, do you?" I smiled prettily. "Matthew has told me so much about you, I feel I already know you."

She looked at me strangely. "No. Kathryn is fine. However, I don't have time for a chat just now. Maybe next time. I wanted to make sure you were settled in and had everything you needed." She moved to leave.

"Yes, I'm quite happy with my office, it feels quite comfy. In fact, after Matthew explained things, I knew these accommodations would work out well for me."

I dipped my head avoiding her gaze. It was hard keeping my composure seeing her eyes widen with each volley I shot over the net.

"Matthew and I have a meeting in about fifteen minutes to run over a few things. And then we're having lunch to discuss my long future here at MTA."

"Wonderful. Maybe one day soon, you and I can have lunch together."

Looking up, I said, "Oh, I would love that. We could get better acquainted. I think it would mean a lot to Matthew. Give me a call, we'll set up something." I bit my tongue to keep from adding *mother*, but knew that would be a bit premature.

She gave a distracted smile. "I'll do that." Katherine shut the door and was gone.

What would Matt think of my little chitchat with his mother?

I never got a chance to tell him about her visit. All through the two and half hours of discussing reports, what he expected from my position, and how he wanted to execute the merger, he never once brought up our engagement charade. I expected and dreaded he would, but he never did. And now we were on our way to lunch.

Un-com-fort-a-ble!

"I thought we'd try my all-time favorite, Tex-Mex." Mr. Speed-Racer shifted gears, tromped the gas, then moved into the stream of traffic, squeezing between two cars. He gave a quick glance in my direction before turning his attention back on the road to maneuver in front of a Corvette trying to block him from changing lanes. "You do like Mexican food, don't you?"

"Who doesn't?" I pulled on my seatbelt to make sure it was secure.

He saw my reaction and laughed. "Point taken. I'll slow down. Herrera's it is. One of the best Tex-Mex places I know. Everything is homemade." He weaved into another lane, merged onto the off ramp, and came to a screeching halt at the red light. His little Porsche was a sweet ride, but he drove a mite too fast for my taste.

When I realized I had a death grip on the armrest, I relaxed. "Are we in a hurry?"

His charming grin brought about a smile.

"No. Just want to beat the crowd, and I heard your stomach growl back there in the office, whether you did or not."

I grimaced wishing he hadn't.

"Don't let it be said I don't take care of my girl. When she's hungry, I feed her."

"I'm not your girl. And I can take care of myself. Have been for ten years now."

"I know." He looked sheepish.

"What do you mean *you know*? What exactly do you know about me?"

"I figured, if you were going to be my fiancée—okay, okay."

He held up his hand seeing I was just about to take his head off.

"Don't get bent out of shape. If we were going to be intimately close—"

"Our contract clearly states *no intimacy except for those times when it is absolutely necessary to convince an outside party we are engaged, e.g. holding hand, a quick hug, and an occasional kiss, without tongue, to seal the deal we are a couple.*" I gave him a hard stare, which he missed entirely with his gaze on the road.

"You're right. And I didn't mean it the way it sounded." Mr. Driver-On-Steroids whipped his car around a corner and then into a parking space that didn't look big enough even for my bug, Agnes. "Here we are."

Before my hand could open the door, Mr. Speed-Racer touched my arm. "Don't move."

I wasn't sure if a serial killer was lurking outside my door or what, so I stayed put.

He climbed out of the car, came around to my side. After opening the door, he helped unfold me from the Porsche.

"Thank you." I adjusted my top, smoothed the front of my pants before turning to follow, only to find Mr. Eyes checking me out. "Is something wrong?" I twisted looking backwards.

"No. Everything is perfect."

He raised his brows, and smiled. His light emerald eyes turned my insides to jelly. I blinked then realized he must be practicing his ability for acting.

Reaching for my hand, he led me across the street. His touch made me almost forget this was a game we were playing. And like a real date and proper gentleman, he held open the door, allowed me to pass through, and then, with his hand on the small of my back he led me to the hostess desk.

Before speaking to the girl, he bent down and whispered in my ear. "I believe you'll be great for the job of convincing everyone my search is over." Then without missing a beat, he smiled at me like a man besotted.

"Two please, Rosa. And tell Maria, her favorite adopted son is here with a surprise."

He turned and winked at me, then continued to ply his charms on the pretty Rosa, who was no match to withstand Mr. Studley's charms.

Instead of watching my companion as he chatted and flirted with little Ms. Teeny-bit, I looked around the quaint, sparkling restaurant. The colorful piñatas hanging from the ceiling and mariachi music fed through the overhead speakers, helped to set the mood. My stomach rumbled and my mouth watered as the delectable smells of Tex-Mex wafted through the restaurant.

Behind Rosa were some impressive autographed photos of people, some I could name and others I couldn't. The wall of fame was remarkable. I figured with the stamp of approval by the rich and famous, I was in for a treat.

"Shall we." Mr. Manners' hand was there on my back again, warming me inside-out. I did my best to ignore the quiver racing through every inch of my body by his mere touch, but it was next to impossible.

We followed a young woman in a skin-tight t-shirt and skinny jeans with a butterfly tattoo peaking at us with each wiggle of her small derrière.

I smiled as I imagined the butterfly taking flight. Averting my eyes, I began to wonder where Mr. Debonair's gaze might be—*the butterfly?*

She led us to a corner booth. Our table looked out onto the patio surrounded with beautiful flowering plants, wrought iron chairs and tables holding colorful umbrellas fluttering in the warm breeze.

Before we sat down, a woman in her fifties, and by the looks of her, the same short, dark-haired beauty in some of the photos I'd seen earlier, walked toward us.

"Matthew, you rascal, come give me a hug." Her rich alto voice rang out, causing other patrons to turn and stare as she advanced on us, her arms outstretched. She was almost as round as she was tall, with an inviting smile.

"Maria." Mr. I'm-Just-Your-Average-Joe bent down as the woman enveloped him into a full bosom hug, seemingly enjoying the display of his attention.

"Look at you." She held him at arm's length. "You're too puny. You're wasting away." She dropped her arms to her side. "You haven't seen me in such a long time. If you would come more often, I'd fatten you up with my enchiladas and tacos, but no, you don't come."

"Skinny Rosa says you have brought a surprise." Her assessing eyes landed on me, gave a thorough inspection, before returning her gaze on Mr. Puny. "Is this the surprise?"

She poked her thumb in my direction and shook her head back and forth several times before pouncing her hands on her hips.

"Matthew, Matthew." She wagged her head. "Why don't you marry one of my girls, have plenty of babies, and I feed you every day. Real man food, not that fluff stuff."

"Maria, you know I can't marry one of your daughters. Before I could turn around once, the authorities would have me in jail with a noose around my neck for marrying a girl half my age."

A cackle of laughter filled the restaurant. "Okay, so you can't marry one of mine." She threw another look my way. "She's not half bad, for a gringo, not like that other one you brought around who had her nose in the air. If you can't marry a good Mexican girl,"—she crinkled her nose in my direction—"she'll do."

"Maria, shame on you." He smiled down at me, then turned back to the woman. "We're not engaged … *yet*." The *yet* was supposedly for Maria's ears only.

I colored up and both, Mr. I-Don't-Marry-'Em-Young and Maria dissolved into laughter.

"Maria Herrera, may I introduce you to Tiffany Gates. She hasn't said yes yet, but she will. You'll keep my secret, though, won't you?"

Speechless, I stood there looking like I had been beamed up to another planet. What was Captain Kirk thinking? I thought we were going to take it slow, instead of warp speed ahead. I smiled with a tad of shy in the mix—most of it for real.

"You know me." Mama zipped her lips with her fingers. "Pliers couldn't pry your secret from my lips."

Before I knew what was happening, she had me pressed to her bosom, squeezing me so tight I thought a couple of my ribs might crack. She released me, held me away from her. "Welcome to the family. You make my boy happy, you make Maria happy."

I stood there dumb-founded.

"Come. Sit. I'll fix you something special. It's on the house."

"You're too good to me."

Astonished, I watch Mr. GQ bend down and give Maria a peck on the cheek. "Maybe I should marry you instead."

"You couldn't keep up with me. And what would my Josè say about that, què?" She shooed us toward the booth. "You don't stay away so long, or next time I'll turn you over my knee. Now enjoy your dinner."

Mr. Maria's-Boy ushered me into the booth, then scooted in next to me instead of sitting on the opposite side. I moved to scoot on around. He grabbed my arm, trapping me.

"What would Maria think? You over there. Me over here." He nodded his head in both directions. "Stay put. This is the first of many to convince the world we are a couple."

I stayed put. But I didn't know if I would survive the close proximity. This new side of Mr. Boss-Man had me reeling with images of a caring and loving man that could laugh and tease with the best of them. If only he weren't quite so rich, I just might consider working toward making this pretense real.

What am I thinking? We wouldn't fit together in a million years—opposite ends of the polar cap, or something like that. And you're the hired help—don't forget that for a minute, Tiffany.

A waiter came to the table balancing chips and salsa and a basket of hot, homemade tortillas with small silver wrapper pads of butter. "Hey, Matt. Long time no see."

"Rico." Like the waiter was his long lost buddy, Mr. Surprising stood, did a knuckle, fingers, hand thing, then a bear hug. "How've you been?"

"Okay. Maria said you were to get the royal treatment. Something about a new gal, one you might keep this time." Rico grinned as he took a slow perusal of me, or at least everything he could see above the table. "Thought I'd check her out."

So much for those pliers and keeping her lips sealed. Rico probably used a jackhammer.

"Don't get too fresh or I'll take you down a size or two." Mr. Friendly laughed, then sat down beside me again. With little or no thought, or at least that's what it seemed, he took my hand in his, moved it to the top of the table. Mr. I'm-In-Love interlocked his fingers in mine, gently squeezed, then kissed the tips before placing our hands back on the table.

The buzz going through me must have shown on my face. *Man, he was good at playing pretend.*

Rico laughed as he winked at me. "She's a pretty chica. You'd better latch on to her before someone else does."

"I'm trying, friend, I'm trying. I've just got to convince her."

"No foolin'? I guess Maria was right. Mr. Matt hasn't sealed the deal yet. *Whew!* What's that, a first for you?"

Matt shrugged. "Hopefully, not for long."

He gave me a look that nearly had me melting on the spot.

Rico took our drink orders. When finished, he leaned toward me and in a low voice said, "If you don't want him, I have several friends that would love to set you on fire."

My world is already on fire, including my body.

I managed, "Thanks," despite the shock.

Rico looked at Mr. Seize-the-Moment and said, "She doesn't say much. I like that in a woman."

"Outta here, before I call Rosa." He was a natural—his growl playful, with the right amount of serious. His performance could even win an Oscar. He certainly had my vote.

Rico laughed, and just before he disappeared around the corner, he looked back at us. Mr. Debonair slipped his arm around my shoulder, leaned in, his breath tickling my ear.

"Don't look surprised. Smile. Remember you're on stage."
He pulled me up tight to his side and nuzzled my ear.

As soon as Rico disappeared, I pulled back and asked,
"What is there about *no public display of affection* that you
don't understand." My temper flared, and I thought for sure
steam might be coming from my ears because my face was
burning hot.

"Calm down. This is all part of making them believe
we're an item. You do remember I hired you for the job,
which you accepted. Now act the part."

"Yes. But isn't this a little fast?"

"Maria and Rico don't know how long we've been
dating." He removed the plate of butter and then lifted the
top to the warmer of hot tortillas, making my mouth water.
I could already taste the warm tortilla smothered with
butter and dunked into the salsa.

"We haven't been dating."

"That's the point. We are now. We are a couple, a man
and a woman in love. See if you can't at least act like you
like me a little or you'll ruin my image."

Act! If I'm not careful, I won't have to act.

I laughed, unable to reply.

Placing a tortilla on a plate, he handed it to me. Then I
watched as he juggled another hot tortilla in his hand, set it
on another plate, slathering butter over the top before
rolling it up.

Watching him was hypnotic, and not because I was
starving. This—being here with Matt—would be wonderful
if it were for real.

"Sorry, if I gave the impression I don't like you … I
do."

"Could have fooled me."

He dunked the warm tortilla into the salsa and then
chomped down on it like a starving man eating his last
meal. When he looked at me oddly, I averted my eyes.

"It's just that I didn't figure you would move this fast. For a moment or two there, I lost my equilibrium. I'll do better." I smiled at him, which he didn't see.

For the next few minutes, we didn't converse, just fed our mouths like we were ravenous. My eyes kept straying to him, wondering how I could patch the hole I had torn into our working relationship, but couldn't come up with an answer.

Before I knew what was taking place, a napkin was being swiped across my chin, and Mr. Seduction was leaning into my personal space smiling into my eyes.

"You had a little sauce there. I would have licked it off, but knowing how you hate the show of public affection ..."

His actions flustered me, taking my breath away, at the same time making me want to kick him in the shin. I choked out, "Thank you." He certainly knew how to get to a gal.

"You're welcome, love."

Almost buying the endearment and his loving gaze, I noticed out of the corner of my eye Rico coming towards us with a tray laden with food and Maria dogging his tracks. I leaned into Mr. Romeo playing my part but not knowing what to say or do. Holding up my rolled tortilla, I took a small bite, chewed. "Mmm. Perfection."

Mr. Boss-Man had a devilish glint in his eyes. "Yes, Sweetheart, you are."

He dipped his head toward me. Just when I thought he would kiss me, he took a bite of my tortilla. I did a slow burn as he turned toward the approaching duo.

"Maria, you've outdone yourself. I told Tiff that your place was the best in all of Texas, and this"—he swept his hand in the direction of loaded trays—"is perfection personified."

I shook myself mentally. If I didn't get a handle on our charade, I'd be sunk. But if he could play this game, I was determined ... so could I.

Chapter 21

I didn't come up for air until I was halfway through the food on my plate. Satiated and knowing there'd be no way I could eat another bite, I glanced toward my companion. Watching him eat was amazing and at the same time hypnotic. How could a man look so handsome wolfing down Mexican food?

He looked at me and grinned, pointing his fork at my guacamole. "Are you going to eat that?"

"Incredible! Where are you putting all that food?" I pulled the tablecloth up to peek under the table. "You got a hollow leg down there or what?"

"Funny." He smirked at me, eyeing my small glob of guac like a hungry wolf. "Well, are you?"

I wanted to ask, *am I what,* but figured he wouldn't take my humor lightly. "No. Go ahead." I shoved the plate closer to his.

"If I don't make a good showing, Maria won't feed me next time."

"I guess her food is worth gorging until you're sick."

When he finally slowed down and pushed his plate away, I figured it was time to forge forward. Mr. Sated needed to answer some questions.

"What did you mean in the car that you knew about my past?"

He avoided looking in my direction. "I didn't say that exactly—"

"Don't mince words with me, Mr. Ainsley. I want answers."

"So we're back to Ainsley again, huh? Am I to expect this each time you get upset with me?"

"No, Matt, I'll remember to hold to our bargain." I tapped my fingers on the table. "You were about to explain?"

"Can't this wait until we're back at the office?"

"No. I believe this is the perfect time and place." Again, I tapped my fingers.

"Let's get out of here, and then we can have this conversation where we won't be overheard."

I figured I could at least give him this one concession, but once we left the restaurant, he would answer my questions or else. *Or else what?*

After saying goodbye to Maria and a few others who stopped by to get a look at Matt's girl, he stood and helped me out of the booth. His hand at the small of my back, sending chills all the way up my spine, he led me to the car, opened the door, and then waited while I slid in and buckled up.

He was silent as he maneuvered the car out of the parking spot, then down the street. I thought he was going to ignore my request for answers. However, I wasn't going to allow him to get away without answering.

After turning into a small park—a little quaint spot with plenty of flora and fauna and loads of shade—he parked and turned to look at me.

Though I wanted to jump right in, I held back until he stopped the engine, ready to wade into the fray.

"After I loaned you our company car, I did a little background check. I had to make sure you were who you said you were. Not that I doubted you for minute."

His sheepish look almost made me laugh. "Of course not." I added a look of *skepticism* for good measure.

"No. Really."

"And ..."

"That's when I found out you'd lost your job at Hadley's."

"Lost my job! How did you come by that information?"

"The day after the wreck, I stopped by Hadley's and you weren't there. Several of the clerks said you had a run-in with some Stewey character. Who is he anyway? Someone I should know about?"

"No. He's not anyone you need to be concerned with." I looked everywhere but at him.

"Are we or are we not engaged?"

"Not for real. Pretend."

"Close enough. I take care of my girl and anyone that tries to harm her."

There was a spark of something in his eye that made me glad it wasn't directed at me. "Get on with what you found."

"Let's begin with you're an only child, both parents deceased. However, you lived with your mother and grandmother up until their fatal car accident ten years ago."

My temper rising, I wanted to ask, *who gave you the right,* but knew I would have done the same, if I were in his position. With a little less simmer, and a pleasant look on my face, I said. "And ..."

"You had to work your way through college, and upon graduation, were unable to work in your chosen field, that is until now." Mr. Smug smiled after the last revelation.

"As you had already told me, you took a job not of your choosing because the bottom had dropped out of the market and you needed income. However, before I offered you, or I should say my mother offered you a job, you were barely making ends meet." He gave me a questioning look. "How am I doing so far?"

"Quite well."

Peeved this man knew so much about me and I knew very little about him, I had the overwhelming desire to knock his lights out. Never one for violence before I'd met Mr. Wonderful, I found I harbored the beginnings of sadistic nature.

Thoughts of torture were foremost in my mind. Thankfully, ones I would never act upon—the rack and drawn and quartered were two of my favorite choices.

Mr. Megabucks had the assets to research, while I had nothing more than the Internet and news articles to investigate him, often unreliable sources.

That was it! I'd had enough! My temper wouldn't stay capped. "Who gave you the right ..."

"No need to explode. I didn't do anything that any ordinary employer wouldn't do."

I worked to keep my voice level without a hint of what I'd like to say and do to Mr. CEO.

"Ordinary? Do you do this type of background check on all of your employees, or just with your pretend fiancées?" I threw in a smile so tight I could feel my face on the verge of cracking.

"Not always. But in your case, I couldn't have an unknown rise up from your past and bite me in the rear. If I place a person in a position of trust, like I have placed you, then I want to make sure they are trustworthy."

"And ...?"

"You're here, aren't you?"

Peaches 'n cream couldn't have looked any sweeter than the smile he gave me, but I wasn't buying it for one minute. He was up to something. What? I didn't know, but it was up to me to find out.

This whole thing had me walking a tightrope over a canyon. If I took one miss-step I'd end up at the bottom in a million pieces.

Mr. Sauvé gave me a quick look with a quirky grin. "You're doing a remarkable job of holding it together." He chuckled under his breath.

My hand itched to give him a facer. He didn't realize just how fragile the hold on my temper was at this moment.

"As I mentioned, I had to know who I was up against."

"Up against, *my foot.* You were just afraid I'd sue the pants right off your backside after you hit my little Agnes."

"Agnes who?

My face turned hot. "My bug."

"Your VW?" He had a hardy laugh at my expense. "You named your car?"

I swiped my hand to cut off his deviation of topic. "At the moment, you're getting off point. You were saying."

"And … there was that odd chance you would sue me. It's been done before."

"I don't go around suing people."

"I know that now. But you must know, from the first there was something between us—what, I'm not sure, but now I'm willing to invest some time to find out. Agnes? Really?" He shook his head.

I saw no need to answer, so I waited for him to continue.

"At any rate, when you came to MTA, I ordered a thorough background check. Mind you, nothing out of the ordinary or that we haven't done before for all new employees in high level positions. However, I realized I had to put a stop to my mother. What I was about to offer you—both positions, ELS and fiancée—well … I put the ball into motion."

"And did you …?"

"Did I find any skeletons in your closet?"

"Yes."

He shrugged. "You wouldn't be sitting here with me now if I had. From all accounts, you are the very pillar of society, or at the very least, a well thought of individual. And if the reports are true, someone I can trust."

"But can you be sure?"

Why I wanted to shake his resolve, I didn't know. My guess, I wanted to rattle his cage as badly as he had mine.

"Yes."

I wouldn't allow my eyes to turn from his strong gaze.

"You, Tiffany, I would trust with my life."

I studied his strong profile and saw no signs of mockery or deceit.

Mr. Persuasion couldn't have said anything at that moment that would have affected me more than his words of trust.

One thing for certain, when this farce was over and Mr. Pretend-Fiancé and I parted ways, his incredible face would be indelibly etched upon my mind. No man would be able to live up to his image nor be able to replace what I felt at this moment.

The agreement I'd struck with Mr. Matthew Thomas Ainsley the Third was turning out to be far more complicated than the original bargain. I was in deep trouble.

Chapter 22

"You're here. Well, it's about time"

I looked up to find Lucy Bell pointing her bejeweled finger at me, her jingling jewelry flashing.

Without asking, she advanced into my office then planted herself in one of my side chairs. Her rhinestone glasses sat perched on the tip of her nose in the precarious position of falling off. Her rosy cheeks, whether from makeup or exertion, looked remarkably like pictures I'd often seen of Santa's cheeks, making her more endearing than threatening.

"I have a few questions I want answered and I'm not leaving until you do."

As professional as I could, I folded my hands on top of my desk and asked, "What may I do for you, Ms. Bell?" For some reason, I knew what was coming next, and my inner conscience made me feel like a heel.

For the past week and a half, Matt and I had been seen together leaving for lunch, dinner, staying late, even in the lunchroom a time or two. I knew there was talk and speculation going around the office, even heard gold-digger on one occasion in reference to me, but I hadn't figured anyone was taking it seriously. Apparently, they were.

"You can begin with the engagement that everyone from the thirteenth floor down to the first is talking about. Are you a gold-digger? An opportunist? Or just along for the ride for what you can get out of Matthew? It certainly can't be love."

Her personal attack set me back wondering why she felt it her duty to confront me.

"You hardly know my grandson, let alone had the time to fall head over heels in love. *Humph!* Preposterous. You've done no such thing." Her faded blue eyes blazed with fire as brightly as the stones on her glasses as she scrutinized me.

Grandson? Why hadn't Matt told me Lucy Bell was his grandmother?

Not quite prepared for such a straightforward attack, but certainly up to the challenge, I charged into the fray like a demented woman on a shopping exposition.

"What engagement?" Then I prayed she couldn't see through all of the falsehoods I was about to engage in to sell this sham her *darling* grandson had hired me for.

"Don't give me that poppycock. You know perfectly well of which I speak."

"Really?" I smiled sweetly, knowing all the while I would have to tell a lie to Lucy Bell, the very woman that came to my rescue, an ally on my first day here at MTA. "And what did your grandson tell you?"

"The same such dribble I am likely to receive from you, it seems. But I won't stand for it, do you hear me?" Her sparkling hand fluttered up and down as she pointed and wiggled her index finger at me. "I want answers, and I don't plan on leaving here until I get them."

"All I can say, Ms. Bell, your grandson is quite headstrong—"

"I already know that, so tell me something I don't know." She looked at me like a mouse eyeing a piece of cheese.

"Then you will also know, when Matthew sets his mind to something, it's very difficult to change it, especially when he's so persuasive."

This time I tried for the smile of a besotted person in love. I didn't want to deceive the sweet old woman, but neither did I feel I could betray her grandson. My heart pounding, I waited for the hammer to drop.

"That's true. But what I want to know, are you or are you not engaged to Matthew?"

The worry in her face made her look every bit her age and then some.

"I don't want you hurting my boy or taking advantage of him. He's had a life full of gold-diggers. He doesn't need another one. Knowing Matthew like I do, he probably hasn't even asked for a prenuptial."

Shocked, I tried for bewildered. "A prenuptial?"

"I thought not. And don't act so coy with me, young woman." Lucy Bell shook her head.

"We really haven't gotten that far yet."

"What do you mean by that?" She scrutinized me.

I could feel her eyes peeling away my pretense layer by layer and getting to the truth.

Not knowing what Mr. Boss-Man had said to Lucy Bell, I prevaricated. "Just that. He's a wonderful man, but …"

"But what? What are you holding out for? You won't find anyone better than Matthew."

Inwardly, I laughed, realizing Grandma was now trying to convince me of her grandson's fine qualities.

"I realize he's a wonderful catch. But like you, I want to make sure this is the right move for both Matthew *and* me."

The woman sat quietly watching me. After some thought and heavy breathing, she gave me a beady-eyed stare. "Do you love him?"

Stunned, I gathered my wits about me and swallowed before answering. "There are many fine, redeeming qualities that I love and admire about Matt."

"Oh, stop mincing words. You heard me. Do—you—love—my grandson?"

"I don't believe this is something I should be discussing with you." I smiled sweetly. "However, just like you, I want to make certain what I feel for Matthew is love."

Each word pounded like a nail in a coffin—mine. How could I be so deceptive and say what she wanted to hear? I buried my nervous hands below the desk in my lap hoping this inquest would be over quickly.

"Are you—?"

"Grandmother, so nice of you to visit Tiffany. I hope you are becoming better acquainted. "Hello, darling."

The man himself strolled in, pecked grandmother on the cheek, then moved to where I sat. He dipped his head and gave me a full on-the-lips kiss—our first I might add.

I sat speechless, stunned to my very core.

"What do you think of Grandmother Bell, sweetheart?" He looked at his grandmother and winked.

At first, too shaken to answer due to the effects left behind by his lips—mine ablaze—a nudge from Mr. Actor got me rolling.

"Don't you remember? I told you I met your grandmother the first day I came to work and she was most helpful with the loan of her shoes."

What did he want me to say? I didn't know she was your grandmother. She's giving me the inquisition and is about to stretch me on the rack for the truth? Indignation and guilt washed me.

"That's right. Well, Grandmother, I hate to intrude on your little chat, but I need Tiff to go over some last minute details for the benefit tomorrow night. You don't mind if I steal her away, do you?" He smiled sweetly at Grams, which said person promptly bestowed an *I'm not through with you yet* look in my direction.

"If you recall, Grandmother, Tiff and I will be to Sunday Dinner. You will have plenty of time to visit with her then. And ..." He gave a pregnant pause and gazed at me like some besotted idiot. "I might have an announcement to make to the family."

He smiled down at me before he turned and bestowed *I'm a busy man and I need to get on with it* look at Grams.

Like flipping a switch, she smiled a little too brightly at me and said, "Welcome to the family—I guess. We'll talk later, Matthew." She rose and sailed out of the room leaving me stunned and not looking forward to exchanging words with her again anytime soon.

"What did you two talk about?" Mr. I-Have-It-All-Together looked a little disturbed.

"Nothing much. She asked if I loved you, and if there was a prenupt in the offering."

To see his stunned expression was priceless, then he laughed. "That's all?"

A worm had to feel better than I did for all the deception I knew would be ahead. I turned and glared at him.

"You expected more?" I raised my brows. "If you want my opinion that was more than enough. You came in the nick of time. Otherwise, there is no telling what lies I would have committed."

"You lied? About what?" I saw that same determined look I had witnessed in Lucy Bell's face moments earlier. He wanted answers.

"Not much, because I didn't know what you had told her. Believe me, I was dancing around her questions. You would have been proud of my footwork." I gave a half-hearted laugh. "Just exactly how did you expect me to answer *Grams*?"

I stood and moved to the window, looking down on the front entrance. A car went around the circle that held neatly hedged MTA before heading out toward the street, escaping. Inwardly, I wished I was that person.

Heaving a sigh, I turned disgusted. "What's this about a benefit anyway? And, what about Sunday dinner? Were you going to tell me about either or wait until the last minute and spring it on me?"

I didn't wait for his answer, just turned my attention back to window, anger and disappointment building. A flock of sparrows took flight as white fleecy clouds skipped across the heavens.

How had I gotten into this mess. All I wanted was a job, but not as an actor.

I heard him come up behind me, then lean his hip against the credenza facing me, hardly any distance separating us.

"I'm sorry I wasn't here for you. I should have warned you about Grandma Bell."

I felt his eyes watching me as I stood staring, saying nothing.

"The benefit was a ruse to get my grandmother out of your office. But we do need to talk about it. Do you have something appropriate to wear to the banquet? It's a formal affair."

"I believe I can manage to find something presentable."

He dug into his pocket, pulled out a credit card, and held it out to me.

I shook my head, knowing if I took the card I was in for the long haul. There'd be no jumping off the boxcar till the train stopped.

"If you remember our agreement, I pay for your clothes in the line of duty. And since this is black tie affair, don't go cheap on me—dress, shoes, purse, jewelry, whatever is necessary to make a good showing. Neiman's should have what you need.

"Also pick up something spring-like, yet casual for Sunday."

When I didn't reach for the card, he shoved it in my direction. "Here, take it. That's yours to keep for occasions like tomorrow night and Sunday."

Taking the credit card didn't seem right somehow. But a bargain was a bargain. And what would I do with all the fancy clothes once this farce was over anyway. Wear them while I do the laundry?

Inwardly, I laughed. It wasn't as if he couldn't afford the expenditure. Yet, what did that make me?

With a deep intake of breath, I took the card and asked, "If your grandmother hadn't made her impromptu visit, when were you going to tell me about the benefit or Sunday dinner?" This time I look him square in the eyes.

"As to that, I was going to tell you this afternoon. Grandma Bell just preempted me." He pulled away from the credenza. "By the way, what did you tell her?"

"About what?" I feigned ignorance, but he saw through my ploy.

"Do you or do you not love me?" His grin covered his face.

"Are you serious?" I gave him an incredulous look.

Although, his question did touch a chord in the pit of my stomach. For the last several days, we had been going along fairly easy with the pretend infatuation. Now he was ramping it up and going in for the kill.

He turned me toward him. His knuckle tipped my chin upward. The sparkle in his eyes … mesmerizing. I couldn't move.

I knew what he was about to do. But I couldn't stop him, and I wasn't sure if I wanted to. Not a rational thought could be found in my head except him.

Our lips met for too brief a moment before he pulled back, his gaze locked with mine, then he shook his head as if to clear it. "Don't answer that yet."

What was he doing? No one was in the room. No one was listening. It was just him … me. Practice?

That could only be the reason for such a display of affection. For certain, he almost had me believing we were a couple, and that he felt something for me other than as a hired fiancée.

"You've broken our agreement. This isn't a public place. And we don't have an audience."

"Ahh, but I enjoyed it, didn't you?" Not waiting for my answer, he left the room chuckling.

The man was infuriating. He could take a saint and turn them into a raving lunatic. Me? He had me completely off kilter.

I knew now I wouldn't be coming out of this bargain unscathed.

Chapter 23

"Oh, my dear, you look absolutely beautiful. And I can't imagine how you've stayed single for so long. Men today certainly aren't like my Edgar, God rest his soul. He would have taken one look at you, scooped you up and off to the minister." Mrs. Mac tittered, beaming a brilliant smile and preening like a young schoolgirl.

"That's what Edgar did when he first laid eyes on me. My, we sure made a handsome pair." Her eyes were misty with thoughts of yesterdays.

"Thank you, Mrs. Mac. I'm sure I could never be as pretty as you were."

I looked at my reflection in the mirror by the front door. The black satin, floor-length gown with a demi-jacket fit me to perfection, yet I wondered if it was right for the occasion.

I didn't want to be overdressed or underdressed, yet I had never attended a gala benefit before. And though I tried to reassure myself, I was way out of my comfort zone.

Shoving the thought from my mind, I said, "My ride should be here any minute now."

Mrs. Mac pursed her lips. "Well, I hope he's a gentleman and not like some of the boys today, honking the horn, expecting the girl to come a runnin'"

"Oh, I'm sure he's not a horn honker." I barely kept from laughing. At least I hoped he wasn't.

Hearing a car door shut, footsteps on the porch, and then a knock on the door, I picked up my black satin handbag.

"There. You see. He's a perfect gentleman." After another quick glance in the hall mirror, I turned to answer the door and almost collided with Mrs. Mac, eager for her first glance of Mr. Mega-Bucks.

"Hello, I'm Mrs. MacIntosh. Tiffany is right here. But I must say, you're not quite how she described you."

I heard a burly laugh that wasn't Mr. Boss-Man's. "I'm sorry if I disappointed you."

"Lands, no. You're handsome enough, to be sure."

Gently prying the door from Mrs. Mac's hand, I moved between her and my ride and got my first look at my date.

"James. Are we all riding together?" I hoped he hadn't detected any lack of enthusiasm on my part.

He laughed. "No. Matt had a last minute overseas call. He sent me to fetch you. Hope you don't mind. He'll catch up with us at the benefit later."

Not knowing how I should feel about Mr. I'm-Too-Busy having someone else do the fetching, I decided to make the best of the situation. After all, it wasn't like we were *really* engaged. And James was good company and would make any girl proud to be seen with him—*why not?*

"I don't mind at all." I turned to Mrs. Mac. "Mrs. MacIntosh, this is James Foster. He's Mr. Ainsley's cousin, and also an executive at MTA. James, this is my landlady and friend, Mrs. MacIntosh."

Mrs. Mac simpered like a southern bell. "So nice to make your acquaintance."

"The pleasure is all mine." James smiled while looking around the hall. "You have a lovely home."

She simpered some more. "Why thank you. My dear Edgar, God rest his soul, had it built for me a few years after we were married. Wouldn't think of living anywhere else."

"I can understand why." James had completely won Mrs. Mac over.

"We had better be going." I turned to my landlady. "Don't wait up. I have my key and can let myself in."

"Unless you arrive home after midnight, I'll be up, dear, so don't worry about waking me. You know I must watch my late night talk shows." She shooed us with her hands. "You go on now. Have a nice time."

Not much exchange occurred until we were well on our way, and then James entertained me with stories of Matt and him when they were little boys. The tales revealed a great friendship, but also the competition that went on between them. I figured they were much like the present, trying to push one another's buttons, except they were grown men now.

"By the way, you look absolutely stunning in that dress. Tonight, you'll put the rest of the women to shame. In fact, you quite took my breath away."

I was glad it was dark and he couldn't see my blush. I cleared my throat and said, "Thank you. You don't look half bad in your tux either." I laughed trying for a lighter mood and tone.

"I'm glad my cuz was too busy to pick you up."

"And why is that?" I wasn't sure if he was flirting or what. I wondered why the sudden change in topic. One thing about this family, they played by different rules.

"It gives us some time to get to know each other a little better." He glanced over at me. "Shall we forgo the benefit and go out on the town? You'll only meet a whole lot of stuffy folks. Not much fun. What do you say?" He winked at me.

"You're outrageous. I believe your cousin would have something to say about us not showing up. He'd not be too happy with me." I laughed. "I believe you're trying to get me fired."

"I guess that's a no then, huh?" He flashed a bad boy smile at me.

"I believe you hit it on the nose."

"All I have to say, my cuz is plain stupid if he doesn't realize what a prize you are."

Too stunned to comment, I glanced out my window at the approaching Dallas skyline. Was James playing a game, trying to win the prize—me—away from his cousin? What would Mr. Busy say to that?

"What does he have that I don't have?" He chuckled. "Okay. Several millions more, but I'm not a bad catch. And financially, I'm doing all right for myself. And I think you and I would work well together. How 'bout it? Dump my cuz and date me."

I sputtered out laughing. "What is this, cousin one upmanship? I'm afraid that wouldn't set so well with my present employer."

Was this entire thing nothing more than a big joke between cousins with me caught in the middle? Or did James want what big cousin had—me?

He shot a curious glance my way before exiting off Woodall Rogers onto Pearl. "Last chance. A boring benefit and Matt, or me and the time of your life. Which will it be?"

I laughed. "You're impossible, James. What would you do if I said yes?"

"Try me and see."

With a shake of my head, I noticed the mischief lurking in his eyes. "You're trying to stir up trouble. Tonight it will be the benefit."

He gave a bark of laughter. "You're right. But you'll never know what you missed."

He shifted gears, then hooked a right into the drive of the well-lit entrance of the Fairmount Hotel. Young men in uniforms ran up to the car and opened my door. My heartbeat accelerated.

What have I gotten myself into?

James walked around the car, took my elbow, and guided me through the doors. Inside the lobby, he bent and whispered in my ear, "Don't worry. I'm not giving up so easily."

I laughed and shook my head. "You're impossible."

"You and I will have our date yet."

To say I wasn't affected by his comments would be a lie. However, his touch didn't affect me like Matt's.

I felt relieved when we began to mix into the crowd. My escort, though still attentive, didn't remark further about the two of us making an escape. Instead, he became the perfect companion.

He slipped my arm through his as he guided me in and out and around the throng of people talking and moving slowly. He stopped occasionally when someone spoke to him and introduced me as an executive of MTA, nothing more.

From time to time, he'd bend his head close to my ear to shed little tidbits of information on the rich and famous attendees, many times making it hard for me to contain my composure.

"Oops ..." He turned me in a different direction around a small group of people. "Don't want to go that way. We'll be waylaid by Mrs. Upchurch. She'll want to tell me all about Herbert."

I glanced up at him, my eyes questioning. "Her husband?"

"I wish." He grinned, his eyes sparkling. "No, her dog."

Doing my best to conceal my humor, my hand covered my mouth, but my laugh came out in sputters.

"It's not a laughing matter. The little imp nearly took my leg off. He's a ferocious little pug, with horrible manners." He rushed us quickly away as Mrs. Upchurch frantically waived to gain his attention.

After several more introductions, an escalator flight up, then down a side hall, we reached our destination, the ballroom. James motioned toward stairs that led to a platform where a long line of tables butted together with white table linen. Artfully arranged flowers flowed from containers and trailed along the table with candles strategically positioned throughout.

"Am I sitting up there?"

James gave me an apologetic smile. "I'm afraid so. You're Matt's date. He's expecting you to sit next to him."

I pointed to one of over a hundred or more tables in the room. "Oh, but I'd much rather sit at one of those. Maybe one of the front tables where he can see me, or the back?"

"What and leave Matt without a date? I don't think that will work for him."

He gave me a nudge and we moved up the stairs behind people who were already seated. Each time we attempted to pass someone, they would waylay James, and in turn, he would pull me to a halt and make introductions. During these interludes, I felt like an imposter waiting for someone to say *she doesn't belong here. Evict her.*

Not wanting to be the object of stares and speculations, yet knowing that the problem already existed, I moved down the line, a smile frozen in place, answering with obligatory responses. Spying a place card with the name *James Foster* in beautiful calligraphy, I saw his was the third seat from the podium, then *Tiffany Gates,* and lastly, *Matthew Thomas Ainsley, III.* Though I sat in the spotlight, I gained a little courage knowing two good-looking men would be flanking me on each side.

"What happen to your date?" I asked as James pulled out my chair.

"My cuz beat me to her."

I passed it off as a joke and averted my gaze to the sea of tables that were filling up with people. Noticing a very attractive, model-like brunette, dressed in black with a long strand of pearls hanging low over her well endowed and much in view cleavage, I saw her stare at James and then at me with a look of loathing.

Her head turned, and she spoke with her companion before sliding out of her chair and heading in our direction.

"James, do you know the woman who is walking toward us?" I wasn't sure if I needed to take cover or what. With a menacing look, she was headed straight for us.

His frown, quickly replaced with a bored look and artificial smile. "That's Candace Hill, a friend of the family. I'll speak with her."

He stood, walked around our table, and then squatted on his knees, eye-level with the young woman.

Unable to hear the conversation, yet privy to a perfect view of her face, I could tell Candace was letting James have a piece of her mind. After a few more heated words, the woman flounced off toward her table, and a disgruntled James returned to ours.

I touched his sleeve to gain his attention. "Is everything all right?"

"Perfect." James' carefree attitude had disintegrated into surly.

"It's none of my business, but sometimes it helps to talk. Maybe this is one of those times." By his hardened features, I thought he might tear my head off my shoulders. I mumbled, "Or not."

Not privy to the story behind his changed attitude, I gave him a sympathetic glance. A waiter came up and asked if we would like coffee or tea, then left with our orders, breaking the tension.

"Sorry about that." He gave a nod in Candace's direction. "She thought you were my date and was none to happy about it either. She got more upset when she found out you were Matt's."

"Why would that bother her? Are you two an item? Or is Matt and she an item?" I looked in her direction. Candace's stiff body language betrayed her animated expression.

"It's a long story. Suffice it to say she wanted exclusivity, but only one way—mine not hers, just in case something better came along, which she hoped it would—Matt."

My heart jerked to a stop. I wanted to ask if Matt and she were still an item.

Since we were a pretend couple anyway, I didn't figure it was any of my business, yet it still galled me thinking of Matt with her. Instead, I touched his arm and managed to say, "I'm sorry."

"Don't be. I've moved on." His expression said differently. "Apparently, she still wants to keep her options open, meaning Matt and me. But she doesn't have a chance in h—sorry." He took a deep breath, smiled, and then the carefree James I knew and liked was back. "Enough about her."

"Sorry I'm late." Mr. Man-of-the-Hour bent over my shoulder, his lips lightly brushed my cheek. "Hey, Gorgeous, where have you been all my life?"

The sensation of his touch and his words went straight through me, making me feel warm inside.

He pulled out the chair beside me and sat down. Without ceremony, he traced his finger on the top of my arm, then locked his hand with mine, giving it a gentle squeeze.

Without a doubt, Matt Ainsley knew how to charm his way into a girl's heart and make something look real when it wasn't.

The mere sensation of the brush of his lips and our interlocked hands set a blaze rushing through me, turning me on fire. Then I remembered the game we played. The feelings turned to ashes as I gave myself a good scold.

This was all an act, and I, one of the actors. I glanced over at my supposed fiancé, smiled besottedly, and then ever so gently tried to pry my fingers from his grasp—a useless maneuver on my part.

Mr. Hardy-Grip leaned into me. "I truly am sorry about not being able to pick you up tonight. I'll do my best to make it up to you."

His whispered breath fanned my cheek and set my pulse to racing. His words struck a chord in my fanciful mind, turning me giddy. Once again, I remembered this was all part of the act. I landed back on solid ground.

"Don't worry about it. James was the perfect escort."

He gave me a bemused look as he leaned forward to look at his cousin. "Thanks for delivering my date."

"Don't mention it. My pleasure entirely."

James gave me a huge smile and a wink.

Mr. Handsome gave my hand another gentle squeeze, and then lifted it to kiss the tips of my fingers.

This man knew what he was about and how to make our romance look real. My emotions had no protection against him.

Cheeks blazing, my heart beating wildly at his intimate act, I felt as if we were the only two in the room.

My defenses to his charms were being breached. If I weren't careful, I'd be in a downward spiral and would be irrevocably lost forever.

Chapter 24

"Darling, don't you look handsome in your tux."

I didn't have to turn to know that Mr. CEO's mother was the voice behind the words. Nor, did I need to be a detective to know the words held a twinge of displeasure, for what, I was uncertain.

"Mother."

Mr. Manners stood and gave his mother a peck on the cheek similar to what he'd given me earlier. A good thing I hadn't taken much stock in his overture minutes before.

"I didn't know Ms. Gates would be here. Is she your date or James'?" She held her gaze on her son's face, her expectant look speaking volumes.

Now I know why the displeasure. How could one not come straight to the point but still deliver that point with such a sharp edge?

Apparently, I was no longer the favored one, which was to be expected.

"James is flying solo tonight. Tiffany is my date and a very beautiful date, I might add." His eyes leveled on me with appreciation.

Uncomfortable under the scrutiny of a displeased mother and satisfied son, I wished myself anywhere but here on this dais and at this banquet with the Ainsley clan. I managed to mumble my thanks.

He gave me an audacious wink before returning his gaze to his mother. "You look lovely, Mother. A new dress? Or is it the hairdo?"

"Thank you. Yes, on both accounts, but for a good cause. You know how much I support Big Brothers and Big Sisters and education."

James rose from the table, moved to where Ms. Owens stood and then bent to give her a quick peck. "Good evening Aunt Kate. I agree with Matt, you look stunning. The men will be fighting over you tonight."

She laughed and then began a discussion of the banquet.

James moved behind me and placed his hand on my chair. His fingers touched my shoulder reassuringly for a brief moment, as if to say he was my ally. Unfortunately, James wasn't Matt, and I wasn't falling for him.

When did I start thinking of Mr. What's-His-Name as Matt?

I needed to remind myself, this was a game with Matt. Or could he truly feel something more for me than a casual partner in crime? Just my luck. I was falling for the wrong guy.

Here I was, eyes wide open, and I promised I wouldn't let my heart get involved, but that was exactly what was happening. Now how would I extricate myself from these unplanned, unexpected emotional responses to Matt?

Best to keep it on a level playing field, that way, no one would get hurt, especially not me. *Stay the course, Tiffany. Take no prisoners. Who's the prisoner here?* I wanted to laugh knowing I sounded too much like Mrs. Mac.

Watching the by-play between mother and son, I could see a definite resemblance in their strong features. And for whatever reason, I knew by the set of Ms. Owens' stiff posture, the playing field had changed. She had taken a dislike to me, or at least had altered her mind about me being suitable for her son.

"Mother, you better find your seat. They are beginning the first course. I believe you will find you are sitting by Candace."

"Thank you darling. But first, promise me you will speak to Candace before the night is over. She will be so disappointed if you don't. You know how much she adores you. She's such a lovely, refined young woman."

For a brief moment, her gaze darted to me, then flittered away.

"I'll do my best."

"Please do. She'll be expecting you. I'll speak to you later then."

Ms. Owens looked at me again. "I hope you enjoy the evening, Ms. Gates." However, the sentiment didn't quite reach her eyes.

I dipped my head in thanks. "I'm sure I will."

What would the two women have to say about Mr. Man-of-the-Hour and me? How much of an item had Candice and he been? How long ago had Mr. Handsome moved on? Weeks? Days? Hours?

Maybe I was overreacting.

Without being obvious, I kept tabs on my one time supporter. Ms. Owens arrived at her table and greeted everyone before taking her seat next to Candace. I saw the two women's heads come together with a few nods and glances in our direction.

There wasn't a thing I could do. The course had been set, and I for one refused to worry about Matt's mother. This was my job, one I would do well, or die trying.

Smelling the delectable food, I knew I could occupy my thoughts with something other than what Ms. Owens and Candice might be cooking up. Thankfully, Mr. Wonderful struck up a conversation, and the evening held more promise than what I had originally imagined.

Dinner over, plates removed, a speaker stepped to the podium.

I could finally allow my mind to wander. My responsibility, for at least the next few minutes, was to smile and look interested, which I could do while I daydreamed.

Judith could feel someone staring at her and knew who. Rolf's mother, Lady McPherson. She could feel the woman's disapproval crawling across her skin.

After the initial shock wore off that Rolf was truly interested in Judith, Lady McPherson made it clear Judith had not gained a friend but a foe. The Lady had chosen a mate for her son, and it wasn't Judith.

The door opened and in walked a laughing Rolf and the beautiful Lady Meredith wearing a radiant smile. The ugly head of jealousy rose up, causing Judith to doubt her place.

Meredith pulled Rolf to a stop, leaned up on her toes, pressing her body up next to his side, then whispered in his ear.

Judith wanted to snatch the woman bald-headed. Seething, she motioned for a servant to pour more water.

"There you are, my love." Rolf bestowed a look of love in Judith's direction. "I wondered where you had gone."

He led the dark-haired beauty to her place at the table, bowed over her hand, and then strode to where Judith sat, slipping onto the bench beside her.

He bent his head to whisper. "Why did you leave me with that boring and simple woman? She is no match to your wit and beauty. Don't ever do that again. I missed you."

Rolf's breath tickled Judith's ear, but his words warmed her heart.

"There didn't seem to be any reason for me to stay. Lady Meredith occupied your time. I felt I was in the way."

"I wanted you by my side, not her. Promise me you will never leave me alone with that woman again, or I may go mad and do her bodily harm." The last was said on a deep-throated chuckle. "Promise me, Judith."

"Aye, Lord, I promise. I would hate to have Lady Meredith's blood on my head." She smiled, noticing the laughter in Rolf's eyes. The love he had declared and shown her in their chamber earlier that morning still warmed her heart.

From the corner of her eye, Judith saw Lady Meredith's hateful stare. The woman whispered something to Lady McPherson. Both women fixed their gaze upon her. Neither offered a look of friendship.

How could she counter their divisive machination?

Startled back to the here and now by Matt squeezing my hand, I looked over at him and smiled.

"I hope I won't bore you."

The sparkle in his eye had my heart racing.

He stood, then stepped up to the lectern.

My whole body on *Matt alert*, I realized I would have to be extremely careful with Mr. Boss-Man. He knew how to treat me as if I were the only woman on earth. He made our relationship seem desirable and real, even to me.

This will never do. You can't allow him to affect you so. Stay detached.

My whole attention, though I did good not to drool, was directed at Matt as he spoke. Proud to be a part of this wonderful evening and cause, I marveled at how his speech was flawless and moving. Even I could see the sincerity of his words and how strongly he felt about the charity.

When he sat down beside me, he reached for my hand. "Do you think I convinced them, or should I have tried a little harder?"

I had never seen this side of Matt before—vulnerable and anxious. "Your delivery was moving. Your presentation with much conviction. I for one am convinced to support the charity even in my limited capacity. Before I heard what you had to say, I had never thought of this organization in the same light as what you presented."

His smile took my breath away, melting my insides.

"Thanks, Tiffany. Coming from you it means a lot."

The evening continued and ended without further interaction with Matt's mother, for which I was thankful. However, it did get a bit dicey when Candace came to the front determined to speak with Matt. She gave me the cold shoulder, or I should say her cold back.

I stood by, not at all surprised the woman would be so bold and callus to ignore me.

When Matt noticed the oversight, he moved around to stand next to me, placing his arm around my waist. The ploy was so obvious, I almost felt sorry for the woman. She must really love Matt to be so eaten up with jealousy.

"Candace, let me introduce you to Tiffany Gates."

He pulled me up close and I smiled graciously.

"Nice to meet you, Candace."

She nodded without speaking as her gaze raked over me.

Odd how I could feel the heightened tension in Matt's tight muscles and the almost strained sound to his voice. Did she mean more to Matt than I originally imagined?

He ended the conversation abruptly and ushered me away, heading for the exit. The closer we got to the lobby the less tension I felt coming from my companion.

His car arrived and when the door attendant would have opened my door, Matt waved him off and did the deed instead. If I hadn't known this was all a ploy, I would have been thrilled by his devoted attention.

I thanked him, as I reminded myself—this is part of the act.

As with the other times I had ridden with Matt, soft music played in the background filling in the silence, yet tonight seemed more awkward than usual, at least to me. We traveled some distance before I felt his gaze. When I looked, he was focused on the road.

"Sorry about that."

"About what?" I knew what he meant, or at least thought I did.

"Candace."

"Does she mean something to you?"

"At one time. Not now."

"Do you want to tell me about it, or shall we play twenty questions?"

His laughter released the tension. "You're good for me."

Though simple, his words effected me greatly.

"At one time Candace and I dated. However, I didn't know she had been playing James to get to me. Once I found out, I broke it off, but not before … well, let us say, she has a way of using a man, wringing his heart till it's dry, and leaving no feelings left."

I touched his arm, hoping he would know I understood.

A similar situation happened to me in college, but I wasn't about to bare my heart to Matt, at least not tonight.

"I'm sorry, but I'm sure you made the right choice. I think James still has feelings for her though."

"You're right. What she did to him nearly broke him and our friendship."

"I could see how that could happen, but at least it seems to be okay between the two of you now."

"At times I wonder." He let out a breath. "But enough of the past. I'm sorry that I was unable to pick you up tonight. And as of yet, I haven't told you how beautiful you look."

"I do clean up pretty well, don't I?" I figured, might as well keep it light.

"Better than pretty well."

"Thank you."

I felt self-conscious, his stare was doing unfathomable things to my insides. I didn't know what to say so I decided quiet would work best.

The buildings and houses zoomed by shadows in the dark as Mr. Speed-Racer sped south on I-35.

Leaning my head back against the headrest, I closed my eyes allowing the music to settle in around me.

Up until now, I hadn't realized how being on display all evening had taken its toll. Wound tight and feeling exhausted, I needed this time to chill out—to clear my head.

"About tomorrow."

I jerked upright, my heart pumping into overdrive. Tomorrow would be a different kind of playing field. Would I survive or be eaten alive by the many members of Mark's family.

If they all took an aversion to me like his mother had, I'd be a goner for sure.

"Yes? Would you like to tell me why we are moving up this little charade? Since we agreed it would be at least four weeks before I would meet your family, not two?"

He grinned at me like a kid being let out of school for the summer. "Well, tonight, if you didn't notice, my mother seems to be on the hunt for your replacement."

"Ya' think?" I exhaled heavily. "She's fickle. Her love for me was very short lived."

His laughter made me smile.

"Don't feel bad. It was bound to happen. My mother is never satisfied for long. She's double minded. She may want me married, but, no woman is good enough, not even the ones she picks out. Sorry." He shrugged.

"Now I understand why you were so quick to jump on the bandwagon and offer me a pretend engagement. I'll do my best to make her and everyone else believe ours is a love match—love at first sight, so to speak."

His wrinkled brow made me think he wasn't convinced I could do the job.

"Hey, I'm not a magician. I'll do my best and hope they can suspend belief."

With a man like Matt, it wouldn't be hard to convince them we were madly in love. I was practically head over heels in love with the man already.

What was I thinking when I agreed to his plan?

He turned onto Hwy 287 heading west. I would be home soon and would be rid of pretense and fake smiles, with no one to please but myself. And, I'm supposed to do this for another six months to a year?

I knew now, I wouldn't do my time unscathed.

Chapter 25

Today, the cat will be out of the proverbial bag, and our charade could well be over. Matt was going to tell his family what the rumor mills have already been hinting at—he and I are engaged … or at least that's what they're to believe.

We discussed the engagement of convenience at great lengths after the banquet, sitting in the car outside of Mrs. Mac's, or I should say, I appealed to him … please call it off. However, his argument was more persuasive. Matt persuaded me to continue with our little charade to give him the time to make his mega buck deals without mama worries or courting a real fiancée.

He's a very persuasive guy. Now there's no way to get out of Sunday dinner with the *family*.

To tell the truth, I'd rather face a pit of vipers than what was about to take place in less than an hour. Come to think of it, I just might be facing a pit of vipers.

"Tiffany Ann Gates, how do you get yourself embroiled in these situations? Stewey or Mr. Hadley weren't this bad."

Who are you trying to kid? They were horrible! At least you don't cringe from Matt's touch.

My dubious nature rose up to plague me as I turned from side-to-side before the mirror on the closet door. Uncertain if I should wear the pale pink slacks with a white knit pullover, or the vibrant colored sundress with the little capped sleeve jacket, I opted for the dress.

Adding the single strand of pearls Grams presented to me for high school graduation seemed to bolster my confidence and went well with the outfit. I prayed for strength and resolve to see this through, though my conscience still pricked.

I polished off my ensemble with pearl chandelier earrings, hoping they would give me a polished and sophisticated air.

Why should I care so desperately? It's not as if our engagement is for real. I don't have to convince anyone to like or love me—although it would be nice if they did.

I did care. I wanted them to like me for myself. Not this pretend person. And not only his family, but I wanted Matthew to actually see me and love *me*.

When did Mr. Boss-Man become more than my employer and acting partner?

He was too well equipped. He knew how to slide under the radar of any unsuspecting female. Unfortunately, I was no match for him.

With a look of futility, I turned from the mirror and noticed my ride would be here in less than five minutes. I snatched my small handbag from the bed, looked the room over, and without thinking, I hurried down the stairs.

Halfway down, I stopped. Mr. Boss-Man and Mrs. Mac were standing in the hall talking. I hadn't seen him dressed in chinos and a sport shirt before, but he certainly did them justice. He looked as at ease in casual clothes as he did in a suit and tie. And he took my breath away.

I stood observing and studying this man I had partnered with. My wayward thoughts gave way to emotions I didn't want to examine. In an instant, I knew my heart was irrevocably lost to Matt. I also knew he wouldn't return my affections. In fact, he would scoff at my sappy feelings.

My chest constricted, and I experienced pain as I had never felt before. Until today, I knew I had never been in love.

I wanted to weep for allowing this to happen. I knew I would never be the same. Would never encounter a love like this again. All men from this day forth would pale in comparison to Matt. I wanted to run back upstairs, shut my door, bury my face in the pillow and howl.

He looked up. A smile lit his face.

My whole body reacted like a hormonal teenager. The blood zinged through my veins as he gave me the once over, his gaze a caress. This was not a good beginning.

How could I keep the love I felt from showing?

Seeing Matt's distraction, Mrs. Mac turned and looked up at me. "My, Tiffany, you look beautiful." Her compliment broke the spell Matt held over me.

"My words exactly."

He didn't take his eyes off me, but continued to watch as I self-consciously walked down the stairs.

My legs shook. My steps halting. My body in stages of meltdown. I wasn't sure I would make it to the bottom rung without tumbling at his feet.

When I stood within two feet of him, I noticed little specks of light in his eyes I hadn't noticed before. He looked happy to see me. *Or was it wishful thinking on my part?*

"The way you look, you'll knock my family off their feet."

"Thank you. I hope that was meant to be a compliment."

"Believe me it was."

His gaze turned my insides out and blasted my determination to tiny fragments.

Was he serious or playing a part?

He picked up my hand and kissed the tips of my fingers. His gaze never left my face. Unlike me, Matthew seemed to have a knack for this sort of thing.

I thought Mrs. Mac would have a coronary on the spot. By her breathy *ohhh*, I knew her romantic juices had kicked into overdrive. And with little or no effort, she would be tying a bow on my wedding present—hopefully not the picture of Mr. Mac this time—and pushing me down the aisle to matrimonial bliss. I smiled.

"Oh, how gallant you are. A true gentleman." She turned to me. "I like this one very much, Tiffany. He's a keeper."

Mr. Boss-Man could charm a fencepost. And now there was no doubt in my mind he would convince his family we were the real deal.

Releasing my hand, he turned and opened the door. "Shall we?"

"Yes. I'm ready." I looked at Mrs. Mac who was shining like a sunbeam. "I'll see you later."

"You know me, I'll be up. Tonight is the end of the season for my favorite show. I wouldn't miss it."

"Yes, of course. I forgot."

"It was a pleasure to finally meet you, Mrs. Mac." He smiled at her. "And I enjoyed our little chat. I hope to see you often."

"I'm sure you will." She stood at the door and waved us off.

Settled inside the car, I asked, "What was *our little chat* all about?"

"Nothing. Mrs. Mac is quite a talker though."

"I'll give you that. But she's an angel of a landlady too." Since he wasn't saying, I'd find out tonight from Mrs. Mac what they'd discussed.

The drive into Dallas was filled with deep thought on my part. I wasn't sure if Matt was doing the same, but figured a self-assured man like him wouldn't worry a minute over whether his family liked me or not.

We arrived in Highland Park too soon for my comfort. Mr. Charming turned into one of the palatial estates with a winding drive surrounded by huge oak trees, shrubs, and flowers. I resisted the smile tugging at my lips.

"What's so funny?" The mellow voice shocked me back from my thoughts.

"Nothing." I glanced at him and saw the question in his face. "Well if you must know—"

"I must."

"The thought just occurred to me the trees wouldn't dare have the audacity to drop even one leaf on these well manicured lawns." I watched closely to see if he would take offense.

"Oh, believe me, they dare." The laughter sparkled in his eyes. "My dad, a firm believer his son should know the meaning of work, had me out there raking and bagging nearly every weekend while growing up. And there's a ton of leaves on the family estate. My summer and weekend job was to take care of the lawn. And believe me, it wasn't a simple task."

"Really?" I couldn't imagine Mr. CEO of a mega billion dollar corporation as a little boy mowing and raking.

"*Really.*" He drove over a small wooden bridge. "My dad was a self-made man, and his son wasn't going to be an idle rich kid that squandered the empire he had built."

I drank my fill of his profile trying to decipher the man while he maneuvered another curve. Then I looked back out the front window.

A massive two-story, white-stoned Hill Country house with green shutters came into view. On the second floor, inviting balconies with planters filled with ferns and brilliant flowers spilling over the sides of the baskets, making the house inviting.

"What a beautiful home."

"Thank you." He pulled in front and parked before turning to look at me.

"Are we going in?"

"In a moment. I have something I'd like to ask. But first let me get this."

Unfastening his seatbelt, he leaned over and opened the glove-box, extracted a small ornate box, then flipped the lid open. The sun glinted off the dazzling rubies and diamonds embedded in the ring. Rays of light glimmered from the black, velvet bed.

My breath caught in my chest. My right hand unconsciously moved to my throat and felt the pearls resting against my warm skin.

In a daze, I watched Mr. CEO pull the ring from the box, lift my left hand from my lap before sliding the cool metal over my third finger. Though I tried to stop from shaking, my hand trembled in his.

He bent and placed a kiss on top of the ring as if to seal our fate. When he raised his head and looked at me, I saw those same glints of light I had noticed earlier as he stood at the base of the stairwell at Mrs. Mac's house.

When he unsnapped my seatbelt, my bemused mind didn't react. His features blurred and his mouth descended on mine. Warm, inviting, I lost myself in the moment and believed.

I leaned into him, savoring the feel of his lips on mine. He shifted, put his arm around my shoulders, and pulled me closer, and then deepened the kiss. His smell, clean, manly, with a hint of spicy cologne, saturated my senses. I was lost beyond redemption. Lost to all willpower to refuse the man. Lost in a game we were playing that felt for keeps.

Laughter and a knock on the window startled and yanked me back to earth, away from thoughts that would destroy me. Mortified by the boisterous comments, my face sported at least five shades of pink.

We had a spectator. Mr. Boss-Man and I, willing participants, had put on a good show for our audience.

Desolation filled me as the fire of embarrassment worked its way through my body. I pulled back, cleared my throat as I ran a hand down the front of my dress, smoothing the imaginary wrinkles, giving me time to collect my thoughts. The rubies and diamonds caught the light again and their sparkle mocked and winked.

I prayed a sinkhole would open up and swallow me whole. To meet anyone after what just took place, impossible. Instead of crying, I forced steel into my backbone and a smile in place to hide the shame of my susceptibility.

"Tiff, I'm asking you —"

My door flew open and whatever Mr. Boss-Man had to say was lost in loud, boisterous laughter.

"Come on Matt, you can't stay in the car mauling her all day. They're waiting inside to meet your *new* girl."

The young man looked to be in his late teens, early twenties, dressed in jeans and a pullover. He gave me the once over while grinning from ear to ear, then said, "Hey, Matt, ol' boy, I like this one. If you don't keep her, can I have her?"

"J.R. grow up and act your age."

After giving the young man a disgruntled look, he turned and smiled at me. He held my hand and gently squeezed. "Tiffany Gates meet J.R. Ainsley. This scoundrel is my *little* cousin Jeremiah Reynolds Ainsley."

"Hey, no fair." Jeremiah frowned at his cousin then grinned at me. "You can call me J.R."

I forced myself to look him in the eye, hoping he wouldn't see my stupidity. "Nice to meet you, J.R."

"Believe me, the pleasure is all mine."

He bowed, raised my hand to his lips, kissed my fingertips, as a knight in one of my books would do, and then boldly winked at me.

It must run in the family.

Mr. Boss-Man shook his head at his cousin's antics. "You're asking for it, J.R. Now leave us for a minute. I need to speak to Tiffany alone."

"No way, Cuz. I'm under strict instructions. As soon as you arrive, I am to bring you and *the girl* straightway to Granny. You're here, *sooo.*" He bowed, slinging out his arm toward the front door in a courtly manner.

"And shall I tell grandmother you called her—"

"That's not fair. You're playing dirty."

He released my hand and smiled regrettably. "He'll not let up. Duty calls. Shall we?"

The little by-play between cousins was all I needed to calm me down and acquire the necessary gumption for what was to come.

"Of course." I slid out of the car as a courtly maiden. "Lead on, my knight."

On to the executioner.

Chapter 26

The house, though grand on the outside, was even more beautiful inside. The large entry held a wide sweeping staircase with long hallways on each side. The room reminded me of those old movies where the star would make her grand entrance and all the people below, eyes turned upward, watched as a vision of loveliness slowly descended the stairs. Only there weren't any people standing, and I wasn't the vision of loveliness. Just Matt, J.R., and I were present.

Matt steered me through open double doors on our right. We entered an opulent living room filled with people of various ages and sizes, all staring at me. I wanted to turn around and run out the door, but Mr. Your-Not-Going-Anywhere had me in a death grip, nailed to his side.

"Lots of luck," J.R. whispered before deserting us.

He wandered over by a bored-looking, young girl sitting by the bay windows. She perked up to see what the silence was all about. I wondered if she were a cousin or girlfriend.

For some reason, I thought the grandmother discussed by the cousins earlier would be Lucy Bell, but she wasn't.

Instead, a grey-hair, dignified, much older woman sat in a wingback Queen Anne chair, residing over the proceedings. Her gaze locked on me and remained there as Matt led me like a prisoner to the gallows in her direction. I knew she had sized me up by the time I stood in front of her.

Matt bent and gave her thin, wrinkly cheek a peck, and said, "Hello Grandmother. Hope you're feeling well today."

"I'm as well as can be for a ninety-two-year-old woman."

Matt laughed, as did others in the room.

I did my best to offer a smile but figured it fell short.

"Still got your spunk, I see. And as lovely as ever. Is that a new dress?"

The woman turned vibrant before my eyes. The by-play between her and her grandson had worked miracles.

"Still have enough spunk to keep up with you. And no, it isn't a new dress."

Again, her sharp inspection, with eyes the color of faded leaves, landed on me. "Who do we have here?" She pointed a willowy, arthritic finger in my direction.

Matt's strong arm pulled me up next to him as I quaked in my boots—that is, if I had been wearing boots. I knew if granny didn't buy our charade, no one else in the room would either.

"Grandmother, this is Tiffany Gates. Tiffany, this is Mrs. Charlotte Ainsley, my great-grandmother."

"So nice to meet you, Mrs. Ainsley." I wasn't sure if I was supposed to shake her hand or curtsey. Since I hadn't curtseyed before, except when I was a child playing pretend, I decided a handshake would have to do.

The woman tipped her head slightly in a regal acknowledgement. Her paper-thin, vein-riddle hand felt soft and delicate. Her grip was strong, belying her fragile-looking state.

"Matthew, do you have an announcement you would like to make?" She shot him a piercing stare. "If I'm not mistaken, I believe that is the Ainsley engagement ring I see on Ms. Gates' finger."

I heard gasps, one of them mine. Everyone spoke at once in a chorus of congratulations and *why didn't you tell us.*

My face must have been redder than the Oklahoma dirt where my mother had grown up. A little miffed at Mr. Full-Of-Surprises, I wondered why he hadn't told me last night, or even before we arrived what he had planned for this *little* family gathering.

Suddenly, the room became stone quite. All eyes were on us. That's when I spied James. His gaze connected with mine. He offered a nod and half smile before lifting his glass in the air in silent salute, but he didn't take a drink and his smile appeared strained.

Matt put his arm around my waist. "I apologize for putting you in the hot seat, but this is one of our customs."

His whispered apology didn't give my heart the usual flutter.

"I'll make it short and sweet. Sorry about the audience." He gave me a quick kiss on the cheek and reached for my hand. His gaze held mine.

If I didn't know better, I could easily be persuaded he was deeply in love with me. But of course, his was an act, and a good one at that.

Someone give this man an Oscar!

At a loss for words, I stared into his darkened emerald eyes that reached past my heart into the depths of my soul—I was adrift for all eternity. That's when I realized I had irrevocably lost my heart to this man, knowing full well his was still intact. Once our pretense was finally over, I would shrivel up and die, with nothing left to offer.

Chapter 27

"I was going to wait to make the announcement, but since Grandmother Ainsley preempted me ..." He twisted the ring on my finger, in a nervous, playful way. "Tiffany, before all my family, I pledge my heart and soul to you and promise to do my best to make you happy. Will you be my wife?"

With my gaze glued on Matt's face, I shut my gaping mouth, not knowing what was expected of me, and feeling sure someone would call his bluff.

"Well, young lady, you're wearing the ring. Don't keep us in suspense. Is it a *yes* or a *no*?" The cane the matronly woman held in her left hand thumped on the hardwood floors sending shivers of doom through me.

Matt applied a small amount of pressure to my hand. "Tiff ..." His plea was softly spoken yet so heartfelt. If I hadn't seen his lips move I wouldn't have heard my name.

Nodding like a simpleton, I swallowed the knot in my throat and answered, "Yes."

My body trembled, my knees knocked, and I waited for someone to yell fraud, imposter, throw her out of this house. Instead, we were surrounded by well wishers, men pounding Matt on the back and pumping his arm like one of those old fashioned water pumps.

Women grabbed my hand, *oohing* and *ahhing* over the ring. One elderly woman patted my cheek. She mentioned the Ainsley ring—which at the moment was searing my finger like a branding iron—had been in the family for over six generations, and that I must do it proud.

Oh, great! Now I have the added worry of losing the family heirloom and having to make everyone proud of me.

Chalk one up for Matty.

All during the ordeal of well-wishers, he never left my side. In fact, he kept a tight arm around my waist the whole time. Come to I think of it, he probably thought I would escape the first moment he released me.

Believe me, escape sounded better and better with each passing moment, but I wasn't a quitter. I had a job to do. And by all appearances, my role as fake fiancée was turning out to be a success.

Once everyone got past the congratulations, ribbing Matt, and questioning our quick decision—*one look and I knew she was what I wanted. And you know me, I go after what I want*—and asking when the wedding would be—*sometime after the first of the year*—everything quieted down.

Boy, Mr. Answer-Man was good at fielding difficult questions. All I had to do was smile, look like the blushing fiancée, and say *thank you.*

At first, I didn't realize Matt's mother hadn't spoken to Matt or me. She sat quietly sending calculating looks in my direction and occasionally her son's. This couldn't be a good sign—if I were to believe in signs.

Another one I hadn't seen was Lucy Bell, but then again, I could have missed her in the crowd of aunts, uncles, and cousins galore, but I didn't think so.

"Would you like something to drink?"

I stared at Matt as if he had a few screws loose, then smiled for good measure since we still seemed to be the center of attention.

In an agitated whisper I answered, "Drink? I'd ask for a double if I were a drinking woman, but since I'm not, a glass of water will do."

Mr. Funny-Bones laughed before putting his mouth to my ear. "I'll do one better. Come with me, and I'll find you a glass of iced tea and a breather from prying eyes."

His breath tickled my neck and turned the rest of me to jelly. However, to my ears his words of escape were like bread to a hungry soul. I knew if I ever left the room, I'd do my best not to come back.

I'm not saying I'm a lily-livered chicken, but it's a close assessment. At this moment, handing Mr. Exec his ring and taking the stage out of Dodge sounded like a grand idea. But I'm not Miss Kitty and Matt's not Marshal Dillon, and I need the job—at least until I find another one. In the meantime, it looked like I'd be staying and playing nicey-nice.

I would do just about anything to keep my job, even if it meant selling my … No, I'd never do that, but this was getting close … one big fat lie after another. Did I even have a conscience?

He dragged me through huge, lavishly furnished rooms. This house looked much like the rich and famous I'd seen on TV, sporting the three Ps—posh, plush, and pricy. With my frugal ways, the cost of one place setting of sterling silver flanking the Copenhagen china on the dining room table alone would keep me in tall cotton for a long while.

Thinking we would go to the kitchen, get something to drink, and have that necessary chat, *boy*, was I ever wrong.

A beehive of activity was taking place in a kitchen the size of those reality shows where all the chefs are slinging around raw meat, banging pots and utensils, slathering butter everywhere, all the while cursing their helpers as they cooked delicious food. Except this kitchen was quiet, efficient, and orderly, nothing being slung or cursed, and everyone in the room came to a stop when we walked in.

Once again, we were the center of attention until someone cleared their throat loudly, causing the well-oiled staff/machinery to function as intended once again.

"May I help you, sir?" A plump, little gray-haired woman with rosy cheeks approached us. The others in the kitchen kept busy as they took sly glances in our direction.

"Hi Mary, I'd like you to meet Tiffany Gates, my fiancée."

Mary beamed a welcoming smile. "Nice to meet you, Miss Gates. And congratulations to you both."

At the last minute, I remembered to murmur a polite, "Thank you." And I offered what I hoped looked like a newly fiancée's sincere, excited smile.

"Thanks, Mary. I know you're busy preparing dinner, but could I beg a couple glasses of tea from you?"

"Yes, sir." Mary moved quicker than I thought able.

In no time, we had our tea, and Matt was leading me out the back door into the Garden of Eden. I looked around for the snake but saw none.

For the first time since I entered the house, I felt I could breathe again, and then ... he touched me. All logical thought flew from of my head.

Mr. Attentive slipped my hand in his and began pulling me deep into a wooded area. I wasn't sure what to expect, a chain saw murderer or maybe a Mad Hatter, until he pulled me into a clearing.

Immediately transported back to *Gone with the Wind*, one of the most whimsical, inviting gazebos, framed with huge oak trees, stood begging me to enter, and I did. All that was missing were my corset and crinoline beneath my antebellum dress.

Best of all, I had my very own Rhett Butler attending me. Personally, Matt was much better looking.

He motioned for me to take a seat on one of the floral chintz cushions and held up his hand.

"Before you let me have it, please give me a chance to explain."

I quirked my left brow and said, "You think you can explain why you shoved me in front of a bunch of strangers and—"

"They weren't all strangers. You knew James and mother, and you met J.R. just before—"

"Semantics." I stated emphatically, swiping my hand to cut him off, "You proposed in front of your whole family."

"Not my whole family." He grinned sheepishly. "There were a few absent."

His grin was too endearing, but right now I wasn't buying endearing.

"Again, semantics," I huffed out. "We weren't supposed to be engaged at least for another two to three weeks." All through with my rant, I let out a heavy breath. "Explain away, if you can."

He shook his head and gave me a look that turned my insides to mush and my heart to pounding wildly.

"If you remember, I mentioned after the fundraiser my mother was already looking for your replacement. I needed to work fast to put a stop to her interference in my life." He turned and rammed his hand through his hair. "You would think a grown man who can handle a room full of antagonistic board members could handle one meddling mother."

He turned back staring at me, his eyes pleading with me to understand.

I turned my gaze to the brilliant red bird who took that moment to hop onto the railing and start chirping. A lot safer. Maybe if I didn't look at Mr. Boss-Man, I could pretend this was one of my novels.

Fat chance. I'm in deep, deep trouble.

His ability to turn me to putty in his capable and persuasive hands had me shaking my head.

"I agree with you, pitiful." His voice held a wealth of conviction.

"What? Me?"

He looked at me strangely. "No. Me. I have an interfering mother who won't stop no matter what I say to her."

I took a drink of tea, allowing it to sooth my nerves. It tasted so good I took another swallow.

"Marry me. If you do, she won't interfere in my life any longer."

Bad timing. I choked on my drink, spewing tea like a fountain. Fortunately, Mary had given us some napkins. She must have known I would make a mess.

"Do what?" I mopped at my dress, glad to see I was able to sop up the drops of tea without leaving behind a stain.

Mr. Bad-Idea-Man bent down brushing tea off his shoes. "Marry me. Our marriage will take care of your problem and mine at the same time."

"What problem? I don't have a problem except you." I couldn't believe what I was hearing. "First you destroy Agnes—"

"Agnes? I don't know an Agnes." He scrunched his brows looking at me strangely.

I waived him off. "My VW. I call her Agnes. I told you that the other day."

"Oh, yeah. Do you normally name inanimate objects?"

"Not generally."

"Really?"

"Don't change the subject. You hired me and proposition me—"

"I what?"

"I don't mean that type of a proposition. What's wrong with your mind?"

Shaking his head, he offered an incredulous look. "My mind is just fine, thank you. Yours may need some looking into."

Mr. Looney-Tunes mumbled the last, but I heard him just the same. I continued as if he hadn't spoken.

"You know full well we have an agreement of convenience, to which, I might add, I've held up my end of the bargain. And now, you want to marry me to take care of my problem and yours. The only problem at this moment I seem to have is you."

I stood for good measure, not sure why, but I felt at a disadvantage looking up at him.

Wrong move.

He pulled me into his strong, capable arms, hauled me up against his solid chest before capturing my mouth with his very persuasive lips, leaving me breathless. My heart nearly stopped, then pumped hard as if I had run a five-minute mile, which for me would be impossible.

Mr. Magic-Man pulled back, looking disgruntled.

What? He didn't like the kiss? Well excuuusse me! I heard a buzzing, didn't know if it was a bee or my ears.

Mr. Man-of-My-Dreams pulled out his phone, holding up one finger. "Hold that thought and don't go anywhere."

Where was I going to go? He drove me to this little engagement/announcement party. Highland Park was too far to walk home. I could call a cab, I guess.

Matt swiped his phone. "Yes?" He listened. "Give us a minute." He listened again, this time more agitated. "We'll be right in." He hung up. "That was James. Said the family was sitting down to dinner and our presence was requested."

He pulled me up close again, but this time I *did* resist, but didn't quite get out of the circle of his arms.

"Mr. Ainsley—"

"We're back to Ainsley are we? Matt. Say it. Matt. That's my name." He looked none too happy.

"All right. Matt, I want to oblige you, but you seem to change the playing rules when it suits your purpose. And right now you're falling into the territory of not following them at all."

"Like you said, the rules don't seem to suit me ... not sure they ever did."

"That's what I mean." I pulled. He tugged. He nibbled on my ear. "Mr.–Matt, stop that. We don't even have an audience."

"I like it better without an audience." He nibbled my ear again. "You have the sweetest, little earlobes." He went in for another nibble.

Pulling my ear out of reach of Mr. Nibbler, I did my best to control my emotions and found it impossible. They were tumbling off the chart. I had no control at all.

I planted my hands on his chest to push him away.

Huge mistake. He didn't budge. Matt was solid like a rock and felt so wonderfully strong, I wanted to cave in, let him take care of the problems I would have if I quit my job. Instead, I said, "Did you forget? *Displays of affection only when necessary to show conviction of our engaged status.*"

"I didn't forget, but the rules no longer work for me."

"What is this? A game to you?"

"If it's a game, it's a very serious but delectable game."

He nibbled on my neck this time. I lost the battle of reasonable thought and holding to the rules. I felt so right in his arms.

"Please, Matt." This time I gave a more insistent shove. I needed space to think. I couldn't let him take advantage of my weakened resolve. I am an all or nothing kind of a gal. Not a take it or leave it kind.

He crammed his hands into his jean pockets. "Okay, hands in pockets. I want to explain but right now they're expecting us back at the house for dinner. On the way home, we'll talk, I promise."

I ran my hand down my hair making sure it wasn't mussed after being thoroughly kissed and nibbled on. Hopefully, he didn't … "You didn't leave any marks on my neck did you?"

"Only the kind that can't be seen." Matt grinned devilishly and gave me a peck on the lips. "You look gorgeous, come on." He grabbed my hand pulling me along.

"Don't do that."

"What? Pull you?" He slowed his step.

"No. Kiss me."

He shook his head. "No can do. Your lips are too enticing."

"Matt—"

"All right. I'll do my best to resist. But I won't make any promises for fear of breaking them. And with you, I want to keep all my promises now and all of them to come."

Chapter 28

For the remainder of the afternoon, Matt played the perfect gentleman. He never left my side, for which I was grateful. I didn't want to be cornered by his mother or great-granny, or anyone else—though both women and several others kept staring at me oddly.

I thought the time would never come for us to leave, but it did. We made our enthusiastic show of appreciation, then skedaddled out of the house, making our hasty get-away.

"Matt, wait up."

Not fast enough, it would seem.

I liked James. And I hoped he wouldn't be too inquisitive. Maybe he wanted to give us his congratulations since he hadn't spoken to either of us all day.

"You want to explain what's going on?" He gave Matt and me the eagle eye.

"Nothing to explain." Mr. Cool-Hand-Matt shrugged.

I stood all jittery and ready to cave in, yet knew I had to keep up my end of the bargain, so I smiled doing my best to act natural. James didn't seem to want to buy our little charade.

"You meet and less than three weeks you're engaged. Don't tell me there's nothing to explain." He moved closer and gave me the onceover as if to determine what type of gold-digger I might be. Then, he gave Matt a look of disbelief, as if he had a few screws loose.

What's so hard to believe, huh? You think I'm not good enough for Mr. Richie-Rich? Or because I live in a one-room efficiency, I'm not worthy?

Let me tell you something, buster, I put my pants on one leg at a time, just like you!

"I've known Tiffany longer than two weeks. We met by accident—"

James' laughter cut him off. "Yeah, I know. A car accident two weeks before she came to work for you. Are you sure it was an accident? Other women have tried to snare you, but you have never been so gullible." He nailed me with his glare.

"I'll try to forget you said that." Matt's calm voice wasn't pleasant and bordered on menacing.

Of all the nerve! My inclination was to give James a good piece of my mind and something more to think about. He was really beginning to get on my nerves.

"Matt, you've done a lot of things I may not agree with, but I've never thought you capable of something as crazy as this."

He swung his hand in my general direction, which made me shrivel up inside. Did he think I had snared Matt? Did all of Matt's relatives think the same?

Matt and James were like two mad bulls in a ring, staring one another down while I stood holding my breath. I hoped and prayed it wouldn't come to blows. Cousins, who were also good friends, shouldn't be at odds, especially when this whole thing didn't really matter. There should be a better way.

"What do you know about her? And don't tell me it was love at first sight, I won't buy it for a minute, not with her."

His words hurt and insulted. I wanted to run away. Was this what his whole family thought—I was inferior to him and only after his money?

"It's immaterial whether you wish to believe it was love at first sight or not. Get it through your head, we are engaged. We will be married, with or without your blessing. I expected far better from you. Either give us your well wishes, or go back inside. This conversation is over."

"Matt, James please—" Both men threw me a *don't interfere* look. I lowered my gaze, unable to look at either of them, feeling the prick of tears and sick inside.

"I'll see you at the office tomorrow." Matt took my arm, turned, led me down the remaining steps, opened the car door, and then waited for me to get in.

I expected him to slam the door, but he shut it gently while I looked out the window at James through blurry eyes. The man gave me a cold, hard stare before turning and going back inside.

The ride was quiet. Matt's anger still simmering. I wanted to say or do something to take the edge off the situation, but before I could, soothing music filled the car. My enigmatic partner's face was stoic, yet I saw a troubled sadness in the stern set of his jaw.

Unable to let it go, I turned down the radio. "Matt, I don't believe it's wise to alienate your cousin, who is also your closest friend. Don't you think this is going a bit too far to keep your mother off your back?"

"No."

No what? We're not that close? He was a bore?

"Come on, give me a break here. Please, can we talk about this?"

"No."

"Well, if you won't, I will."

"Drop it, Tiffany."

He didn't sound upset, more like he was bored with the topic. Yet there was an edge to his voice that told me I was treading in boiling water.

Think again, buster!

"No can do. I won't drop it because it directly involves me. And since I'm one of the parties of interest, I think I have a right to speak my mind to tell you how I feel."

"Hold that thought."

"What?"

"I'll answer your questions in a few minutes."

Was he trying to work though the problem? Okay then. I'd give him a little time to think.

Mr. Take-Charge hooked a right, then another right into an underground parking lot. We whipped around a couple walls before he parked in space A1. He hopped out and came around to open my door, smiling.

I didn't see what was so funny, so I sat there and wouldn't budge. I didn't have a clue where I was, what I was doing here, or why he was trying to pry my body from the car?

To be fair, he hadn't touched me, just opened the door. Maybe getting rid of the problem—me?

"Do you plan on sitting there or do you want answers? For answers, you'll have to come with me."

When I didn't move or say anything, he shrugged, and then turned to leave.

"Just a minute." I scrambled out of the car to catch up with him.

I wouldn't have had to rush. He stood with his arms crossed, his hip resting on the backend of the car, waiting for me with a smug grin on his face. He was letting me know he knew what I would do all along, which now had me steaming.

"Where are we and where are we going?" Since my mind hadn't been on Matt's driving, I didn't have a clue where we had ended up—my closest guess, somewhere around downtown—Uptown maybe?

He pulled away from the car and waited for me to catch up. Clasping my hand, he led me to an elevator.

"You wanted to talk? I'm taking you where we won't be disturbed, and you can talk until you're blue in the face."

"For your information, I never talk until I'm blue in the face, Mr. Know-It-Ill." My feelings were hurt. What did he think ... I was a chatterbox?

He chuckled, but dragged me up alongside him again. He seemed to like to do that. In fact, he was a very Hands-On kind of guy, something I hadn't realized until just now.

I wasn't sure I liked it much. *Who was I kidding?* I loved the way his touch made me feel, all mushy and gooey inside, and it seemed like I couldn't get close enough to him.

"Where is this place you're taking me?"

"You'll see, Ms. Impatience."

The elevator doors opened, and Matt pulled me inside. He released my hand and flashed a card across a sensor, then pick up my hand again, seemingly fascinated with my fingers.

Hmm, could be a finger fixation.

"Did you know, Tiffany Gates, you are one beautiful woman? I'm glad our paths crossed, even if it was a wreck that brought it about."

He thought I was beautiful? His words thrilled me. "I wouldn't call crashing into my Bug as *our paths crossing.*"

A deep chuckle was his answer as he lifted my hand and proceeded to kiss the top of each finger, while looking deep into my eyes.

No doubt about it, he had a finger fetish, and I liked it.

My heart nearly leapt out of my chest. What he did for romance was the ambrosia of books. If I could only translate these feelings onto paper, I'd become a best seller overnight.

"A crash that you caused, I might add."

He laughed, something he seemed to be doing a lot of lately.

"I can always count on you to ground my feet. What did I ever do before we met?"

"Probably charmed some other gal outta her shoes."

He gave a grin and a calculating look. "Is that what I did? Charmed you out of your shoes?"

Flustered, I shook my head. "I wasn't referring to me but to other women—"

"Ah, but Tiffany, I don't care about other women. I want to know what I do to you. You see, if you're going to be my wife, I need to know how to please you. How to rock your world."

This time, instead of leaping out of my chest, my heart stopped altogether, and then just as quickly, beat like a drummer in the battle of the bands. Fortunately, the bell dinged and the doors opened, saving me from answering or expiring on the spot.

"Hold that thought."

I could hardly hold myself together, let alone hold a thought.

We stepped off the elevator into an exquisite entryway leading into one of those "Big D Magazine" showcase living rooms. Twelve-foot floor-to-ceiling bay windows with a clear view of downtown Dallas, hand-scraped oak hardwood floors, a plush looking sofa and two overstuffed chairs a person wouldn't want to get up from.

In other words, a pad I could only dream about. *Was that a bearskin or alpaca rug before the fireplace?* I couldn't tell.

This time my heart jumped into my throat. I knew where I was. And of all the places I didn't want to end up, it was at Mr. Boss-Man's pad—*alone*.

Well, not really alone, he was there too, but just the two of us, which didn't bode well with my jittery nerves exploding all over the place. Talk about stupid, irresponsible, totally out of my element … that was me.

And, of course, I had to ask. "Whose condo is this?"

Mr. Spider raised his brows. A sparkle appeared in his brilliant eyes. "Mine."

He was already spinning his web around me. I could feel it tightening. "I need to leave."

"No, you don't."

"Yes, I do." I nodded—for emphasis, as I backed up and bumped into the elevator door.

"No you don't." He shook his head—for emphasis. He looked smug, *too smug* walking toward me. "You want answers? I've got answers, but you'll only hear them if you stay."

Matt turned, moved into the living room, and then stepped out of his shoes. He scooted them under the coffee table, then sat down on the sofa and began patting the cushion beside him.

I was correct. Matt sank down into luxurious comfort I could only dream of owning.

"Come sit down so we can talk. I'll explain and answer all your questions."

"Oh sure, I just bet you can explain."

He patted the sofa cushion again.

I don't know why, but I walked like someone in a trance into the living room. At the last moment, I passed the sofa to look out the window at the night-lights of downtown Dallas, putting off the inevitable.

His window afforded a beautiful, sparkling view of the city at night. The slanted glass windows of Fountain Place, the Perot Museum, which to me looked like the outside still needed to be finished, and even the white, eye-catching, 140 million dollar Margaret Hunt Bridge to nowhere were all there to see.

"Tiffany, stop stalling. Come sit down. I refuse to talk to your back."

I didn't comply immediately, but when I did, I sat down on the opposite end of the couch, making sure to keep a cushion-width between us.

I was right. The couch was *way* too comfy.

"This elaborate plan of yours, does it include your family hiring a hit man to take this little gold-digger out?" I jabbed my thumb at my chest. "And, I don't mean on a date either—like snuff my lights out?"

Laughter filled the room. "What movies have you been watching on TV?"

"I don't have a TV."

"Then what do you read? Mafia hit men novels? Don't tell me you're a PI/sleuth junkie."

He continued to laugh at my expense.

I narrowed my gaze, hoping he'd get the hint I didn't think his little joke was the least bit funny. "No I don't and I'm not … in that order. When you get through laughing, you can take me home." I moved to stand, but he placed his hand gently on my arm.

"Please stay. I'm sorry. No more jokes."

Something in the way he looked at me made me scoot back and get comfortable again.

"Would you like to divulge this plan of yours? It might have been nice to know it beforehand. I could have been a little better prepared today instead of being caught off guard."

"As I mentioned earlier, my mother already had someone waiting in the wings to take your place, which I wasn't at all pleased to hear. The announcement of our engagement was my preemptive strike to keep that from happening."

"Maybe the woman would be better suited for your lifestyle and family, unlike me. Who is she, or is she to be a surprise as I was? Do you even know?"

He acted none too pleased. "Candace. If I remember correctly, you met her last night."

My heart sank. Candace was everything I wasn't. Rich, sophisticated, charming, even if she was rude to me. And … she was beautiful. She would fit into Matt's world far better than I could.

"Yes, we met. She's beautiful. But weren't you two an item once before?"

"Yes, however, my mother seems to think we should be one again, which I disagree." He sounded tired of the subject. "I like our arrangement. But I would like to propose a slight modification."

He raised his hand. "Hear me out before you misunderstand what I'm offering and go into one of your rants." Matt moved closer. Reached for my hand, the one with the family heirloom, and held my fingers in his warm palm. He turned the ring back and forth.

If he didn't have a finger fetish, maybe he was the type of person that needed something to do while he formed his thoughts. However, what his hands were doing to mine was pure bliss. I could feel the tingle igniting every cell in my body.

"I don't know how you feel about me, but I believe you like me, and we get along well together. I know I find you fascinating and irresistible." He stared into my eyes.

"Your quirky sense of humor is refreshing. Your upbeat attitude spills over and affects me in a good way. I also noticed that since you came into my life, I am very possessive where you're concerned."

"Possessive as in controlling, overprotective, jealous, domineer—"

"You can stop right there, and yes, all of them except controlling—well maybe a little."

I waggled my head, letting him know what I thought of *little.*

He did that thing again, kissing my fingers one at a time, gazing straight into my eyes.

Mesmerized, I couldn't look away. The room turned warm.

Hot flashes? ... No way, too young! I couldn't catch my breath. My insides felt like a quivering lump of jellyfish, the kind that cover Galveston beaches sometimes.

Goosebumps covered every inch of my body just before I turned all shaky. My heart beat so violently, I thought I could possibly be in the throes of a heart attack or maybe a relapse of the flu.

"I know we haven't known each other very long."

"Yes, James pointed that out quite succinctly."

"Let's leave James out of this."

"He made a very good point. You really can't count those first two weeks after our wreck. You never called once to see if I was still among the living."

"I would have, if I hadn't been sicker than a dog. I came in contact with a person who didn't have the good sense to stay home when they had the flu, infecting me."

At that moment, I certainly had the good sense to keep my mouth shut. I was probably that person.

"If we're through with James, and if I have answered to your satisfaction my lack of interest in you for the first two weeks, and if you have nothing more you'd like to add ..." He paused, no doubt to see if I would jump right in and bring up something else. "Marry me."

"Do what?" *Well, I didn't see that one coming.*

"Marry me. It would solve our problems."

"Solve our problems? You said that this afternoon. Are you daft? I didn't have any problems until you hit me." I did my best to extract my hand, but he wouldn't let it go. He held it tight, but like it was a fragile porcelain piece that needed tender care.

"Tiffany, if you think about it, you know you had problems before MTA. You were barely making it. And now you're well on your way to becoming solvent.

"As my wife, you will never have to worry. When we marry, you can keep working if you like, or not." He shrugged. "Either works for me, at least until we have children, and then I'd prefer you stay home with them."

Matthew held out our hands. "And look at us. Whether you want to admit it or not, we're good together."

He didn't seem to be affected by my stunned silence.

"You make me laugh, something I haven't done in years. I keep you guessing, which helps to spice up your life." He gave me a cute little boyish grin. "And, I can't think of anyone I would rather marry.

"Look at it this way, you're well on the way to loving me already, so why not marry me?"

"I'm what?" I wasn't well on my way, I *was* head over heels in love with him. Something I wasn't about to tell Mr. Ideas-Man.

"Come on, admit it. We're good together. If you don't say yes, I'll be placed on the open market to be hounded by"—He gave me a look of horror.—"Candace and others just like her."

I smiled before my thoughts turned to his mother.

What does Katherine think I am, an indecent candidate? The woman wanted me for her son, and now just like that, I'm chopped liver?

And who does Mr. Boss-Man think I am ... some kind of easy mark that will roll over and play wife?

"So, let me get this straight. I'm to run into your willing arms to keep you off the market and your mother off your back."

"I didn't mean it—"

I held up my free hand. "And for my trouble."

He scrunched his brows together. I could tell he didn't like how this was going.

"I'll move from my little shanty in Midlothian and live in this huge mansion on top of the world. Sounds like a plan to me." I was just getting warmed up.

He started to say something, and again I held up my hand to keep him silent.

"I've got an idea. Why don't we leave now and fly to Las Vegas. We could maybe find an Elvis impersonator to do the deed, and then fly right back and make your family happy as pie … *in your dreams.*"

This time I extracted my hand from his and moved off the couch.

He stood, his face a myriad of expressions. "Tiffany, I'm sorry. I know I'm not saying this well. I've gone about this all wrong."

"You think!" I felt like smacking someone.

"Truly, I'm sorry. I haven't had experience opening my feelings to others. But what I'm trying to say is, I love you and I want you for my wife."

Chapter 29

I stood there dumbfounded. Why Mr. Incredible was still standing and not in a heap of cinders was a mystery. Doesn't lightning come out of the blue and strike a person down for telling whoppers? *Hmm.* Maybe lightning is selective as to the lie told.

Matthew continued to watch me, waiting for my reaction. Was he expecting me to run into his arms and thank him profusely for saving me from a life of drudgery?

Did he honestly think I would believe him, the man who always got what he went after no matter what, or at least that's what I'd heard?

For some silly reason *to the victor goes the spoils* came to mind. Was he taking that same tack with me?

My heart told me to believe. *How could I?* This was Mr. Eligible-Bachelor-of-the-Year asking me—little-nobody-from-across-the-tracks and a gold digger to-boot—to be his wife. All this love came about in a little more than a month—if a person counted the week and a half I was home sick in bed and he was too.

People don't fall in love that fast … *do they?* Come to think of it, he captured my heart with one look of his vibrant green eyes, even if I were a little stunned by the accident and violently ill with the flu.

My parents, theirs was love at first sight. It lasted twenty years until the good Lord took Dad home. But me?

Surely, that kind of stuff only happens in my novels or in fairy tales with Prince Charming. How could I be certain what I felt for him, or for that matter, what Matthew believed he felt for me, was love and not our hormones operating in overdrive?

What if he was asking me because everyone was opposed, or because he wanted to shut his mother up once and for all?

Oh, to be truthful, it would be nice to have my own Prince Charming, but not at the price of my soul.

Why couldn't life be simple black and white?

Boooriiinnng.

"Matt, I think we need to sit down and calmly talk about what this - this marriage thing is all about." This time I sat down on the couch and waited for Matt to do the same. He started to sit next to me, but I motioned for him to go to the other end.

"You sit there. I want to be able to think straight." With him close and touchy-feely, my thinking always seemed to get mixed up.

"Let me begin with, I think you are an incredible man any woman would be proud to call her husband. But I'm not certain that I'm the right person for you."

"Tiff—"

"Let me finish." I raised my hand. "And though you said the words, I'm not convinced that you truly know their meaning."

"I do where you are concerned."

"I would like to believe you. And it would be too easy to go along with your plan, but I can't. Allow me to offer you a counter proposal."

"I'm listening, but only if it doesn't involve you quitting or leaving or giving back the ring."

This time I twisted the ring on my finger, knowing I didn't have the strength to remove it.

Truth be told, I liked how the ring felt and what it represented. I didn't want to give it back. When he slipped it on my finger earlier, it didn't just brand my finger, it branded my heart.

"No, it doesn't involve any of those options, unless we decide differently."

He shook his head empathetically. "I know my mind. I love you whether you want to believe it or not. And if you will look deep into your heart, you'll see you love me too. I believe you're just too afraid to acknowledge the fact."

"What I propose is we stay engaged for six months. This will keep your mother off your back, which was the original plan and reason for this … you know." I didn't want to say farce because it was way beyond that now.

"This plan will allow us to really get to know each other and to see if we can even stand being together that long. If in the next six month you continue to love me, then I'll say yes to your proposal."

"May I?" He motioned to move closer to me.

I nodded.

He moved up next to me and did that hand and finger thing again. As before, my heart galloped like a horse in a race. My reaction to his touch was way *too* revealing of how I felt about him. I just hoped it didn't show.

"I agree wholeheartedly with your terms, only because I know if I don't, I'll lose you. But let me be perfectly clear. This will be the longest six months in the history of man as far as I'm concerned. To wait will be the most difficult, excruciating thing I have ever done in my life.

"But, know this Tiffany Ann Gates, after six months, we will be married. Because you will see our love will grow stronger and our wants and desires are the same.

"I love you and want you for my wife now, but I'll wait." Matt moved in closer this time, tipping my chin up. "May I?"

Thrilled he had asked and didn't take it as his right, I nodded in anticipation, knowing I wanted his kiss as much as he wanted mine.

His head descended and our lips met. I melted in his arms, not wanting the moment to end but knew it must. For a kiss, it was far too short, yet held an eternity of longing.

For the first time, I knew the definition of love. The stuff of my novels couldn't compare with what I felt in his arms and the promise he spoke with his lips. Love was no longer a word but a commitment, an emotion that went far beyond feelings, settling a sweet satisfaction of wellbeing deep inside me.

"Now that we have an agreement, but not the one I would have liked, I'll take you home." He stood pulling me up next to him. "I'm going to court you as no woman has ever been courted before. And if for no other reason than from sheer exhaustion, you will ask me to marry you."

In a daze, I stood in front of him wondering why he would say something so silly. Courting was good. But exhaustion wouldn't have me asking him. I smiled knowing that he would wait a long, long time before I asked him to marry me.

"That's a moot issue. You've already asked me to marry you, so why would I ask you?"

His little quirky smile appeared. "Only time will tell, Ms. Gates. But know this, your proposal will be something we will tell our children, grandchildren, and great-grandchildren." His smug smile and cocked brow had me concerned.

My mind was set. It would be a cold day in Hades before I would ask Mr. Smug to marry me. And everyone knows it will never snow in hell. Oh, forget it. He'd already asked me and I'd accepted ... or had I?

Yes, I definitely had.

Chapter 30

I didn't know how hard it would be to work for my *real* fiancé.

After our talk and our goodnight kiss at the door—a kiss, I might add, that curled my toes—he came in to work today and said, *Good morning, Tiffany. Please come to my office.*

He was gone before I could form a reply and without a backward glance in my direction. How's that for love?

Mr. Fiancé had to be one of the most infuriating, egotistical, world-revolves-around-me men I'd ever met. And believe you me, I'd known a few.

Well, two can play this game.

Determined to ignore him as he had ignored me, I wondered if Mr. I'm-Not-Interested had slept on his decision and changed his mind. Did he want his ring back? Well, I figured I'd make him ask before I gave up the family heirloom.

Another thing, he could wait a few minutes before I go running to his office just because he snapped his fingers. Come to think about it, he didn't snap his fingers. Yet, I'm not the jump at his beck and call kind of gal.

On second thought, I'd better be. He's paying my salary, and right now I need the job.

Steaming, but trying to put a lid on it, I grabbed my iPad, stomped over to the door, and then stopped long enough to ensure I didn't have any clothing malfunctions.

After planting a peaches and cream smile on my face, I opened the door and sedately walked into Mr. Boss-Man's lair.

A fat lot of good checking my appearance did. His back was to me, the propeller on the small plane spinning. He'd already forgotten he'd asked me to come to his office.

"Shut the door please, Tiffany."

I nearly jumped out of my skin. Mr. Boss-Man was more attune to me than I thought. He *had* heard me.

Nervously, because I didn't know what his frame of mind might be, which at the moment seemed to be very unusual, I turned and shut the door.

I had been behind shut doors with him many times in the last couple of weeks. But today he'd acted so cold, I didn't know if his playing rules had changed. They did seem to change quickly with him.

I turned around. There stood Matt within arms' reach of me making me nearly come unglued. I hadn't heard him, yet he was close enough to smell the delicious, scent of his mind-blowing cologne.

"Good morning, love."

He drew me into his arms and dipped his head. His lips captured mine and rattled my cage and all the other parts of me too.

When he pulled back, it was a good thing he still held on to me. Otherwise, I would have become a crumpled heap on the floor at his feet.

He laughed because he had received a positive reaction from me, *too positive*. I wanted to kick him in the shin because he knew what his kiss had done—blown my mind.

"Did you sleep well last night, dear?"

I pulled away and said, "Yes, *dear,* and you?"

I wasn't about to tell him it took me forever to fall asleep, and then once I had, he was in every one of my tantalizing dreams.

"I didn't," he growled. "In fact, thoughts of you kept me up all night."

He gave me a grumpy look, then pulled me back into his arms, kissing the tip of my nose. "Are you sure I can't convince you to marry me next month?" He kissed me again, but this time, short and sweet.

"No, you accepted my proposal—"

"Did you propose to me already?" He raised his brows, a silly grin in place.

"You know good'n well I didn't propose to you." I hit him, but not hard enough to hurt.

"It sounded like one to me."

I smiled up at him sweetly, slipped out of his arms a bit shaken, then moved to the chair I normally occupied when he wanted to discuss business. "You accepted my terms, remember?"

He came up behind me, nuzzled my neck. "Can we go into renegotiations again?"

Though his touch made me weak all over, I shooed him away like a pesky fly. "No."

"You're no fun. I'll have to remember, you're an evening person and a grump in the morning. But ... on you grumpy looks outstanding."

He moved behind his desk and sat down, watching me as if he was analyzing his next acquisition.

I opened my iPad and asked, "What did you want to discuss?"

"Nothing." There was that little boy-teasing glint in his eyes.

"Nothing? Why did you call me in here?"

"You had me agree to no public affection unless absolutely necessary, so I called you in to get my good morning kiss without public view. Would you rather—"

"No, I wouldn't." I stood. "If there's nothing else you want, I'll—"

"Oh, but there is."

The man was quick, I'll give him that. He came around his desk and had me in his arms faster than I could whistle Dixie. "Marry me before I go completely insane."

I shoved against his chest. He didn't budge an inch. "You're crazy." I smiled up at him so he would know I was teasing.

He captured my lips in a strong, meaningful kiss, before he let me go. When I opened my eyes, the connecting door was open, and Mr. Ainsley gave me a look that reached down to the bottom of my heart, making it spill over with love.

"I love you." He spoke without sound.

Clearing his throat, he turned all business. "I will be out of the office this morning until around eleven. We will pick up where we left off when I get back. That will be all, Ms. Gates."

Like in a trance, I said, "Yes, sir."

I walked out of his office into mine, knowing the next six months were going to be the hardest six months to keep from asking Mr. Sure-Of-Himself to marry me and move up the date.

The week flew by while Matt courted me. He gave me presents. Oh, nothing outlandish like diamonds and furs. I think he knew I wouldn't appreciate those type things. However, simple, love inspiring presents.

A rose bud or a card would be in the middle of my desk. An *I.O.U 3 xxx* on a scrap of paper inside my laptop upon opening the lid. A box of Godiva chocolates, each in the shape of a heart. A picture of him with a note—*so you will remember what love looks like.* Fortune cookies, each note inside asking me to marry him in a dozen different ways. How he did that last little trick, I don't know, and he wouldn't say.

Each day I looked forward to the beginning of my day and Matt. He was a constant in my thoughts. Yet, something was terribly wrong. I hadn't seen Katherine or Lucy Bell, and it was Friday. And James had made himself scarce also, which didn't bother me all that much. I didn't look forward to a repeat performance of what took place at the house after Matt's announcement.

This morning, I had found a note from Matt. Oh, not a love note, but a note explaining he had to pick up some businessmen, take them to lunch, and would see me around two this afternoon. He ended the note with … *can't wait until tonight. I'm taking you to a special place to celebrate, With all my love, Matt.*

Sniffing the note, Matt's cologne delighted my senses. Even though I didn't know what we would be celebrating, excitement filled me at the prospect of being alone with him.

I had it bad, *real bad.* When I wasn't with Matt, I counted the minutes until I would see him again.

In the middle of my work and deep in concentration over a plan for the campaign I'd been hired to do, I was startled by a knock on the door.

James stood there looking unsure. My heart dropped in my lap. I was instantly on guard for his volley of how unworthy I was to be his cousin's wife, to which I knew I had no defense.

"May I come in?" He looked a little sheepish, which put me further on guard.

"Yes, please do. Have a seat." I motioned at one of the chairs, hoping my look was pleasant and normal.

"I came to apologize about Sunday." He sat down, his face contrite. "I would have done it sooner, but I've been out of town."

"There's no apology necessary. I understand how our engagement must have been a shock for you and everyone."

"To say the least, but once you left, I realized I had been offensive and for that I apologize."

"Accepted. Please think nothing more about it."

He cleared his throat. "I know Matt is out this morning and won't be back until later. Would you have lunch with me so that we can become better acquainted?"

I began shaking my head. "I'm not certain that would be a good idea."

"If you're thinking Matt wouldn't like it, I understand. But believe me, it won't be a problem. In fact, he'll be happy to know I have mended the fence, in a manner of speaking." His grin was poignant, his eyes concerned.

"I promise I'll be on my best behavior. I won't act like a jerk. Since Matt and I are so close, I'd like to know you better." He hesitated, his dimples showing. "I'll tell you about some more of our boyhood escapades if you'll say yes. Even tell you some quirky family traits."

He did look eager to mend the breach, and he made it difficult to say *no* without sounding churlish.

"Say yes, *pleeeze.*"

"Oh, all right. But I can't be gone long. I have a report I need done before Matt returns."

"I promise I'll have you back in plenty of time." He stood to leave. "Thank you for understanding. I'll be by to pick you up at eleven. We can beat the rush that way."

As much as I would have rather said no, maybe next time, I said, "Eleven will be fine."

My mind in a jumble of worries, I wasn't sure what Matt would say about my lunch plans with James, but he wasn't here to ask.

If James went on the personal attack again, I could call a cab to come back to the office.

I turned my thoughts back to my work, still a little uncomfortable with our lunch date, but figured nothing he could say would change my mind about Matt. Our engagement hinged on whether Matt truly knew his feelings for me, which only time would tell.

Promptly at eleven, James showed up. Fortunately, I had finished the report Matt needed and had placed it on his desk.

James walked me to his car and assisted me inside before shutting the door. I felt awkward and wished I hadn't accepted.

He slid behind the wheel. "I hope you like Italian."

"I do." My mind was on what Matt might be doing at this moment.

"There's a place over on Prestonwood that reminds me of cuisine found only in Italy. I think you'll like the experience."

I had never been to Italy. I had barely been out of the state of Texas, and that was only a few times to the bordering states. I was uncertain what to expect from authentic Italian.

Did he mean no spaghetti and meat balls? Was James showing me the ocean between me and their family was wide and deep? If so, he was doing a good job chipping away at my self-esteem.

"Do you go abroad a lot?" I figured I might as well help him chip away.

"Once a year. Matt and I did several European tours while in college, stayed over there all summer long a couple of times hopping all over Europe. But once we got our degree, a trip a year has been about all I can manage and less for Matt." He glanced at me. "Do you like traveling?"

"I love to travel, but I haven't done much, and nothing as exotic."

"Matt will have to rectify that once you're married."

What could I say to that? I'll make sure he gives me the grand tour of Europe, even rent an Italian Villa in Tuscany overlooking the vineyards. Or maybe in Venice where we take—

"Earth to Tiffany."

I shook my head, clearing the nonsensical thoughts from my brain. What was I doing playing fiancée to a man who could command the world—well almost the world. I had six months in which to make him see we weren't suited, as everyone in his family already knew.

"Sorry about that. Woolgathering."

"No problem."

He pulled into the parking garage and stopped. I wanted to ask James to turn around and take me back to work, but I didn't. Instead, he left the car running for the valet, came around to open my door, then took my elbow and led me inside the restaurant.

The smell of food turned my stomach. I didn't want to be there, yet, I smiled and followed the maître d´ as he took us to a table that overlooked a courtyard of sorts with a cement pond and water spurting about twenty feet in the air.

I would have enjoyed this place if it weren't for the reminder that I didn't belong here, not with James, not with Matt.

Since I was unfamiliar with most of their dishes, I opted for something light and hopefully quick. James on the other hand must have been starving. He ordered appetizers, a salad, and something totally foreign to me.

He was entertaining and easy to listen to. I didn't have to say much, just nod my head from time to time. However, I enjoyed his tales about Matt when he was a little boy. I kept taking nonchalant looks at my watch. We had already been gone from the office over an hour and still our meals hadn't arrived.

"I'm sorry, but could you ask our waiter to box our lunches to go."

"They won't be any good warmed up, and I'm sure the food will be here any minute now."

"I need to get back to the office, James. I have a ton of things to do before Matt returns."

"I'll ask to see if he can put a rush on our order." James motioned for our waiter, explained the situation, and sent the man on his merry way.

"We'll be back before one. It doesn't hurt to take an extended lunch once in a while."

He dimpled up and entertained me with a story of him and Matt when they were in college. We were laughing over one such story when I felt someone behind me. I looked up and stared into the stormy gaze of Matt, looking none too happy to see me.

"I see you two are having a pleasant lunch. If I'd known you were going to be here, I would have asked you to join us."

He motioned back to a table across the room where several men were smiling and looking in our direction. Though pleasant, the friendliness didn't reach his eyes. In fact, his gaze was colder than an Alaskan glacier.

Was he upset I wasn't at the office working or that I was here with James? *Bingo!* James.

Something was rotten in Denmark. I could tell by the frozen glare he gave James, he didn't appreciate his cousin having lunch with me.

"Did you finish the report?" Matt's question was directed at James.

James raised his brow. "On your desk." The waiter came to the table with our lunch. "Well, here's our lunch. Care to join us?"

"No, I have investors with me. I'll meet you back at the office."

I thought he was going to leave without speaking to me.

He bent down, his mouth next to my ear, his breathe on my skin sending my senses off the charts.

"I'll see you back at the office, gorgeous. Maybe then you can explain why you're here with my cousin." He kissed me on the cheek, then left.

What little appetite I had, deserted me. The food in front of me didn't look appealing.

"If you don't mind, I would like to return to the office."

"Now?" James looked incredulous.

"Yes. But if you'd rather, I could call a cab."

"No, that won't be necessary." Annoyed, he waved at the waiter. "Please box this up, and here's my card for the check."

I pulled out money, which James pushed back at me.

The feeling I had displeased Matt by being here with James had me upset and out of sorts. Surely, he wouldn't hold it against me once he knew I accepted the invitation hoping to patch up the rift between him and his cousin.

James guided me over to Matt's table. Matt stood up, placed his arm around my waist, and then introduced me to the men at the table as his fiancée, making me feel a little better. However, I could still feel the chilly vibes coming from him. He wasn't acting like himself. Even though I had only known him for a short time, I could already tell his mood swings, and this swing wasn't a good one.

"I'll see you back at the office around two or two thirty, once we've concluded our business here."

Again, Matt bent and gave me a peck on the cheek. When he released me, his smile didn't quite reach his eyes—not a good sign.

I walked out with James, feeling as though I had left my heart back with Matt and wasn't sure what he would do with it—take care of it or trample on it on the ground and destroy my hopes and dreams. If he did the latter, I'd be devastated and not sure I'd ever recover.

Chapter 31

James made small talk all the way back to the office, which thankfully I didn't have to answer. I just listened and nodded.

When he stopped and parked, I decided now was as good as any to ask the question that was as pesky as a gnat flying around a face.

"Would you like to tell me what exactly happened back at the restaurant?"

"What do you mean?" He scrunched his brows as though he didn't have a clue.

He squirmed when I gave him a stare any schoolteacher worth her salt would have given an errant child caught in the biggest fib ever. He knew very well what I was asking. And I wasn't buying his ignorance for one minute.

"Were you aware Matt would be eating there with his clients? And did you take me there purposely to needle him?"

He turned a pretty shade of pink and squirmed under my penetrating glare.

I had my answer.

"This whole thing was an elaborate ploy to get back at Matt and put me in my place, right? Well, thanks for nothing." I opened the door to the car and got out.

"I can explain."

"I don't think there are enough words in your vocabulary to explain away what you have done. And furthermore, I am no longer interested. I'm not someone you can play your games with, James. I'm not a pawn on a chessboard you can easily dispose of to become the victor.

"As far as lunch goes, thanks, but in the future don't ask me again. Where you're concerned, I'm permanently busy." I slammed the door for good measure.

James called my name, but I ignored him, rushing into the building. I took the first open elevator hoping it would be the last I'd see of Matt's meddling cousin, or for that matter any of his family, at least for today.

Wrong! There in the middle of the elevator stood Lucy Bell, Matt's grandmother.

Could the day get worse?

She looked down her nose and gave me a *just what have you been up to* look that had me squirming much as I had done to James.

"Hello, Ms. Bell. Nice to see you again." I pressed the button for my floor and faced the door hoping against hope she wouldn't want to enter into conversation.

"I understand I missed the little announcement Sunday at the family gathering."

"Yes, it's a shame you weren't able to come. It was such a wonderful dinner. And Matt has one of the loveliest families I've ever met—so warm and welcoming."

I almost gagged at the falsehood, something I was becoming good at. I knew she was thinking—*what turnip truck did you fall off?* But I didn't let it faze me, *not much.* I'm made of sterner stuff.

"We need to have a talk, young lady, alone."

DING!

Saved by the bell. The elevator doors opened on Lucy Bell's floor.

I looked at her.

She didn't move.

I looked out the open door, then back at her.

Still she hadn't moved.

Then because the door was shutting, I held my index finger on the *Open Door* button, not wanting her to miss her stop. What I really didn't want, her following me to my office for an interrogation.

Blinking, with a look of innocence, I asked, "Isn't this your floor?"

Lucy Bell gave me a look that could have killed a bug. She patted her elegantly bedecked nine-and-half foot on the elevator floor as if waiting for me to say something—*what* I didn't have a clue. Neither was I about to fall into a trap.

Let her ask the questions. I'd answer if I pleased. However, I did keep a stiff upper lip, or should I say, I plastered a smile in place, waiting on the matronly woman to exit.

Lucy Bell huffed loudly, causing the numerous, sparkly necklaces to jiggle on her ample bosom. "At the moment, I have a meeting. I'll give you a call and set up something when we can talk without interruption. I plan on getting to the bottom of what's going on between my grandson and you. And, with you, young lady, I know it's not what meets the eye."

"Whatever do you mean?" I can act the innocent when I have to, and right now, I had to.

"This farce—"

The buzzer on the elevator made a loud, obnoxious noise, drowning out Lucy Bell's words and stopping her all together. She huffed and gave me a no-nonsense look before stepping off the elevator.

I released my finger. But as the doors shut I heard her dire warning.

"You haven't heard the last from me yet. I'll call you. And don't you think I won't."

I fell back against the wall, exhausted and ready to chuck this whole sordid affair to the wind.

By the time I reached the sanctuary of my office, I was going down for the count. I wondered what Matt would say if I went home early. But then I might be pushing my luck or fate, or whatever these horrible things happening to me were since I had agreed to be Matt's fiancée. Yet, what worse could happen?

I could be fired.

Be sure your sins will find you out, and mine seemed to have come to roost, leaving telltale signs of bird droppings all over the place. Apparently, I was an easy prey and quite gullible, if James were any indication. I should have recognized his manipulation, especially after Sunday.

Shoving my purse into the drawer, I decided I needed some tablets for the bruiser of a headache that was beating my skull. Pulling a couple of pills from my purse, I went in search of a bottle of water at the executive's lounge.

Carefully opening the door, I looked inside before entering to make sure I wouldn't run into any family member of Matt's, ready to turn tail and run if I there were. I saw the coast was clear. Snatching a bottle from the refrigerator, I shoved the tablets in my mouth and swallowed, taking a couple of big swigs to wash the pills down.

I sputtered and choked when Katherine walked into the lounge.

How in the world does one escape his family that seems to be crawling out of the woodwork?

"Good afternoon." I moved past her and out the door. "Wish I could stop to chat, but I've gotta run. I'm on a deadline."

The door was closing when I heard my name. I could ignore it, or face it like the strong resourceful person that I am.

This Chicken Little practically ran down the hall as if gaggles of geese were chasing me. I made it all the way to my office, shut the door without mishap, before I collapsed in the chair.

Today it seemed like everything was against me, and regardless how hard I tried, there was no way to avoid a catastrophe. Today was bound to be a day of explanations.

One—explain to Matt why I showed up with his cousin at the same restaurant where he was having a business luncheon, when just last Sunday the guy couldn't stand me.

Two—have a showdown with Matt's grandmother since she wanted to get to the bottom of all this nonsense.

Three—meet with Matt's mother before the day was over, for what I didn't have a clue, unless she was going to buy me off to dump her son.

I loved Matt. I also knew I would be miserable without him. But did Matt really know his mind enough to know he loved me?

James had done his best to show me I didn't belong in their world. It was okay to work for Matt, but marrying him was a taboo, at least where all the others were concerned.

Why did I think after our talk things would change for the better? How did I have the audacity to think that we— Matt and I—might have a fighting chance to see if our relationship was more than an agreement or mere attraction?

The excitement I felt when I was with Matt, was it more stimulation from the thrill of the moment or real?

Well, I have had enough stimuli to last a lifetime.

I felt the tears gather in my eyes and knew I had my answer to what I needed to do. This arrangement might have had a fighting chance if Matt and I didn't come from different worlds and ... if everyone would stop setting landmines for me to walk into.

Who am I kidding?

The trouble with our relationship, there were too many things against us, mainly his whole family. They were all working to tear apart any budding love we had, wishing us to fail.

The moment Matt comes back to the office and before I allow him to grill me about lunch, I'll tell him straight out *this isn't working.* I'll give him back the ring and ask him to send what he owed me by mail to my home address, and then go about finding another job.

I found this one, didn't I? Come to think of it, I didn't find this one? Matt's mother tricked me into the job.

The coward's way out would be to leave Matt a note, pack my things, then go home.

If I took a prudent approach with my finances—skimping, eating ramen noodles, peanut butter and jam—what I'd earned this far could last at least two months, if I was *very* careful.

Good luck with that.

My mind made up, I was going to do the only thing a reasonable and intelligent woman would do ... *take the coward's way out*—leave a note and run.

Writing the note was taking forever. I scratched through several drafts between bouts of tears and regrets. Finally, receiving an inspiration on a way to say the right words that would let Matt down gently and not hurt him—I laid all the blame at my door, not his.

Dear Matt,

You do me a great honor in your proposal. And for a small moment I thought there might be a possibility we could make a life together. However, it has been drawn to my attention we come from different worlds. I would never fit into yours. And you would have trouble fitting into mine.

In a more perfect world, it might have worked, but this isn't a perfect world.

I am so sorry, but I find I cannot accept your hand in marriage, nor, can I play make-believe any longer.

In the small envelope, you will find the family ring, the credit card you were so generous to supply, and the keys to the car that also came with the job. I appreciate the generous salary and all you have done for me. You may send the check for the days I've worked during this pay period to my home address, and count us even.

I do not want, nor do I expect, any severance pay as was previously agreed.

The project proposal is complete, and I hope you will find my work satisfactory and be able to implement my suggestions.

My hope and prayer is that you will find a more suitable person to be your wife, and will find true happiness.

Best regards,

Tiffany A. Gates

P.S. If you are so inclined, a reference would be appreciated.

I called a taxi, which I knew would cost me an arm and a leg, but I didn't want to have to bring the car back and run into Matt or his family. I packed my personal things in a copy paper box, wanting to make a clean getaway from MTA. If I saw Matt again, I might break down and beg him to take me back and marry me.

With the ring and note inside, I sealed and propped the envelope against Matt's desk lamp and placed my proposal for the project in the middle of his desk. I ran my hand lovingly over his chair, knowing I would miss him more than he would me.

I gave one spin of the propeller like Matt often did as tears clogged my vision, then walked out, shutting the door to my future. I sniffed in deeply, wiping the tears from my eyes, knowing my life would never be the same without Matt.

The thought that someone might come in at any moment, mainly Matt, had me taking one, quick, final look around my office. Wiping the pesky tears from my cheek, I hefted the box on my hip and walked out the door without a backward glance, while my heart broke in two.

Chapter 32

No phone call. No knock on my little efficiency door. No Matt.

So much for his protestations of love.

My check, with six month's severance, came in the mail three days later. However, nothing from Mr. Eager-To-Be-Your-Husband. Not even a tiny *thank you* or *sorry about that*. Apparently, he wasn't as interested in sealing a matrimonial deal as much as he proclaimed, which hurt deeply.

Well, what did I expect? From the beginning, my job was for a paid performance, nothing more ... even if it felt like more in my heart.

Eager to send back the severance pay to Mr. I've-Forgot-You-Already, with a note I couldn't accept money I hadn't earned, I made the deposit since he'd sent only one check. I mailed back a personal check in the amount of the severance, and a short note—*Thanks but I can't accept the severance pay.*

For the next few days, I cried. I searched on the Internet for a job. I cried some more. Cried and searched, cried and searched, until I couldn't cry anymore. Without Matt, nothing seemed worthwhile, not even my writing.

When Mrs. Mac handed me the mail, she patted my cheek. "Don't you worry none, deary. That man of yours will come around, you'll see. He'll not let a good one like you get away."

"Thanks, Mrs. Mac, but I don't think it's that simple. If you remember, I'm the one who quit. He's probably already washed his hands of me."

"If he did, he'll soon find out no one is as good as you." She pulled me in for a tight hug. When she left, she started singing, "Onward Christian Soldiers going off to war, in the heat of battle, your job will be restored."

Laughing, I said, "I'm so glad I have you to cheer me."

"My pleasure, dear."

Stepping back inside my room, I looked around. I was glad I hadn't moved to someplace more expensive when I started my job. If I had, I would have been in a world of hurt.

Seeing Mr. My-Word-Is-My-Bond's handwriting, I tore open the envelope, pulled out my personal check torn in half, along with a terse note.

Keep the severance. You deserve every penny for a superior performance. You certainly had me fooled.

Miserable. Wretched. My tears fell. Wishing I could see those beautiful eyes and gorgeous smile of his, my heart broke, and the last ray of hope slipped away. With his terse little note, I knew there would be no going back, and there was nothing left between us.

After a good long cry, I determined in my mind to forget about Mr. Matthew Thomas Ainsley the Third.

Apparently, he had already forgotten about me and moved on.

The watering pot wasn't finished. I cried more and knew I would never forget him. He owned my heart.

Knowing Mr. Mega-Bucks would just send the check back, I knew it was a fruitless effort to send one to him. Postage cost money, and at this crucial point in my life every penny counted.

I hit upon a plan that soothed my conscience. I would put the severance pay into an interest bearing account. Once I was back on my feet, I'd return all the money, plus interest earned, and then take it in person to Mr. I've-Moved-On. Or better yet, to his mother. I felt sure she'd keep the money. On the upside, I wouldn't have to see *him*—less complicated that way.

For over two weeks, my résumé went out to various corporations without mentioning I worked for MTA Amalgamated. For two weeks, I received nothing … nada …zilch. Finally, I figured, *hey, what do I have to lose?*

More résumés went out, but this time I listed MTA Amalgamated as my last employer but with the omission of the length of employment.

Bingo! A company called to set up a time with me for an interview. I prayed they wouldn't check with MTA first, but if they did, I hoped Matt would give me a good reference. My one blessing, the company was in Waxahachie, only fifteen minutes down the road from where I lived. Now if I could just land the job, I'd be in tall cotton.

Feeling quite satisfied with my appointment in the morning, I took my bath to relax and clear my head. Tomorrow, if the person happens to ask why such short term at MTA, the story would be, they hired me for a specific assignment and I finished the project early. It wouldn't be a lie exactly, because it was certainly true on one count.

Did he even use my plan for the project? Oh, well, water through the culvert, and nothing to worry about now.

I smiled. I was sounding more and more like Mrs. Mac everyday.

There'd be no need to mention the *other* project—the proposal of sorts—and my desertion before completion. Nor the fact I had turned tail and run as fast as I could to protect my heart, which I found out too late I had no defense against Mr. Unforgettable.

I hadn't been the same since the day of the wreck, and I knew I never would. However, the heart thingy wasn't any of their business, nor Mr. Ainsley's business either.

If the person were to ask for references, I'll give them Mr. Exec's number. And if he sabotages the job, so be it. I could always get a job at McDonalds or maybe even Walmart as a greeter until something else came along.

Does age matter for a greeter? Surely, someone would be hiring.

Dressed for bed, I sat in front on my computer, determined I wouldn't think of ...

I pulled up my manuscript on the screen and started reading the last chapter to get my mind back into my story. Since quitting my job, I had been entertaining Mrs. Mac each night with portions of my novel. Always so receptive, she gave me the spark I needed to keep writing.

Mrs. Mac really got upset when Sebastian hit Judith, *and with Judith expecting a child, that nasty cur.* I did my best to explain it was only a book and Judith would be all right, but she didn't seem to understand. She fumed for a whole day over *that despicable villain, Sebastian.*

I felt pretty much the same over the despicable villain, James, for sabotaging the false engagement that had turned into a real one, and I had ended. *Enough!*

Her heart mounting with fear, Judith edged her way carefully along the cold, damp wall, one cautious step at a time. She slipped her toe out feeling beyond the step before moving. If only the flint had lit the candle. Maybe there was a rush torch, surely a spark from the flint could take hold. But dare she have such a huge light?

It might be seen beneath the stone if Sebastian came searching for her. Better not chance lighting a torch even if she found one.

Inching her way down the steps until she came to a wall, Judith carefully moved about the room by using the wall until she bumped against something hard. Bending, she found the bed Simon had mentioned. At least if she were sitting, she might be able to light the candle, making her time here less frightening.

For fear that a rat might be nesting in the straw, she waved her hand back and forth, hoping to shoo any vermin away. Satisfied she wouldn't be attacked by any little creatures, she tested the straw mattress. Reasonably content the bed would hold her, she sat down to work on the flint and candle without success.

What was keeping Simon? Why hadn't he returned?

Mumbled voices near the entrance of the tunnel brought fear. The faint sound of stone scraping on stone made Judith's heart lurch in her chest.

Had Sebastian tortured Simon to learn her whereabouts?

She had to find a way of escape. Standing, she fumbled along the wall hoping to find another opening besides the stairwell, an anti-room or chamber where she might hide, or maybe a way to flee.

The distorted voices grew louder, echoing off the wall. A beam of light filled the stairwell, faintly spilling into the room where she stood. Backing along the wall, yet keeping watch for the coming threat, Judith found a relief in the wall— another hall or room she could not tell.

Taking a less cautious step, her foot gave way. Her body spiraled backward. Her scream rent the air as she tumbled into a dark abyss of nothingness. Blow by blow, pain shot through her body as her world turned black.

Matt. Without him, my world had turned dark and bleak. By now, his mother had probably found someone more suitable to replace me.

With a hardy shove, I pushed all thought of Matt right out of my head—well, not quite, but almost. Slipping beneath the covers, my last conscious thought … *what had I done?*

Chapter 33

Jittery and as keyed up as if I had drunk ten cups of double shot espresso, my mind whirled as I drove Agnes into Waxahachie. I found the building, pleasantly surprised it was one of the new ones recently built. Giving one final look into the rearview mirror to make sure I didn't have anything stuck in my teeth and my lipstick looked fresh, I went inside.

All I knew about the company, … they had recently merged with another corporation and were looking for a person with just my skills. Since I had listed many skills, I wasn't sure which they were interested in, but hoped for the best.

Impressed by the welcoming atmosphere of the reception area, I prayed this was indicative of the company. Everything in the large room, from the plush area rug lying on the hand-scraped oak flooring, to the small, inviting groups of furniture, gave off a peaceful ambiance. The room spoke quietly of money and power. My nerves were anything but calmed. If the rest of the offices were like this, it would be a pleasure to come to work every day.

Oh, phooey, who am I kidding? If they were offering a warehouse job, I'd say yes to keep my head above water and the carnivores from my door.

A woman, in her mid-forties, looked up from her computer and smiled.

So far so good.

"Hi, I'm Tiffany Gates, and I'm here for a job interview."

"Yes, Ms. Gates, have a seat, and I'll let them know you have arrived."

Too antsy to sit, but knowing I would look nervous if I didn't, I picked up a magazine from one of the tables and sat down, thumbing through the pages, trying to look interested while taking several well-fortifying breaths.

When my eyes finally focused on the open magazine, I was holding it upside-down. Glancing up to see if the receptionist had noticed, I found her gaze on the computer screen. Hopefully, she had missed my humiliation altogether.

This time, turning the magazine right side up, I stared down at the open page. Just my luck, "How Not to Botch a Job Interview." This really gave my confidence a boost … *not*.

Where was this little gem, like last night, when I could have used it? Skimming over the article, ticking off everything I had done right, my confidence went up several notches until I read …

In this age of instant accessibility, do your homework first. Search the Internet for information about the company before you go for your interview. Be able to ask intelligent questions. This will tell them you have done your homework and are interested in their business. You will demonstrate you are the right candidate for the job.

Just great! I hadn't thought to look up the company. Didn't know a bloomin' thing about them or even the company's name. Hoping upon hope, the name would be posted somewhere in the room, I looked around for a hint.

Nothing. Nada. Zilch.

"Have you worked very long for ..." I paused the appropriate amount of time for the receptionist to fill in the blank.

"For the last three years. But we were just bought out." She smiled sweetly looking over at her computer screen. "You may go back now."

After making sure I put the magazine back where it belonged in its neat little arrangement of magazines, I walked over to the desk. "I failed to ask, what does this company do?"

"You'll learn all about us during the interview."

Shoot, she wasn't going to give me a clue. "And where do I go?"

"It's down the hall and the second door on the right. If the door is shut, please go right in."

"Thanks."

Her friendly face quieted my nerves some. Thinking it a bit strange she didn't mention the person's name, she must have figured I knew it or I'd find out soon enough.

I sent up a prayer the interview would go off without a hitch.

My shoes clacked across the small expanse of hardwood, then softened when I stepped on the deep green runner that ran the full length of the hall. I stopped in front of the second closed door on the right. I took a deep breath to settle my nerves, shifted my portfolio into the other hand, tapped on the door, turned the handle and stepped inside.

My heart was in my throat—*you can do this, Tiffany, smile.*

Like the reception area, the office was well appointed. No expense spared in the decor. The hand-scraped hardwood floors continued in this office, and like the front, a nice, expensive area rug served to make the room inviting and warm.

An executive desk, bookcase, and credenza, along with two comfortable looking chairs, completed the room. The leather executive chair behind the desk faced the window with a view of an open field under construction. Only a small portion of the top of the interviewer's head peeked above the back.

I cleared my throat, hoping it would draw the person's attention, then waited as my pulse raced.

Whoever they were didn't move.

Did she say the second on right or the left? Was I in the wrong office?

The room smelled new, yet also had a slight hint of a man's cologne that gave me a pang of remembrance.

Don't think of him now. You don't need the added distraction.

Yet something about the tiny portion of head I could see seemed vaguely familiar. The chair swiveled around to face me. My gasp reverberated off the walls.

A stoic Matthew Thomas Ainsley the Third, eyes dark, lips tight, stared back at me menacingly.

My heart skipped a beat then stopped altogether before slamming against my ribs and nearly coming out of my chest. A ringing in my ears began with a spreading numbness and tingling sensation.

This can't be happening to me, not here, not now, and not when I needed this job so desperately.

"Shut the door Tiffany. We have a few matters to discuss unless you would rather run away again."

The voice, so endearing, sounded strained as though doing his best to keep from throttling me. His intent gaze didn't waiver one iota from my face.

One look, that's all it took to turn me into a weak-kneed jellyfish. I had two choices, run and not look back, or face the man who had become an integral part of me from the day we'd met.

Without taking my eyes off Mr. *Suuuprize—Suuuprize,* the same who had thrown my world into utter chaos, I reached back and quietly shut the door.

"How ...?" Even to my ears, it sounded weak, like a rabbit caught in a snare.

"Please sit down so we may discuss ... *how."* He waited for me to comply—his elbows on the armrests of his chair, his fingers templed in front of his face.

I knew I wasn't here for a happy reunion. His beautiful, pale emerald eyes were stormy with impatience, or was it anger? Or maybe I wasn't moving fast enough to please him.

This man, who had stolen my heart, was powerful and a little frightening. If he could arrange this farce of a job interview just to talk with me, what else could he do?

I'd bet he could even squelch the Walmart greeter job if I applied for one.

I settled back in the chair, hands on my lap, and looked at him square in the ... *chin.* If I looked him in the eyes, they would rob me of all thought, and I'd be blubbering on the spot. However, my feelings were all jumbled by looking at his chin, so what did it matter?

I lifted my gaze, stared into his eyes, and melted, wondering how I had found the strength to give up so much by walking away. If he loved me, why didn't he come after me and drag me back, or at the very least call to talk?

"What we have here, Tiffany, is a conundrum." He took a deep breath, tapped his fingertips together, then templed them again.

"I agree. What are you doing here? Where is the person who is supposed to interview me for the job?"

Mr. Smug smiled, yet it didn't reach his eyes. "I'm that person. I'll be interviewing you to see if you are the right individual for the position. After our last meeting, I have my doubts."

"Well, we both know how that will end. I won't get the job. I might as well leave now and save us both the trouble." I scooted forward to stand.

"The interview has already begun, and if you want the job, then I suggest you sit back and answer a few questions. When I'm through, I'll answer any questions you may have. How does that sound?"

Swallowing spit that proceeded to get stuck in my throat, I nodded, wondering what harm could there be by staying. I couldn't leave with the chance this was a legitimate job offer. "I'm listening."

By Mr. In-Charge's inscrutable face, I couldn't begin to fathom his thoughts.

"First off, the job available is long term—longer than the four weeks you gave MTA Amalgamated."

"That's un—"

He held up his hand. "Unfair? To the contrary, that's exactly what you did, Tiffany. Gave me four weeks then left without so much as a word."

"I left a—"

"A note? Yes, you were thoughtful enough to leave a cryptic note, and this." He opened the hinged lid and pushed the ring box across the desk toward me.

A lump developed in my throat as my heart sank. The diamonds winked at me as if laughing at my fate. I couldn't take my eyes off the Ainsley family ring. The very same ring he'd placed on my finger. The ring I'd left in an envelope for him to find. I wanted to beg for his forgiveness.

I knew why I was here, and it wasn't a job interview. This was revenge.

Everything within me crumbled. The pain in my heart excruciating because I knew I had wounded him deeply. Now it was payback time. "I'm so—"

Again, he lifted a hand to stop my words. He glanced up at the ceiling as if in thought then back at me. "You are well qualified for the position I'm offering."

His steadfast gaze was unsettling and made me all jittery.

"The salary is negotiable. However, the job will include travel. You will accompany the CEO on most of his business trips, some out of the country. You'll receive four week's vacation, fully paid health and dental plan. The job also comes with fringe benefits–a car with gas and full maintenance included, a house or condo of your choice at no expense to you, an unlimited expense account, and—"

"Wait just a minute. What kind of job is this? It sounds too much like what I had at MTA."

"I'll get to that in a moment." He lowered his hands to the armrests. "The job is within your range of expertise. You will work long hours, some of them demanding. From my previous experience of working with you, I have no doubt you can handle the man you'll be working with quite easily. Are you interested?"

Interested? You bet your life I was interested.

I narrowed my gaze, still unsure if this was a legitimate job offer or if he was yanking my chain for leaving him high and dry.

"Yes, I would love to hear more about the position. But first, who is this mystery man and what job will I be doing?"

He shook his head. "Before I answer, there are a few more questions and answers that need to be completed first. Since MTA owns this facility, and others just like it, if, while you are on assignment or maybe working at other facilities, you by chance meet any of my family, will that be a problem?"

"Of course not." What did he think I would do? Tell them off for ruining my life? To be honest, Matt wasn't aware of the *ruining* part exactly. I ran before his family had a chance.

"Or, as some of my family are often prone to speak their mind, if they say something unkind, are you going to quit, run, and hide?"

Mr. Nosy was starting to get my dander up. "I didn't quit, run, and hide."

He raised his brow to that statement.

"You knew all along where I lived. You could have come by anytime. I wasn't hiding. As far as quit and run, I-I-I, *yeah*, I did do that, but I had my reasons."

"Such as?"

"I knew it was just a matter of time before you came to agree with your family. I felt awful fooling your relatives with our pretense. Most of them didn't buy it anyway. Leaving was my way of letting you off the hook. I gave you an easy out—no harm, no foul."

"I don't remember asking for an easy out."

"Well, … you didn't. But I knew it was just a matter of time." I couldn't quite make out his mood. Was he angry or just probing?

"And how did you come by that astute observation?" His gaze zeroed in on my face. He didn't consider my analysis to our predicament as brilliant.

I was in quicksand, sinking fast. "Matt, listen to me."

"I thought that's what I was doing. Explain away if you can." He leaned forward folding his strong hands on the desk, hands so gentle they could turn me to putty by one touch.

I huffed, a little peeved at having to dredge up what I had *almost* buried. "Your family is very sweet and nice—"

"Thank you."

"But—"

"Let me hear it."

I rolled my eyes. "—but, they don't believe I'm good enough for you."

"They wouldn't think any woman is good enough for me."

"Yes. But someone like Candace, they wouldn't believe she was a gold digger out to steal the family jewels."

"Candace? Is that what your leaving was about, Candace?" His brows pulled together causing an adorable deep wrinkle above the bridge of his nose.

"No. Weren't you listening?" I didn't want to rehash all the reasons I had left. However seeing Mr. Exec wasn't going to let it go …

"Candace is everything I'm not. Unlike me, she would fit in with your family quite well. I'm a nobody who lives on the opposite side of the tracks, who your mother and others think is after your money. Which I am if it means I can work for you and do a decent day's work for my pay. But otherwise no … I don't want your money."

"Please, don't tell me I've just spent two of the most miserable weeks of my life because of some nonsense about my money and Candace?"

"No. Yes. No." I shook my head. "Stop confusing me."

"Which is it no or yes?"

"For Pete's sake, you're not listening to what I'm saying?" *Did I hear him correctly?* Hope soared. "What do you mean you spent two miserable weeks?"

"Just that."

"Would you like to explain?" This time I was eager to hear what he had to say. I took in the tiredness of his face I had missed earlier and saw the sadness in his eyes.

He stood, moved around the desk, and then knelt in front of me, picking up my hands.

"You heard what I said. I have been more miserable in the last two weeks without you than I have ever been in my entire life. I'm down on bended knee, Tiffany, begging you. Marry me. You make me crazy—"

"Crazy?" I narrowed my eyes. "Why would you—"

"—crazy in a good way. I love your zany sense of humor. Your wit. Even love how you find enjoyment in the littlest of things." His green eyes were pleading his case. "I have missed being with you. Can't sleep at night. Can't even think straight. I love you beyond reason." His gaze searched mine.

His nearness was driving me wild, but I couldn't allow my emotions to run away with me this time. That's what happened before, and it broke my heart.

"Didn't you hear anything I said?"

"Yes, and didn't you hear my response?"

I let out a huff. "Yes, but Matt, really, you're not thinking straight. You'll live to regret this."

"How can you say that? You are all I think about, all I want. You are in my dreams, my waking thoughts, and I'm miserable without you."

My heart told me to believe, but I was afraid.

"Matt, you say this now, but when your family tells you we aren't a match, what will your answer be then?"

He laughed and kept on laughing, hurting my feelings a little. I hadn't said anything that would cause such levity.

"What's so funny?"

Smiling, he tweaked my nose. "You."

"Me?" Was he making fun of me?

"Before you get all hot and bothered and stomp out of here and leave me to wallow in my misery, let me explain."

Probably afraid I'd jump up and leave, he stood and pulled a chair over next to mine. What he didn't know, I wasn't going anywhere. I had to find out if he truly loved me and wanted to marry me.

Hoping and praying what he said was true, yet unable to believe Matt could fall for someone like me, I wondered if it were possible.

He leaned in close, his elbows resting on his knees as he held my hand. His gaze roamed my face as if memorizing every inch. I wondered if he could see all my little flaws, the chicken pox mark on my left cheek, or if my lipstick was smeared, or my mascara smudged beneath my lashes.

His touch warmed my heart. His spicy cologne enveloped me. His endearing smile was driving me wild. One look from Matt caused my whole body to react, longing to believe what he'd said was true.

The feel of his warm breath on my face, his nearness, was drawing me like a magnet, snatching all reasonable thought from my brain, turning my will to mush. And, yes, I wanted Matt.

"Ask my family. They will beg you to marry me and put me out of my misery. You can't believe what a tyrant I've been since you've been gone. I've been unbearable. No one wants to be around me." He gave me a little crooked grin.

"At work, since you've left, I've snapped at everyone, even bitten off several heads. No one will get near me. I threatened to fire all my staff. It's been a nightmare, one I don't want repeated. Behind my back they call me *the beast*."

I shook my head laughing. "Matt, how could you?" The love I felt for this man was more than I thought possible.

"It's all your fault."

"My fault? ... Not hardly."

He smiled mischievously, squeezing my hand. "Even my mother, when she sees me in the hall, turns and runs in the opposite direction to get out my line of fire. So you see, you have to marry me and put a stop to this insane madness that has possessed me since you walked out of my life. I don't want to live without you."

"Are you sure?"

He stood, pulling me up with him, gathering me in his arms. "You, Tiffany Ann Gates, drive me to distraction—a good distraction that is." He hugged me close, breathing in deeply before pulling back and looking into my eyes.

"I find I can't live ... No, let me rephrase that. I can't and don't want to live without you."

Matt gave me a little boy wounded look. "Please take pity on me and the rest of the world and put me out of my misery. Say yes, because if you don't, you will turn me into a tyrant who will be greatly hated and feared by all.

"Marry me, please." He bent his head toward mine.

The anticipation of his kiss had me weak in the knees. His eyes were filled with the intensity of his love.

Our lips met. His kiss was everything I had remembered and more. We didn't have an audience. No one to convince. But he was doing an excellent job persuading me to listen to my heart.

When he broke the kiss, he hugged me tightly. "Tiffany, you have driven me insane." Again he looked at me smiling. "At first I was so angry I wanted to strangle you within an inch of your life. Then my anger turned to rage, which I took out on anyone who came near me. It's a wonder I have a company left."

I laughed.

He pulled back trying his best to look serious. "You think it is funny. Lucy Bell asked for your telephone number and address. I told her *no.*"

"Thank you." I sighed with relief.

"You better be thanking me. She said she was going to give you a good talking to, make you see sense. And if that didn't work, she would drag you back. She was tired of me moping around and snapping off everyone's head."

"Surely not you, Mr. In-Control."

He growled then nipped at my neck causing gooseflesh to cover every inch of my skin.

"I'll make you think in control."

He zeroed in on the target—my lips—planting the biggest, most mind-blowing kiss I could ever hope to experience.

My body reeled with emotions, emotions I had no idea existed, yet I knew I would want to experience them again and again with Matt. One delicious sensation after another exploded inside me, shattering any hope of ever living without him.

Would I ever get my fill of Mr. Matthew Thomas Ainsley the Third?

Not likely.

Chapter 34

Matt looked as shaken as I felt when he pulled back and stared into my eyes.

"I hope that's a yes, because if it isn't, you might as well bury me here and now, because I won't be fit for human interaction if you don't marry me. I can't lose you."

"Matt, let's talk."

"Sure." He acted like a man being lead to the gallows as he motioned for me to be seated.

"First off, I think you know how you affect me, but in case you don't, let me explain. I love being in your company. And I certainly like the way you make me feel when I'm around you, or when you … kiss me, but—"

Matt reached for my hand. "I have never liked *buts*. They often mean something I don't want to hear. What can I do to convince you that I love you?"

"I'm convinced you *think* you love me. I certainly feel a strong attraction to you. But what you feel for me, will it last? Or is it because I walked away?"

I could feel my heart hammering in my chest. I knew what I wanted. Without a doubt it was Matt. But I was uncertain if he knew what he wanted, or if his reason for being here today was because he didn't like losing.

Well, come to think of it, he didn't exactly come after me. He kind of tricked me into coming to him. But it still mounted to the same thing.

"Do you want me to answer that question, or show you?"

I shook my head. "If you show me, I won't be able to tell you what's on my mind. And right now, knowing what's in my heart is very necessary for our next step."

"All right, I'm listening." His gaze was strong, intent, and filled with emotion.

Not sure I could continue if I looked at him, I looked out the window he'd been staring at when I first walked into the room.

"Sometimes when a person as strong as you has something taken from him that he isn't quite finished with, that thing, or in this case me, becomes more desirable.

"I want you to be certain what you're feeling for me is love and not just because I walked away. I don't want to be an acquisition or a prize to be won for the sake of winning because I left on my own accord."

Matt looked wounded. "I have never thought of you in that manner. I'm not asking you to marry me because you left. I want you because I love you. No other reason."

"If we marry, I want our marriage to last a lifetime."

"That's what I want also. Nothing less will do." He squeezed my hand gently.

"For me, marriage isn't a trial run, it's a lifetime commitment. No redos. No loopholes. No get-out-quick clause. I want to be first in your life, after God, of course."

"Of course, and you are and will continue to be even after we're married."

I looked around the room, anywhere but at Matt, doing my best to gather my scattered thoughts. It would be so easy to say yes, and my heart begged me to, but something held me back.

Matt's eyes reflected the depths of his worry. The short time I'd known him I had never seen him act so scared and unsure about anything, yet here he sat, expecting me to say no.

That's it! I knew what was holding me back. "If you will agree with my plan, I'll accept your ring."

"Anything. You name it, I'll do it." He wore a silly grin. "Well, within reason."

"I'm never unreasonable."

He raised his brows as a smile played about his lips.

His willingness to comply let me know he was serious.

"For the next three to six months, I would like for us to really get to know one another. At this moment, all we know about each other is very little, mainly surface information. I need to know your likes and dislikes, how you were when you were a kid, learn about your failures, aspirations, disappointments—and I don't mean your acquisitions in business but your personal life.

"Are we compatible? Do you even want children, a house—"

"Yes, to all of the above, as long as it's with you." His eyes brightened. "Together, we'll make such beautiful babies."

The heat rose to my cheeks. "Be serious."

"I am serious. I know my mind and heart. However, I'm willing to court you so you'll know when I say *I love you,* I mean it. And I don't plan on changing my mind either." He dipped his head, gazed at me, as he raised my hand.

My body felt live-wired by the touch of his lips on my flesh. Shivering, I said, "Don't do that, I can't think straight."

His look of innocence wasn't fooling me one bit.

"Don't do what? This?" He lowered his lips to my fingers again, then he turned my wrist over and kissed the sensitive spot there. His touch sent sparks shooting up my arm, robbing me of what little coherent thought I had left.

"Yes, that. Don't do that." I pulled my hand away, missing his touch immediately.

"Ah, but I love to kiss your hand and your ..." He moved in, his breath mingling with mine as he proceeded to show me.

This time, I was more shaken than before.

When he pulled back, I took a moment to catch my breath.

"I propose we date for three months, giving us a chance to become better acquainted. This will also give your family a chance to get used to us as a couple. Then if you still want to marry me, we'll set the date for our wedding. Will that work?"

"It'll only work if I can get you to lower the time limit to a month."

I shook my head. "No. We need time. And I don't think three months is asking too much."

"Not to you maybe, but me ..."

He breathed out heavily, gave me a drop-dead smile that caused me to want to change my mind, but I didn't.

"You drive a hard bargain, woman. Three months will seem like an eternity." A speculative look appeared in his eyes along with a quirky grin on his handsome lips.

"If, at any time, during the next three months you want to move up the date, let me know. I'll be happy to oblige."

"You're impossible." I smiled, shaking my head.

He stood. "Now, will you take your old job back, because I need you in the worst way."

"I like the sound of that—you need me."

"I don't think you could ever know how badly I want and need you."

I wanted to tell him the feeling was mutual but thought I'd save it for another time.

"Yes, I'll take my old job back. I guess it really isn't so old. I was there less than four weeks. What about the job here? Don't you need to fill the position?"

He gave me a sheepish grin.

"That was a ruse to get you to talk with me. I didn't think you would see me if I showed up on your doorstep, so I went for broke. I'd either win you back or leave a wrecked man."

"You're impossible, but in a good way. What if I had said no?"

"I was hoping you wouldn't." He shrugged. "But if you had, I was willing to offer you a position here regardless.

"You're good at what you do. The plan you left behind for me to implement was flawless. We executed it without a hitch. So you would deserve a job regardless if you married the boss or not."

To hear Matt's praise made me feel valued. His validation of my work certainly went a long way with my deflated spirit.

Matt pulled the ring from the box. He slipped it on and then sealed our engagement by kissing my finger.

"Tiffany Ann Gates, I love you with all my heart and soul. Wear this as a token of my love and know I desire you above all women."

This time the ring felt right, not like it branded me, but like I belonged to Matt. I was proud to have it back, and I was happy to know Matt loved and wanted me as much as I did him.

Matt leaned his forehead against mine. I closed my eyes, relishing the moment.

"You ever hear that old song *Anticipation*?"

His deep voice rumbled through my chest, causing all kinds of sensations.

"Once or twice."

He breathed in deeply, then lifted his head. "You're driving me wild, Tiffany. And that's what I'll be singing if I can't convince you to move up the date."

"Let's take one day at a time."

He tweaked my nose. "I'm sure I love you. However, I'm willing to wait until you're convinced I'm sure." Shaking his head, he wrinkled his forehead and laughed. "Does that even make sense?"

"Perfect sense to me."

I turned and picked up my purse, and then handed him the useless résumé.

"You can throw that in file thirteen. It seems I won't be needing it after all. I already have a job."

"Yes, you do." Matt tossed the folder into the trash can.

"Would you like to follow me home? Then you can give me a ride to the office."

"Yes, ma'am. I'll follow you anywhere."

Matt drove behind little Agnes in his Beamer to Mrs. Mac's house where I dropped off my car.

"Well, Matthew, it's about time you came to your senses." Mrs. Mac gave him a beady-eyed stare. "You took way too long to come after Tiffany. You should be ashamed of yourself. My girl was plum down in the dumps. She hardly did any writing on her book."

"Mrs. Mac, Matt doesn't want to hear about that."

"Don't stop the sweet woman." He raised his brow. "I'm sure she has plenty to say." He smiled at my landlady. "You were saying?"

"I was afraid you weren't going to be smart enough, young man, to see the nose in front of your face. For a while there, I thought I'd pegged you all wrong. I see you came to your senses. Good thing too."

She gave him a big wink. "You do know a good thing when you see it. And Tiffany is the cat's meow, let me tell you. None finer."

He looked at me smiling. "You're right on that score, Mrs. Mac. Tiffany is a gem."

"Well, as long as you remember that, you'll be all right and so will my girl."

She waved at us like shooing a fly. "Now go on with you. I've got cleaning to do." She stepped inside the house, but stopped. "Maybe if you have time when you come home, Tiffany, you could read me some more of your story. Matt might want to hear some of it too."

"See you later. We've got to be going." I tried to usher Matt toward the car, but he wouldn't budge. Instead, his gaze was glued on my landlady.

"What story is this, Mrs. Mac?"

"She hasn't read you any of her novel yet?"

Matt's eyes sparkled as if he'd just found the prize in the cereal box. "Not a word."

"Oh my. You are in for a treat. Tiffany is a splendid writer. She's writing a story—"

"We need to leave." I began tugging on Matt's arm, hoping he would get the hint. He was unmovable, like his feet were glued in place.

"Sweetheart, don't be rude." He latched onto me, hauled me up next to his side, and snaked his arm around my waist. "I'm very interested in what this lovely lady has to say." He smiled kindly at Mrs. Mac.

"Well, like I was saying, Tiffany is writing a story about Lady Judith and Lord Rolf, with a nasty villain, Lord Sebastian, who wants to have his way with Lady Judith, and her a married women, can you imagine that? And she's his sister-in-law to boot. Well—" Mrs. Mac pursed her lips.

"You wouldn't want to ruin the story for him, would you?" Again, I pulled on Matt to leave.

"Oh, dear no, I don't want to do that." She turned to Matt. "If you get home early enough, we'll have her get her book and read to us. You'll see what I say is true. Tiffany is a marvelous writer." Again she shooed us with her hands. "Get along with you now. We'll see you tonight."

"I'll make sure we get home early for Tiffany to read. Thank you, Mrs. Mac.

Matt's hand rested on the crook of my back. He leaned down, his mouth next to my ear. "And when were you going to tell me about your little sideline? Before or after we're married?"

Chapter 35

I changed the subject while on the way to the office, not wanting to bring up the matter of my book. Fortunately, Matt didn't bring it up again either. In fact, I hoped he would forget all about the thing, but knowing him, he probably wouldn't.

When we arrived at MTA, I didn't quite know what to expect, but receiving a wide berth with cautious looks, and staff turning around to take a different route or popping inside an office and shutting the door, wasn't it. Matt must have been a real ogre. And now they were looking at me as if I was the cause.

Come to think of it, I probably was.

I chuckled under my breath.

"And you thought I was kidding."

He bent, whispering in my ear before laughing and sending chills over my skin.

"You see what you did to me and my staff? You almost single handedly took down my company."

"Now wait just a minute. You can't blame that on me"

"Oh, but I do." His whispered teasing continued. "And by the looks of them"—he nodded in the direction of some staff turning around and heading off down a hall—"so do they." He laughed.

Heat began at my throat and worked its way into my cheeks. "They don't really believe that, do they?"

Matt put his arm around me and brought me up close for a gentle squeeze and a peck on the cheek before releasing me. It was the first time he'd ever given me a spontaneous show of affection while in the office, which thrilled me to no end. He wasn't playacting for an audience, which was refreshing.

"No, I'm teasing. They blame me totally for my actions and for not going after you."

He steered me into my old office and shut the door. Pulling me into his arms, he kissed me soundly on the mouth. When he pulled back, he looked as shaken as I did.

"I'll give you a few minutes to get settled in, then come to my office. I want to discuss your next project."

His silent footsteps took him to the adjoining door. Before he stepped through, he turned and stared at me. "Just so you won't forget ... I love you, Tiffany, and my love will never change."

Matt shut the door behind him, leaving me dazed and wondering if I would be able to last the three months. He was one persuasive guy. The fact I was head-over-heels in love with him didn't help my resolve any either.

I walked behind my desk, but instead of sitting down, I gazed out the plate glass window at the tiny cars and people below. How did I become so blessed to be the recipient of Matt's love? If it hadn't been for him running into my little Agnes, I might have missed this altogether.

"Hey, gorgeous, I heard you were back. May I come in?"

Startled, I jerked around and saw the man I met on my first day here—smiling, teasing James, my friend, my confidant, and yet I put up my guard. His dimples were just as deep, his smile just as genuine, but he practically called me a gold-digger. Could I trust him?

"Sure, come in. Sit down." I motioned at a chair and took my seat behind the desk, my arms crossed protectively. "I just got here. How did you know I was back?"

"The whole company was alerted the moment you stepped one foot on MTA soil. Everyone is abuzz with your return, and hoping you will tame the beast."

"They can't be calling him the beast. Tell me they aren't." I felt horrible I was the cause of Matt's ill temper.

James laughed. "I'm afraid so, and worse." He glanced down at his hands, his countenance somber.

He looked down at his hands and cleared his throat. His reticent behavior was a different side of James never seen before.

Glancing up, he grimaced. "I didn't come here to discuss Matt, but to apologize. This time, I am sincerely sorry, and I mean it. I know you have every right not to believe me and to hate me, but I hope you can get past what I did to you and we can become good friends again."

"There's no need for your apology."

"Oh, but there is. I wronged you, for which I am sincerely sorry. No excuse, just bad judgment on my part."

"Apology accepted and forgiven." Though I heard the words, my heart was still guarded.

"Thanks." James pointed to the Ainsley diamonds on my finger. "Congratulations, and this time I mean it." His deep dimples appeared again.

I nodded, not wanting to vocalize my thanks.

"I will be on my best behavior. Matt and I were practically raised together. I don't want anything to come between our friendship. And I'd like to include you in that friendship."

His sorrowful, little boy look did a number on me, but still concerned he would turn against me, I sat silent.

"What do you say? Can we become friends?"

Doing my best to choose my words carefully, I said, "If you are willing to accept me into the family at face value, I am more than willing to accept you at face value also. Matt would want us to be friends, and I'm willing to make the effort."

"Thanks, Tiffany, that's all I ask. And know this, anything you need, I'm your man." He stood. "I'll let you get back to work."

I rose from my chair. "Right now, I'm in a holding pattern." I nodded in the direction of Matt's office. "The beast, as we speak, is getting together a project for me."

"I'm sure he is, especially after that last proposal you submitted." James shook his head. "Man!" He moved to the door and stopped, looking back at me. "Great job. That was one of the best plans I've seen implemented. You're good at what you do, and I believe you're good for Matt too."

A twinkle was in his eyes. "I only have one last question."

"Ask away."

"You wouldn't happen to have a twin or maybe a friend who's like you to introduce me to?"

I smiled. "No siblings. But I do have a dear friend in San Antonio that will give you a run for your money."

"If she's anything like you, I would love to meet her. See ya later."

How odd. Today, James was his old self but more mellowed.

A light tap came from the connecting door. Matt stuck his head inside my office. "Hey, beautiful." Seeing that I was alone, he walked over to where I stood. He placed keys on the desk. "Those are to your new car. Some business just came up, and I have to leave for an hour or two. So you're on your own until later this afternoon. When I get back, we'll go over the new project, and then tonight I'll take you to dinner. How does that sound?"

"Sounds great. Where is the car parked?"

"Already thinking about escaping?" He gave me a conspirator's smile.

"Yes, but only for an hour. I didn't bring my lunch."

"It's in the space next to mine. Park there from now on. Here's a credit card." Matt pulled out his wallet, slapped down a card with my name on it. "That's yours to use. Put it in your purse and use it for lunch."

"I can't."

"Yes, you can. I insist. I virtually kidnapped you and hate that I can't take you to lunch. It's the least I can do. Also, while you're out, take an extra hour or two and go shopping. We have a family thing on Saturday." He looked kind of sheepish. "That is, if you're free."

"I am. And thank you for being so considerate to ask."

"I hope you won't mind. My mother wants to officially announce our engagement to the world at large and welcome you into the family. And she never does anything by half-measures. So make it dressy-dress."

"My, news travels fast around here."

He grimaced. "Someone told her you came in with me. She called and asked one question."

"What was that?"

A rather pleased look appeared. "My answer ... you were wearing the Ainsley ring. I'm afraid she took it from there." He bent and gave me a peck on the cheek.

Disappointment filled me. I wanted more.

"You don't mind, do you?"

His gorgeous, questioning eyes were so close to mine I felt like I would go cross-eyed or melt in their depths. "No. I don't mind."

"Good." He leaned in and kissed me properly.

My senses went on overload. I wasn't sure I'd recover. I wondered if I'd be able to hold out for three months.

Matt leaned back. "I think that should last me for two or three hours." The small indent in his cheek appeared. "On second thought …"

He pulled me up close, gathered me in his arms, breathing in deeply. "I love how you smell. You drive me wild. I can't seem to get enough of you."

As if his last kiss hadn't affected me enough, Matt dipped his head and gave me one that made the last one feel like child's play.

Too quickly, he released me and gently helped me down into my chair. His green eyes sparkled as he gave me one of his drop-dead smiles. He knew full well the affect he had on me.

"There that's better. That should do the trick."

Gathering what breath I could find, I did my best to act normal. "Yes, it works for me."

He winked. "That's my girl. See you in about three hours." He walked back to his office whistling a cheerful tune.

I don't believe I will ever tire of Matt's company, nor will I tire of his kisses.

Chapter 36

Apparently, Katherine was too busy to drop by my office, or maybe she was avoiding me. Whichever, it didn't matter. I was rather glad for the reprieve. Even though Matt said his family was in favor of our match, I wasn't sure if it was entirely true. They could be placating him so he wouldn't take their heads off.

After lunch and the shopping spree Matt insisted I take, I came back to the office and checked to see if he had returned. He hadn't.

No sooner had I sat down at my desk, Lucy Bell came barging through the door. The sparkle of jewelry on her chest snagged my gaze. I heard the jingle of bracelets as she shut the door behind her and then moved in my direction.

My heart nearly stopped, wondering if this might be the beginning of World War III, and if it were, would I be able to withstand her open fire and live.

Matt's grandmother was huffing like a loaded freight train pulling out of the station. If reason hadn't prevailed, I would have thought the woman had run up two flights of stairs instead of riding the elevator, which was more the case. However, to have arrived so quickly, she must have posted someone in the hall or downstairs to watch for my return. I feel certain, the woman was determined to catch me before Matt came back to the office.

"Hello, Ms. Bell. Have a seat please." I motioned to the chairs in front of my desk. "Nice to see you again."

I displayed my most pleasant smile, determined to be amiable even though she had been less than cordial the last time we met. After all, I would be married to her grandson and a part of her family soon if everything went according to plan.

Lucy Bell chugged to the chair and sat down, eyeing me the whole way as if I might disappear from the room.

Running seemed like a good option, but I stayed put.

How many points would I score if I told her I loved her grandson beyond reason or hope of recovery? Best leave that unsaid. No need giving her any ideas Matt could twist me around his little finger, just because he could. She might think it her duty to impart that bit of news to her grandson, which he didn't need to know, at least not yet.

One thing I did know about her visit, hers was anything but professional. She was here most likely to ferret out what had happened and what were my intentions toward Mr. Matthew Thomas Ainsley the Third.

If Lucy Bell was anything, she was loyal to a fault … and protective too. Her appearance here today proved that much.

"I want to know what you thought you would accomplish by running off and leaving my grandson? You nearly broke his spirit. What were you thinking?" Her blue eyes were paler than what I remembered, but snapped and sparkled with fervency.

"Frankly, I didn't think to accomplish anything by leaving."

"Then why did you leave? It almost killed him, not to mention the fallout that occurred."

Smiling inwardly, knowing the fallout was Matt's ill temper that trickled down to everyone—family and staff alike—I played ignorant, my emotions mixed over her statement.

I never meant to hurt Matt, but Lucy Bell wasn't the one I needed to say that to. Matt was. Yet here she sat with tears clouding her eyes, wanting to make sure her grandson would be okay with my coming back and I wouldn't hurt him again.

"Lucy … may I call you Lucy?"

The older woman nodded with a hint of a smile.

"I left because I knew most of the family didn't agree with our engagement. Also, I didn't want Matt to be placed in the position of having to choose sides, or worse yet, tell his family it was his way or the highway."

Lucy Bell's lack of denial proved my point. "I knew if I left, he wouldn't have to choose. Nothing or no one should come between family."

Lucy Bell's necklaces winked at me as she took several quivering breaths. I witnessed the glint of moisture in her eyes.

"I'm beginning to change my opinion about you, Tiffany. I think you just might be a good match for my grandson." Her head bobbed. "As long as you treat him well and make him happy, you'll have my blessing." She cocked a brow. "The first sign Matthew is in an upheaval, you and I will have a little chat. Do I make myself clear?"

She gave me a stern look for good measure, but I could see her words were mostly bluster.

"I don't think you'll have a thing to worry about. You see, we've discussed the matter thoroughly, and we are both in agreement. This time, I don't plan on letting anyone run me off."

Lucy Bell leaned forward, nailing me with her keen gaze, her bejeweled arm and hand resting on the edge of the desk.

"Good girl. But be truthful with me, Tiffany. Do you love my Matthew, or are you in love with what he can give you?"

My first reaction was to tell her it was none of her business. Then I took a good look at Lucy's face.

Concern was written across her wrinkled brow, as her anxious eyes watched me closely and her compressed lips quivered. This was a woman who loved her grandson deeply and wanted what was best for him and nothing less would do.

I could do one of two things. Alleviate her worst fears, or give the older woman many nights of worry. To me, it was a no-brainer.

"Lucy, to ease your mind, from the very beginning Matt's money and position were a drawback to me, not an asset. I didn't seek him out. In fact, your daughter-in-law was the one who found me and offered me a job, which I might add, without a hint the job included working for her son.

"You can rest assured, if I was after his money, I would have never left in the first place. The choice to get married is ours to make." I paused for affect, allowing my words to sink in. "When we get married, it will be for love only and not the family money or jewels." My pointed gaze drifted to her arm and hand. "I would marry Matt if he were a pauper."

Lucy Bell stood and gave me a long satisfied stare.

I stood also and smiled at her, because I wanted her to like me, especially if I was going to be part of her family.

"I believe you will be a good match for my Matthew. But if you break his heart again, I'll come looking for you, and it won't be a pretty sight when I get through."

Her stern lips turned into a smile that grew to cover her whole face. She walked around the desk, engulfed me in a perfume-scented bear hug, and then just as quickly released me.

She sailed out the door leaving behind a very shaken and bewildered ... Tiffany Ann Gates.

I would be telling Matthew what took place with his grandmother, but not today, and not for quite some time. When the time was right, I would tell him how he held a special place in his grandmother's heart, and it was one of great love.

Chapter 37

Little family gathering, my foot! This wasn't a small family gathering. This was an all-out, full-fledged, bring-everyone-but-your-dog party. Much to my chagrin, there were a couple hundred plus guests milling around the banquet hall of the Glen Oaks Country Club to take a look at Matt's fiancée—*me*.

I shook in my stylish looking Jimmy Choos—more money than I had ever worn on my feet in my entire life. Fortunately, they were low-heeled, sensible shoes that went well with my ankle length black, slinky dress, never realizing I'd bless my choice of shoes over and over during the night.

My trepidation of the gathering wasn't because I thought I would come across like a country bumpkin. I might be a bit rusty, but I knew how to mix and mingle with the best of them. And when it came to the buffet, I wouldn't have to ask what hummus and pâté was, *yuck,* on both accounts, or what those teensy, weensy black pearls everyone was spooning over fancy crackers were, *again yuck.* Also I knew how to eat little and fill my glass half full so that I was less likely to spill.

However, when I was expecting family and a few close friends and then ended up with a mammoth crowd, it became a bit overwhelming and earth shattering, to say the least.

One thing I could say about Matt, he stayed by my side all evening long. He knew everyone and with each meeting, he introduced me as his fiancée, even pecked my cheek on several occasions, or gave me a squeeze, which gave me quite a buzz. He even leaned in close and whispered into my ear how gorgeous I looked and how I was driving him to distraction.

His hand was either at the small of my back, or he placed my arm in his. A gal couldn't ask for a more attentive fiancé.

And Matt ... he looked every inch the man of the hour, and far better than any Mr. GQ I'd ever seen. Even better looking than anyone appearing in one of those *most-handsome-man-of-the-year* magazines, purporting the ultimate stud muffin. If it wouldn't end up sounding so corny, I would say Matt was beautiful.

"There you are, darling." Matt's mother floated up beside us, looking quite pleased. "I believe your engagement party has turned out to be a grand success. Everyone is simply beaming with goodwill. They're saying how you two are so perfectly suited for each other."

Matt bent to give his mother a peck on the cheek. "You look lovely tonight, Mother."

"Oh, thank you, darling." Her distracted smile hadn't quite reached her eyes, which at the moment were gazing over the crowd.

I had to wonder if she was pleased with her son's choice or waiting for Matt to get bored and dump me. No matter, my plan was to work hard at mending the broken fences between Katherine and me, and the rest of his family, especially since Matt and I were to get married. I didn't want anyone sending up flares and disrupting our lives once we were.

"Kathryn, you look stunning and certainly don't look old enough to be the mother of this tall, handsome guy." I wasn't telling a falsehood. Matt's mother was a beautiful woman who at the moment looked vibrant and truly in her element.

"Why thank you, darling. You look quite lovely also. I think you and Matt will make beautiful babies together." Her eyes twinkled.

Blushing, and not wanting to think that far ahead, I mumbled my thanks.

"Oh, there are the Taylors. Excuse me, dears. I'll go welcome them."

Katherine flitted away, and I wondered if I would ever feel as confident and collected as she, or if I would always feel a little awkward in her company?

Matt leaned close, his mouth next to my ear. "Let's not wait. Marry me, and let's start on those beautiful babies my mother is anticipating."

To hide my embarrassment, I glanced away and cleared my throat. "Matt, behave. I want you to be sure, and not find out later this—us—isn't something you will regret."

I felt him stiffen next to me. "Tell me, Tiffany, what do I have to do to convince you I want to spend the rest of my days and nights growing old with you?" His tone held a wealth of hurt.

I felt awful. "I'm sorry. Please forgive me."

Matt pulled me up close to his side and gave me a squeeze. "Sweetheart, I'm not about to change my mind. But if three months will convince you, then I'll wait. I want you to recognize, you're the only one for me." He kissed my temple. "I love you, and that won't change."

"Matt, *daarling*, won't you introduce me to your little fiancée? I've heard some interesting things about her. I'm just dying to meet her."

Standing too close to Matt for my comfort and practically draping herself all over him was none other than Ms. Candace Hill. Though she smiled, I could feel the heat of her gaze doing its best to turn me to ashes.

Figuring this was truth or consequence time, I stood by helplessly watching while Ms. Hill leaned in closer to my fiancé, doing her best to mash her body into his side as she slipped her arm through his. Her cherry red lips puckered into a pretty little pout a baby would have been hard put to match.

"Candace …" Matt huffed out as he pulled his arm free.

Then, with a maneuver most self-defense teachers would have been proud to see, Matt extricated his body from the clinging octopus and stepped around, shoving me in the middle of the two of them. I stared straight into the eyes of hate.

"This lovely woman is Tiffany Gates, who is soon to be my wife." He turned to look at me. "Darling, this is Candace Hill, an old, *old* friend of the family."

"Really, Matt, I'm not *that* old."

"Nice to see you again, Candice. We met before at a banquet."

Candice wrinkled her nose as if she smelled something distasteful. "Oh, really? Sorry I don't remember you."

"No worry. However, since you are a long time friend of the family, I hope we will become friends too." I held out my hand.

Candace looked at it as if it were some kind of poisonous snake ready to latch onto her. Then as if she knew it would be bad form not to accept my gesture of friendship, she grabbed my fingers, but let them go as quickly as she could.

"One day, Matt, when you have time, I'd love to have lunch with you to discuss a few matters."

"Tiffany and I would love to have lunch with you one day. Give my office a call and we can set up a time and place to meet." He turned to me. "Darling, I see an old friend of my father's I would like to introduce to you."

He slid his arm around my waist, pulling me up close.

"Thanks for coming, Candace. Enjoy the party. We'll no doubt run into you later."

As I was ushered to the far side of the room, I felt the woman's glare stabbing my back. "Really, Matt, was that necessary? Given another minute or two, I believe I could have brought her around. I really think she was beginning to warm to me."

He looked down at me with a straight face but a glint in his eyes. "In that case"—Matt stopped—"shall we go back?"

I pulled on his arm. "Not on your life. Where's that friend of your father, or was there such a man?"

"You do me a great injustice by not thanking me from saving your hide. She has some very long claws that can do real damage."

"Ohhh, was that what was about to happen—a cat fight? Well let me say here and now, I am eternally grateful for your saving me once again. Lead on, love." I squeezed his arm, my cheek resting on his bicep for a brief moment.

Matt stopped, looked deep into my eyes, then before God and sundry, gave me a kiss that would have melted Niagara Falls in the dead of winter. He hugged me up close. "Thank you for that." His voice sounded choked and emotional. "I believe that is the first time you have called me love."

Chapter 38

Matt pulled up in front of Mrs. Mac's house and shut off the engine. Instead of getting out of the car, he picked up my hand and began turning the Ainsley diamond back and forth on my finger.

"We need to talk."

I looked into his indiscernible eyes, and my heart constricted. Was he having second thoughts? Did he think I didn't fit into his world?

I believed I hadn't done too badly tonight. Everyone seemed to like me at the party. Maybe I was wrong.

My heart beat so fast I could feel the blood rushing through my veins. Was I on the verge of a heart attack? I'd heard of people younger than I having heart attacks. Maybe this was one. I know it sure hurt.

"First off, thank you for tonight. I hope you realized how well you were liked and received by my friends and family—Candace excluded, of course."

I chuckled as relief flooded me. He wasn't breaking the engagement after all. The fast beat of my heart slowed to a leisurely hum.

"I love you."

My pulse shot right back up there again, racing faster than someone in a police car chase but in a good way this time. I opened my mouth to say … what? Protest that he couldn't be sure? To say I love you too? I started to speak.

Matt raised his hand. "No, I have more to say, so let me finish. I believe I have loved you since the day I smashed into the backend of Agnes.

When I saw you looking lost and helpless with blood running down your forehead, something happened to me. When you gazed up at me, and I saw the shock in those beautiful golden brown eyes of yours, you nearly snatched my breath away. And if love didn't happen at that exact moment, then it certainly did when you fainted in my arms and I carried you to my car."

"I didn't faint in your arms."

Again, he held up his hand. "If you want a say-so in this matter, then wait your turn."

Laughing, I said, "Ok."

"As I was saying, I might not have fully recognized what I felt for you as love that day. However, when I held you in my arms and placed you in my car, I knew there was something about you that if I allowed you to, you would turn my world upside down. And you have."

His gaze searched my face. "I fought the attraction at first. I figured if I didn't see you again, I would get over you, but that didn't happen. When I saw you that first day at MTA sitting in the boardroom looking like you'd seen a ghost, I couldn't let you go until I probed deeper for the answer to why. After that morning you were necessary to make my life complete.

"Tiffany, believe me when I say, what I feel tonight I have felt the same about you almost from the first moment we met. My love is beyond anything I could ever imagine. I love you with all my heart, mind, and soul, and the only way that will ever change is when I've taken my last breath. And still, I haven't expressed half of what I feel in my heart for you.

"I don't want to live without you. So please put me out of my misery. Marry me."

I sat speechless. Sir Rolf couldn't have put the words together as beautifully as Matt.

When I'm old and gray, my mind is half gone, Matt's words of love will still be with me. One day, I might even use Matt's beautiful, convincing speech in one of my books. The world could certainly use such a love as this.

"Tiffany, you're scaring me. Say something."

His anxious face caused my heart to twist, then leap for joy. My Matt, the man who lit the sun, moon, and stars in my world was afraid I was going to refuse him.

"Matthew from the first time I saw you, I was a goner. So let me put your fears to rest. I love you. Will you marry me?"

"Finally!"

He pulled me into his arms. His lips covered mine in a passionate kiss that zinged through me like a comet racing to the moon. I felt the tingling effects from my head to my toes.

WOW! Matt made me feel like I was the match that set his world on fire.

He lifted his head, his eyelids heavy and filled with so much love, I almost cried.

"Yes, I will marry you, Tiffany. I will do everything within my power to make you happy. Your battles are mine to fight, your worries mine to handle, your heartaches mine to heal."

This time, I couldn't hold them back. Tears filled my eyes and ran down my cheeks. "Oh, Matthew …"

All I could do was blubber and cry all over his shirt. I had never in my entire adult life had someone want to take care of me, and now I had the most wonderful man in the world ready to do just that.

He held me gently, soothing me until my hiccupped sobs subsided.

"I didn't mean to make you cry, sweetheart."

Sniffling, and trying to stop the water works, I said, "I'm not crying."

"Oh? So what's this wet stuff on my shirt and what are those black streaks running down your cheeks, if not tears?"

"Ohh, wellll, that ..." I fanned my hand in front of my overheated face, then gave him another watery smile.

"Sorry about your shirt. I believe I got it dirty with my mascara, and apparently, as you pointed out, I have black tracks running down my cheeks. I must look a mess." I brushed my face with the heel of my hands.

"On you, black streaks look wonderful." His smile warmed my heart.

Pulling a tissue from my teeny, weenie, clutch purse that held only a tube of lipstick, a tissue, and a breath mint, I put forth a valiant effort to repair the damage to my face. I knew my stab at making myself look presentable was useless. Hey, it was dark, hopefully he couldn't see much.

After we are married, he would see me in worse conditions than this anyway. Might as well get the bad and the ugly out of the way beforehand.

"When can we get married? Please don't tell me in three months. I'd wait but be miserable."

His innocent look didn't fool me for a minute. Tomorrow is what I wanted to say.

"Matt, you are everything I've ever dreamed of in a husband. In fact, you're like Sir Rolf, the knight in my book, only far better."

"Ah, that elusive book. When will you allow me read it?"

"When we're married."

A chuckle slipped out. My mind conjured up an image of Matt reading one of my sappy historical romances. "But then you will grow faint of heart because I will want you to read all the books I write."

"Hmmm, in that case, we better get married tomorrow, so I can begin inspiring you more."

He raised his eyebrows grinning teasingly. "How about Las Vegas? I have a plane. We can fly there and be back in a day or two or more."

"You'd be shocked if I said yes."

"Try me."

"Mr. Sure-of-Yourself, I would love to marry you tonight but …"

"Haven't I told you, I don't like *buts*. They always seem to get in the way of progress."

"Talk first with your family. Make sure they are on board with us and our marriage. And if they are, how about a wedding one month from today?"

"You sure I can't convince you to marry me sooner, like tomorrow or the next day?" He gave me a pleading, little boy look.

I smiled at him, shaking my head. Me being made of sterner stuff, I could resist …*barely*. Giving him an uncompromising look, I said "I have a question for you."

"Ask away. My heart is an open book."

"Would you like to explain the part where you said I wasn't your type when you hired me?"

"Ahh, that." He looked at me sheepishly. " I wondered when you would get around to asking. That first day, I was afraid I'd scare you off. I couldn't let you go without at least seeing if what I felt for you was real. I knew if I said you weren't my type, you would be more willing to take the position. So you see, I said what I had to because I needed you to stick around. Otherwise, how would I win the heart of my fair maiden. And it worked."

"You're impossible." I took hold of his tie and pulled him up close. "I love you anyway."

"You better." He grinned.

I surprised us both. I pulled Matt closer, our breath intermingling. "What would you have done if I'd walked out on you?"

"I would have come after you, courting you, until I wore you down."

"Well, then, that's okay." His love gave me the power to be bold. I kissed him, shocking both him and me.

I'm not sure what my kiss did for him, but it gave me the freedom I needed to revel in his love. I knew life with Matt would always be full of discovery and our love would last a lifetime.

Chapter 39

I couldn't have wished for a more beautiful day for our wedding. Matt's great-grandmother's backyard was a virtual paradise. Hanging baskets and flowering pots were everywhere. A white runner ran up the middle aisle dividing the covered white-cloth seating for two hundred guests. It stop beneath an archway of gardenias and baby's breath. The exact spot where Matt and I would say our vows.

I wasn't sure where all the people were coming from. There would only be a handful of my friends. No family on my side were coming since the three-week notice to attend our impending nuptials was too short for the few relatives I had left to travel.

Beneath a white canopy, serving tables were laden with food accompanied by round tables for the guests. One table at the front held a fountain, surrounded by glasses, sending cascading golden punch over the edge and into a bowl. Next to it was another table with a huge three-tiered bride's cake on one end and on the other a two-tiered chocolate ganache groom's cake with dark Hersey shavings and chocolate dipped strawberries.

In my wildest dreams, I never would have imagined a wedding as grand and beautiful as ours would be today. Everything seemed surreal.

In a little over an hour, we would stand before the minister. We would say our vows, and I would become Mrs. Matthew Thomas Ainsley the Third. Surely, I was dreaming.

Little time had passed since our fender-bender, and yet that incident seemed light years away. And Matt … I felt as though I had known him all my life.

Maybe this was what others meant when they said we were destined for each other. That's how I felt about my Matt—we had been made for each other. God in his infinite wisdom had us meet at just the right time, when our hearts were ready for love.

"There you are." Sally, my best friend and maid of honor, walked up beside me.

Fortunately, she had been able to take the week off from work to help me prepare and to serve as my maid of honor. I would have been a basket case without her.

"I wanted to see it all before everyone arrived. Get a picture in my mind of how beautiful everything is. Once the wedding starts, I know I will hardly remember anything except for Matt."

"Well, that's how it's supposed to be, isn't it?" Sally hugged me. "But right now, you better come inside or the guests will be arriving and they'll catch you in your jeans and t-shirt. And you don't want Matt to see you before the wedding, do you?"

"No. Thanks Sally. I'm so glad we've had this week together."

"My pleasure. And thanks to you, I've met James. Who knows what will come of that, but right now I'm having fun. You ready?" Her look was filled with love.

I nodded.

"Then let's go." She tugged my arm.

James and Sally seemed to have hit it off from their first meeting, but time would tell if their relationship was meant to be. There was that little thing of distance—San Antonio and Dallas. However, Sally deserved someone good in her life, and maybe James would be that man.

Before heading upstairs to dress, I took one final look around the backyard and marveled at my storybook wedding that was far better than any I could have written about.

Inside the bedroom, set up for me to use as a dressing room, Mrs. Mac fluttered around, muttering her sweet nonsense as Sally helped me dress. Though I'm not superstitious, I went along with Mrs. Mac, knowing she wanted me to hold up years of tradition.

She handed me my grandmother's small Bible as something old to carry beneath my bouquet and to represent that our union was blessed by God.

"For something blue and something borrowed, I killed two birds for that one." She pointed to the lady's handkerchief bordered by blue tatting she'd placed between the pages of the little Bible.

"Why would you kill two birds? Were they bluebirds?" Sally gave the woman an incredulous look of disbelief and horror.

I laughed, knowing she wasn't used to Mrs. Mac's penchant for twisting the meaning and sometimes not hitting the mark or making sense.

"Kill two birds? I would never kill one of God's creatures? I wouldn't—"

"That's all right, Mrs. Mac, Sally misunderstood." I patted her shoulder as I looked behind her and did my best to convey to Sally to keep silent.

Mrs. Mac continued to mutter under her breath about killing animals and other such things, but I didn't quite catch all her mumblings.

"Well, let me tell you"—she moved to pick up a box— "it wasn't easy to get you that little bit of something borrowed and something blue. Ms. Charlotte, Matt's sweet great-grandmother, wasn't about to give up that hankie with the blue hand-tatted lace. But after I explained, she was quite pleased that you would want something of hers.

"However, I must say, it was touch and go for a moment when Lucy Bell said she might have something you could borrow. I feared she was about to offer her boats to wear. Though everyone knows they are certainly old, they positively wouldn't do. No. Not at all. Not after the mishaps you told me about."

"I agree. Thank you for taking care of everything."

I smiled at the sweet woman who had acted like a grandmother to me for nearly ten years, and I knew I would miss her and the nightly ritual of reading my stories and talking about our day. But now I had Matt.

I bent and kissed her wrinkled, soft cheek. "Thank you, Mrs. Mac. You being here means the world to me."

"Well, of course it does, my dear. And where else would I be? I wouldn't have missed this for all the tea in Chicago." She had a small catch in her throat. "Now for something new."

I heard Sally laugh, but she quickly covered it up by coughing.

Mrs. Mac pulled out a stunning diamond heart pendant and handed it to Sally to fasten around my neck.

"This is from your young man. He made me promise not to tell you about our little surprise."

My gasp and loss for words didn't do the necklace justice. In the mirror, the pendant winked and sparkled as it came to rest around my neck, symbolizing Matt's love for me.

"Now for the penny in your shoe."

Though I didn't want to hurt her feelings, I had to stop at the penny. "Mrs. Mac, I'm sorry. I can't put a penny in my shoe. It would drive me crazy."

"Oh dear, oh dear, oh dear. I'm afraid Matt and you will not be prosperous in your new life together."

"What if I place the penny here in the Bible along with the hankie? No one will know but the three of us."

"I've never heard of such a thing, but I suppose it might work."

She fussed and fumed for a few more seconds, then stopped. "I know."

Bending over and digging into her bag of tricks, she pulled out a saltshaker. "Here, throw a pinch of salt over your left shoulder, or is it your right, I always get that confused. Well, just throw it over both shoulders. It should ward off any bad thing from happening and give you many children, or is it money. Oh, fiddle sticks, I forget." She huffed, her brow wrinkled in worry.

"Everything will turn out just fine. Here, give me the salt." Not wanting to hurt her feelings by telling her I didn't believe in bad luck or luck of any kind, I took the pinch of salt and then threw it over first one shoulder and then the next.

Sally stood over by the window looking out at the view, her shoulders shaking from silent mirth.

Once I did the salt thing, Sally moved to my side, swallowing hard to keep from laughing. She placed the veil on my head.

"I believe we will be late if we don't go down now. And I for one don't want to see Matt coming up here after you."

She gave me a hug. "You make a beautiful bride, Tiffany."

"My, my, yes, you do dear." Mrs. Mac gathered her things. "I'll go down now. My job here is done."

She stopped at the door, her hand on the knob before looking at me with terror in her eyes.

"Oh no. Oh my. Oh my goodness!"

What's the matter, Mrs. Mac?"

"I failed to give you the *what to expect on your wedding night* talk. Oh dear. Oh dear. Oh dear." She wrung her hands.

Keeping my face as straight as possible, I said, "Thank you, Mrs. Mac. But it won't be necessary. My mother talked with me a number of years ago on what to expect."

"Oh, well, then, that's all right. I'm off." She sailed out the door. The moment it shut, Sally and I dissolved into peals of laughter.

"That woman is priceless." She shook her head wiping her eyes. Gathering my train in her arms, she turned me to face the door. "Let's get you down those stairs and married."

My hand shook, not because I was uncertain, but because this moment was something I had dreamed about since I was little—marrying my prince.

In the hall, just short of the door to the veranda, Sally poofed out my veil. "There. You're all ready." She turned to James, a sparkle in her eyes. "And don't you dare step on her dress, James. If you do, you'll answer to me."

"Yes, ma'am." He smiled at Sally, his gaze never leaving her. "I'll answer to you anytime."

"Don't be silly." She turned and winked at me. "And make sure you wait until I'm all the way to the front before you come to the door. That's my cue. I'm off."

Standing by the terrace doors next to James waiting for our signal, the strands of the stringed quartet and harpist playing Mendelssohn's "A Midsummer Night's Dream" caused my eyes to fill with tears. Today was a day for new beginnings. Our day. A day to share and remember for a lifetime.

"Are you ready, beautiful?" James' question seemed to settle and excite my nerves at the same time.

I looked up at the man who almost destroyed this day for me. We had come a long way since then, and now I felt nothing but kinship well up inside me for my soon-to-be cousin.

"Yes. I've waited for Matt my whole life. I'm more than ready."

"Well then, let's get the show on the road before Matt comes a-lookin' for us." James' grin was infectious and had me smiling.

Nervous, at first I didn't think my legs would cooperate. Yet, knowing who waited at the end of the white runner, I lifted my head and walked out into the beautiful evening sunset.

Matt stood by the minister smiling, looking so handsome, he astounded me. I moved toward him in time to the music, knowing I would remember this moment forever.

The sky held a smattering of fleecy clouds streaked of purplish hues, the sign of the end of a perfect day and the beginning of our journey together.

Matthew's gaze drew me forward. I made it to the front without mishap. No broken heel. No flying shoe. And, thankfully, no misunderstandings to blight our day.

James released me and slipped my hand into Matt's, and then took his place across from Sally, yet, not before I saw him wink at her. And then I was lost in the moment.

"Hello, beautiful. You are the most dazzling bride I've ever seen, and you'll soon be mine."

"And you, sir, are my handsome knight who came to rescue me. So if this is a dream, when I wake up, I'm going to be put out with you."

"It's no dream. This is here and now. I love you with all my heart. Thank you for agreeing to be my wife."

"My pleasure entirely." I smiled up into the face who had turned my world upside-down, then righted it for a lifetime.

The music ended as we turned and walked the few steps to stand before Pastor Crawley. We said our vows, exchanged rings, and received the pastor's blessing.

"You may kiss your bride."

This was the moment I had waited for since I was a little girl playing dress up and make believe, using one of my mother's old lacey curtains for a veil and dandelions for a bouquet.

Matthew raised the flimsy material of my veil, his look promising me everything. He gave me one of those to-die-for kisses that went on forever and curled my toes, with a promise of more to come. When he pulled away, I knew I was his.

"Do we have to stay for the reception?"

His words in my ear made me turn pink. I wanted to say no. Instead, I said, "Yes. So behave yourself."

I gave Matt's arm a playful squeeze.

"Just thought I'd give it a try, Mrs. Ainsley."

The sound of my new name thrilled me with excitement. His enticing smile had me wishing we could forgo the reception.

For the second time since I had met Matt, I took the initiative. I leaned up on my tiptoes, hooked my fingers around his neck. "Come here, husband." I pulled him toward me. I gave him a kiss that startled and pleased both him and me. My cheeks warmed when we received wolf whistles and clapping.

"Mr. Ainsley, I intend to enjoy this moment and all the lifetime of moments with you to come."

We turned to face the guests as Mr. and Mrs. Matthew Thomas Ainsley the Third. That's when I knew I couldn't have written a storybook romance that would have ended as perfectly as the real thing.

Mr. What's-His-Name meets little Ms. Miserable-Nobody, and turns her world upside down to become Mr. Man-of-Her-Dreams to live happily ever after ...

But, unlike fairy tales, this was not the end of the story, it was only *the beginning.*

Dear Reader,

If you have read any of my books, you know my stories are set in Texas. Most of the towns are real, some fictitious, however, set in the general vicinity of a real town. I try my best to give you a real flavor of the true Texas culture.

Most times, I pick small towns for my settings. The people are often laidback, easygoing, with a true downhome flare for friendliness. During my research, I visit the local establishments and attractions, and take pictures where I envision my story takes place. Many of the towns still offer a glimpse into Texas history, where men and women had to be resilient and tough to survive, and still are.

If you would like to learn more about Waxahachie, Texas or other the cities featured in my other novels, please visit my website. And while you're there sign up to receive my free newsletters and updates for my latest releases. Also, each month, you may enter the drawing for my monthly give-away where a name is drawn to receive a free book and/or other valuable prizes.

Please help me promote clean entertaining reads by leaving your comments, ratings, and likes where you purchased my book and by posting on social medias. Also, tell your friends and family.

And as always, if you find errors in this book, please email me so that I may improve the quality for all my readers.

As in keeping with the spirit of Texas, *ya'll come back now, ya' hear.*

Blessing,

Janice Olson
www.JaniceOlson.com
Janice@JaniceOlson.com

Other Books By Janice Olson

Romantic Suspense:
  "The Texas Sorority Sisters" Series ~ Romantic Suspense
> *Serenity's Deception*
> *Lethal Intent*
> *Chameleon*

> Soon to be released:
> *Run … You Can't Hide*

Romance:
  "Texas Serendipity" Series ~ Romance with a twist of humor:
> *Mr. What's-His-Name*
> *Singletude – Release Winter 2015Í*

> Christmas ~ 2015
> *Plus-One Christmas*

Mr. What's-His-Name

Scripture taken from the Holy Bible, New International Version.

Printed in the United States of America

First edition published 2015 ©
Lyndon Publishing

You may write Janice at:

P.O. Box 382380
Duncanville, Texas 75116

or by email: Janice@JaniceOlson.com

And please sign up for Janice's Newsletter and Book updates at: www.JaniceOlson.com

www.ingramcontent.com/pod-product-compliance
Lightning Source LLC
Chambersburg PA
CBHW062114170626
46813CB00002B/441